A NATURAL DEATH

"With Fran Kirk, Ruthe Furie has created
a smart, funny, and competent female detective.
This is a terrific page-turner.
Ruthe Furie has a real winner."

Warren Murphy, Edgar winning co-author of *The Forever King*

"Furie delivers a good, fast-paced read.
Fran Kirk is gutsy and real enough to touch."

Camilla T. Crespi, author of *Trouble with Thin Ice*

"*A Natural Death* establishes Furie's Fran Kirk
as a P.I. to be reckoned with!"

Annette Meyers, author of *These Bones Were Made for Dancin'*

IF LOOKS COULD KILL

"Furie's got a tiger by the tail in this new series."

Meritorious Mysteries

"Especially noteworthy for its central theme—
the abused wife problem—explored with
insight and intelligence."

The Buffalo News

"A nifty story!"

Toronto Star

Other Fran Kirk Mysteries by
Ruthe Furie
from Avon Books

IF LOOKS COULD KILL
A NATURAL DEATH

A
Deadly Pâté

RUTHE FURIE

AVON BOOKS ◆ NEW YORK

VISIT OUR WEBSITE AT
http://AvonBooks.com

A DEADLY PÂTÉ is an original publication of Avon Books. This work has never before appeared in book form. This work is a novel. Any similarity to actual persons or events is purely coincidental.

AVON BOOKS
A division of
The Hearst Corporation
1350 Avenue of the Americas
New York, New York 10019

Copyright © 1996 by Ruthe Furie
Published by arrangement with the author
Library of Congress Catalog Card Number: 96-96030
ISBN: 0-380-78475-0

First Avon Books Printing: August 1996

AVON TRADEMARK REG. U.S. PAT. OFF. AND IN OTHER COUNTRIES, MARCA REGISTRADA, HECHO EN U.S.A.

Printed in the U.S.A.

RA 10 9 8 7 6 5 4 3 2 1

For Cheryl Olds, with love

Acknowledgments

My daughter Cheryl Olds, with whom I lived in Vaudoy en Brie, France, while writing this book, is the first of many to whom I owe gratitude. She not only gave me a roof but was available for research at all stages of preparing the manuscript.

The fictional village of Vaudoy en Brie is somewhat like the real one, but I have taken liberties with some of its topography. There are no people like the ones who inhabit the fictional Vaudoy, nor is there an *épicerie* like the one in the book or a restaurant called Chez le Rouquin.

There are some fictional people with borrowed names who do not at all resemble the real folks. I must thank my grandchildren for the use of their names—Clarisse, Jefferson, and Clement—and also for their frequent corrections of my feeble French.

My former son-in-law Jean-Pierre Malsert was invaluable in the matter of things French, especially on those evenings when he visited bearing a lovely champagne to go with a foie gras.

I must also thank Jean Larmurier, one of the pillars of the community of Vaudoy, for information about the church, Église de Saint Medard de Vaudoy en Brie, which is rendered factually in the book.

My agent, Janet Manus, is ever in the pantheon of those whom I must thank, as is John Douglas, until recently my editor at Avon Books. That is not at all to slight my new editor, Ann McKay Thoroman, who is walking tall in the shoes she had to fill.

My dear friend Ronnie Klaskin read this manuscript as well as all previous ones in this series, and I am grateful for her help and suggestions. I'd also like to thank David Stout, who was an interested and helpful party to my efforts when this book was being written.

One

She was almost old enough to be my mother, this Frenchwoman whom I had never seen before, but who at one time was one of my in-laws. Her eyes gave me a jolt, the same eyes I had fallen in love with, the eyes of my departed ex-husband. The blue that I got lost in. And now I couldn't stop looking at them. They made me uncomfortable and at the same time gave me back something that was lost.

Madame Rien was my ex's aunt Annee, part legend, part pariah in the family history, because she had gone off to France in her early twenties and abandoned her career in her brother's detective agency. My ex had told me that she sometimes had been held up as an example of what not to do and, just as often, had been referred to as an example of personal strength.

And there I was at her doorstep in the little village of Vaudoy en Brie, looking into those blue eyes, which were smiling a greeting, but which wore an expression of grief.

She was welcoming me and my ex-mother-in-law, Marsha Kirk, after our trip from the U.S., a trip that Marsha had spent twenty-four hours begging me to take.

The grief was why we were there in the first place. It was for her husband, who had crumpled and died during dinner three days before. The cause of death was poisoning; the instrument of death was a pâté.

According to Marsha, Annee had another reason to be distressed, for she was on top of the gendarmes' list of

1

suspects. They had already hinted that they would pursue the case against her.

After all, she was the wife, and, according to Marsha, their domestic situation had not been the best. And hadn't Annee had the best opportunity to administer the deadly pâté?

That was one of the reasons that Marsha had invited me to come along on this trip to France. She thought I might be able to help keep Annee out of jail by finding out who had poisoned the pâté. How I was supposed to do that with the little bit of French that I had learned in high school was a mystery to me.

Guilt was what had finally persuaded me to accompany her. Guilt because I had mostly ignored her in the year since her son's (my ex-husband's) death, and guilt because she had recently been very ill. I knew nothing about her illness for months because I hadn't returned her calls, or I had returned her calls when I thought her answering machine would pick up.

But guilt wasn't the only thing nudging me. I have to admit I was swayed when she said she would pay my way. I had never been to France. I guess you could say I can be bought.

If that sounds hard-nosed, it's because you don't know Marsha. She is persistent to a fault, and drove me crazy after her son's death trying to pretend that all the things he did to me, including trying to kill me, had never happened.

From what I'd heard of Marsha's sister-in-law, Annee, she was perfectly capable of keeping herself out of jail. Dick, my ex, would repeat the tales to me about what a crackerjack sleuth she was, how she never missed a thing. He, of course, was too young to have worked with her in the detective agency. But that didn't stop him from making comparisons, when I helped him in the office, between my work and her legend, comparisons that found me lacking.

So you might say I had another reason to be reluctant to come to France to help her out. And before I met her, I was harboring the idea that I would take the trip to France, learn what I could, enjoy the views and the food, and let Annee go hang. However, I didn't mean hang literally. Besides, I looked up capital punishment before I left the States and found out that the French haven't executed anyone since 1977 and had abolished capital punishment under Mitterand in 1981.

But all the spiteful thoughts I'd had about Annee were before I saw her eyes.

"Annee," Marsha squealed.

"Oh, Marsha," Annee said with just a trace of a French accent, "it's so good to see you. It has been so long."

"You look so, so French," Marsha said, adding a small giggle.

"Well, I am," Annee said. "I've been here for twenty-one years. And I married a *Français*—Frenchman. That in itself makes me French."

"Is it that long?" Marsha said. "I can hardly believe it."

During most of this conversation, they were kissing each other, first on one side of the face and then the other. But they were kissing the air, not skin or hair. Annee started it, and Marsha went right along with it, as if that was the way she always greeted people.

When their necks got tired, they acknowledged my presence.

"This is Fran," Marsha said. "Dick's widow."

I usually corrected Marsha when she called me Dick's widow, because I had been divorced from him for six months before he died. This time I didn't. Maybe it was that slight lift of Annee's eyebrow that told me I didn't have to. Anyway, Annee grabbed me by the shoulders and started the pecking routine with me. At first, it was hard to get the rhythm of it and I almost kissed her smack on the lips, which, I am sure, would have been a gross breach of etiquette.

"Ah, Fran," she said. "It is good to meet you at last." And then, in a voice low enough so that Marsha could not hear, "You have had your troubles, too, yes?"

My eyes bugged out, and I said nothing. When she looked straight at me with those blue lasers, I nodded.

When I found my voice, I said, "I'm really sorry to hear about your husband. It must have been awful for you."

"Poor Annee," Marsha said. "How horrible."

"It was more horrible for Denis. He was in such pain."

Annee was in tears, her face expressing the agony of the words.

At that moment a hugely fat woman came into the hallway, where we were still standing next to our suitcases. She said something to Annee in French and then smiled and said, "*Bonjour*," to us.

Annee introduced her as Madame Morvel, and she was gone as fast as she had come, which wasn't that fast, because she had a lot of tonnage to cart. But apparently she had reminded Annee, in a not-very-polite way, that it was impolite to keep guests standing in the hall, because Annee said something to that effect and immediately showed us to our rooms and helped us to get settled.

I didn't see Annee again until she came to my room just before dinner.

The house was large and very old, made of stone and mortar, with a tile roof, shuttered windows, and walls that were two feet thick. The ceilings were high and the floors were tiled, which made me glad that we were visiting in warm weather. The place looked like it would chill to the bone in winter. The amenities, such as electricity and heat, had obviously been added after the house was built. Wires and pipes, painted to match the walls, ran along the walls near the ceilings and around the frames for the doors and windows. Everything looked clean and well maintained, but old, and there were few frills in the decorating or the furnishing.

If I'd had to guess at the age of some of the chairs, tables, couches, lamps, desks, and bedroom suites, I would have said the stuff was at least fifty years old. It looked to me as if Annee as a young bride had not furnished her own house. But I hadn't yet seen much of the downstairs.

Perhaps, I thought, Madame Morvel, the old, fat woman who had made a brief appearance in the hallway, was responsible for the decor. I had not yet been in her company for very long, but at that point I didn't think I was going to like her.

The room I was to sleep in was simply furnished, with a double bed, an armoire, a bureau, and a desk and chair. The pieces were all of dark wood and the style was not one that I had seen before: very straight, very plain, but well made and polished to a soft patina. The windows were hung with straight lace curtains, which seemed to be there to furnish some privacy during the day, a function that was taken over by shutters after dark.

In the corner of the room opposite the bed, there was a three-paneled screen with pale yellow fabric stretched across each panel. Behind the screen were a sink and a bidet, but it took me a few minutes to figure out what the second item was. I was also confused as to what it was used for. It was low, like a toilet, but it had a drain and faucets in it, like a sink.

The bathroom was down the hall from my bedroom. But there was no toilet in the bathroom, either. The bathroom was for bathing, period. The toilet had its own closet next to the bathroom. It would be an adjustment, I told myself after I had considered the cultural gap in the plumbing.

Marsha's room was two down from mine. The room between ours was occupied by Madame Morvel. As soon as Annee had shown us the rooms that we needed to know about, she went back downstairs and Marsha came into my room all agog.

"Isn't this fun?" she said. "Do you have a bidet in your room, too?" She looked behind the screen to satisfy her curiosity. "I don't think I've ever used one," she said. "Do you suppose that at night when you have to get up, you use the bidet?"

I told her I didn't have any information on the subject but that she could ask Annee and then set me straight. "In the meantime," I said, "I'll just go about things the way I've been doing."

Marsha seemed to want to continue the discussion of the plumbing, but I left the room to use the plumbing that I was sure about. Marsha went back to her room, probably to ponder the uses of the bidet.

I had hung up most of my clothing that I wanted to put in the armoire and was about half done putting the folded clothes in the bureau when Annee knocked on my door.

"Are you finding what you need?" she said. "Enough hangers?" Although her voice was pleasant, her thin face had a pinched expression, as if she were wincing.

"Yes, plenty," I said. "I probably brought too many

things with me, but I really didn't know what I would need.''

"Most of the time, people dress very casually. You'll see. When I first arrived here, people were more formal, but the American influence has made itself felt, despite the French protests that they are the home of culture and fashion.''

I thought for a second that she was going to cry when she mentioned her early days in France.

"America has changed a lot, too, in twenty years.''

"Twenty-one,'' she said with a small, tight smile.

"Even more,'' I said. "Haven't you been back at all?''

"No, never. Denis wouldn't hear of it.''

Funny, I thought, here was a woman who had defied her family and gone off to France, and this same woman could be told by her husband that she couldn't go back to her country even for a visit. But as I was going over this thought, I was reminded of my own behavior. Hadn't I gone against my mother's wishes when I married Dick Kirk? And hadn't I lost control of my life?

"So you and Marsha have kept in touch all the while?'' I said, feeling on safer ground.

"Ah, yes,'' she said. "Marsha has been my link to America. Of course, I do watch some American news that we can get now on the television, but not very often. I am usually busy.''

Marsha had mentioned to me when we were on the flight to Orly Airport that Annee had to work very hard. She not only had a big house to clean, but she had to help with the running of the inn at the edge of town, which was called Chez le Rouquin. Marsha said that meant The Redhead's Place, and was named for Denis Rien, whose hair had been flaming red.

"Marsha said you have a restaurant or hotel called Chez le Rouquin,'' I said.

She immediately corrected my pronunciation and kept at it until I said the words well enough to suit her. It was peculiar to make those sounds in my nose. I didn't mind being corrected, though. I had promised myself to learn some French while I was there.

"That's one of the things I want to talk to you about,''

Annee said. "I would like you to help me. I need your help. A lot of help."

Helping her was starting to sound daunting. "What can I do?" I said, wondering what I was getting myself into.

"I will pay you," she said, and my vision of a vacation in France went up in smoke. "I want you to watch some people who come to the restaurant. And I will give you a job there and pay you for both jobs."

"Both jobs?" I was slow on the uptake.

"The work that you do at the inn and the work that you do as a detective."

I didn't have much opportunity to protest, or to list my reasons for not wanting to take the jobs she was offering.

"I know that this is sudden," she said, "and Marsha knows nothing of this."

Hmm. I wondered whether that was true. I got the sneaking suspicion that they had cooked up this deal. But she had offered to pay me. Maybe Marsha didn't know. Maybe pigs had wings.

"I need someone I can trust," she said.

Why did she think she could trust me? Unless Marsha had told her that I return money to clerks who give me too much change. I had done that once when I was with Marsha and she couldn't believe it.

Annee sat down on the chair by the desk, her shoulders slumped forward. "I may not have much time," she said. She was biting her lip, and repressed sobs were shaking her chest.

"What do you mean?" I said. I had visions of some poisoner stalking her or of some disease eating away at her life.

She took a minute to calm herself before she said, "Our friend Jacques, who is a police inspector, has told me that the gendarmes are going to arrest me soon. How soon, he said, depends on when the tests come back from the laboratory."

I didn't know what to ask her first. "What tests?" I said.

"They are testing the rat poison the gendarmes found in the garden shed. Jacques said that the poison that killed Denis may be the one used to kill the rats."

"And why is this Jacques telling you this? Isn't he supposed to keep a professional distance?"

"Jacques and his wife, Niki, were our friends. He is not working on this case, but he told me what he knew because he knows I have so much to do."

That last remark about there being much to do caught my attention, and again I thought about Marsha saying how hard Annee worked. I began to think that I, too, was going to be working hard.

This was definitely not sounding like a vacation. Marsha would never get me to go anywhere with her again.

My spirits thoroughly dampened, I said, "Like what?" and steeled myself for the list of things she expected me to do.

"I must arrange for someone to see to Madame Morvel," she said, "and I must hire another cook for the restaurant or else close it and run only the cafe."

I realized that all she was thinking about was her usual responsibilities and that she was going to hire several people to do the work she usually did.

"Have you hired a lawyer?" I said.

"No," she said, a surprised look on her face.

"That's the first person you should hire. Take care of yourself first. Let the other stuff go. Save your own skin." I couldn't quite get into this argument, because it wasn't mine. It was one of the harangues usually delivered by Polly, the woman back in the States who ran the battered women's group that I attended. She was always trying to get us to take care of ourselves. I was happy that the argument had come to my mind so readily. Maybe it was sinking in at last.

Annee covered her face with her hands for a few seconds and then rested her hands in her lap and straightened her neck. "I suppose I shall have to do that. I think I have been avoiding it. I just can't believe it."

"Believe it," I said. "Even in the States, the spouse is the first suspect. You ought to remember that." I certainly did.

She looked at me intently and nodded her head. "Yes. I do remember. You are just what I needed, Fran. A breath of fresh air. Someone who will speak her mind. Someone who will tell me the truth.''

''Surely there are friends who will speak honestly to you.''

''I haven't got many friends,'' she said. ''There is always so much to do.''

''But what about the police inspector? You said he was a friend.''

''A friend of Denis, and me, too, because I am, I was, his wife. But not my friend. Not really.''

''And his wife? I forgot her name already.''

''Niki. She is his wife, and so we are friends. No, I have no friends of my own. Except Marsha. She was the only one who continued to write to me after all these years. Others went their own way, stopped writing. We didn't share anything anymore.''

Damn. She sounded so alone, so isolated. She reminded me of me when I was still married to her nephew. But maybe she had more friends than she thought, people who valued her and would want to help her. It seemed that she needed to be pushed into getting a lawyer. She was definitely giving me a lot of reasons why no one could help her.

''Okay,'' I said, ''let's say you don't have any friends. Who could give you advice about getting a lawyer?''

She inhaled deeply and let her shoulders droop. ''Madame Morvel might know someone, or perhaps I could ask Jacques.''

''Great,'' I said. ''Now, what do you want me to do?''

''Would you mind coming to the restaurant tonight— after we eat here, of course? And I will show you the place, and you will see if you can help me. I wouldn't blame you if you didn't want to get entangled.''

Sometimes she used peculiar words when she spoke, like ''entangled'' instead of ''involved.'' I guess it was because she spoke French most of the time and the English words didn't come to her as readily as they once had.

''Would it be easier for you if we ate at the restaurant, since you have to go there anyway?''

''That's very good of you, Fran, but I must prepare a meal for Madame Morvel.''

"Can't she come to the restaurant, too?"

Annee laughed out loud. I didn't think what I had said was funny, and I guess my face told her that.

"You see with what difficulty she moves," Annee said. "Walking to the inn would kill her."

I wanted to say that a little walking and less eating might be just the ticket for Madame Morvel but, for once, I held my tongue. I just said, "Oh."

"Besides, I have already prepared dinner. And you will get a chance to speak with Madame Morvel while we eat."

"Does she speak English?"

"A little. And she will be glad to correct your French."

"Great," I said, thinking that it wasn't going to be fun having that rude woman telling me all through the meal what rotten French I speak. And then, because I like to know about the emotional terrain, I said, "Is she related to you?"

"She is Denis's aunt, his mother's sister. She has been staying with us for ten years. She has always been generous to my son, Vincent."

Kinder than she is to you, I'll bet. That's what I thought, but I said, "I had forgotten that you had a son. Will I meet him tonight?"

"I haven't been able to reach him." She frowned and blinked a couple of times. "He lives in Paris."

We called Marsha then and as we descended the stairs, Marsha asked her many questions about the bidet, which Annee answered with a smile playing at the corners of her mouth.

It was unusual for bidets to be installed in bedrooms, but not in hotels, she told Marsha, "and I would have removed them, but Denis wouldn't permit it."

"You can use them for whatever you want," Annee said when Marsha asked the crucial question. Thank goodness Marsha's curiosity was sated before we got to the table.

TWO

Madame Morvel was seated in the living room when we got downstairs. She had changed her clothes and was now wearing a maroon silk dress with a lace collar. Her shoes looked like good leather and had sturdy heels and laces and numerous little cut out designs. Her hair, which I remembered being held in a snood earlier, was styled in tiny waves with a roll at the bottom, which fell to just below her ears, and was covered with a hair net that was very fine and almost the same grayish brown as her hair. She definitely looked like someone from another time.

"*Bonsoir, mesdames*," she said. "Good evening. Would you like an aperitif?"

I didn't know what to say, but Marsha was ready for her. "Have you any Pernod?" she said.

"*Mais oui*," Madame Morvel said, looking pleased.

When she looked at me, I smiled and said, "I'll have the same." But I didn't have the slightest idea what I had asked for. Annee caught my eye and decided that an explanation was in order.

"In France," she said, "Pernod tastes sort of like licorice." I guess it could have a different taste in different countries, but probably not. That was just Annee's way of telling me what it would taste like. "If you'd rather have vermouth, we have some of that, too."

"Oh," I said, "maybe some vermouth would be better."

Annee then spoke a few words of rapid French, among which I heard my name mentioned.

Madame said something like "dacore" and poured two

glasses of green stuff and two of brown stuff. She handed Marsha a green one and me a brown one. I assumed that I got the vermouth. Marsha poured water in her glass, as did Madame Morvel, and the green stuff turned milky white.

Then we all sat stiffly with our drinks until Annee said, "*Salut*. To better times."

We drank, and much to my relief, the vermouth tasted like vermouth. There was a minuscule bowl of peanuts, and another of about the same size filled with some yellow bits that looked like corn chips. I waited what I thought was a polite minute or two before reaching daintily for the peanuts.

"*Les cacahuètes*," Madame Morvel said. "Peanuts."

I looked up from the bowl of peanuts and tried to repeat what she had said. Annee stepped in and clarified, for which I was grateful, but which Madame Morvel didn't think was necessary, if the frown she wore meant anything.

The conversation didn't get any easier when we went from the living room into the dining room for dinner. But at least we could talk about the food. Madame Morvel, following the task she had set for herself, gave us the French name for everything we ate, and Marsha and I dutifully tried to pronounce each one. After we had had some wine with the courses, white with the escargots and red with the *bifteck* (beefsteak, which wasn't anything like an American steak, but which, I gathered, was on the menu in honor of our arrival, because Americans are supposed to like beef), our attempts started to seem funny, even to Madame Morvel. And by the end of the meal, over a lovely custard dessert that followed a cheese course full of cheeses like I had never tasted in my life, we were muddling through a chat as if we were old buddies.

Madame Morvel told us her first name was Laurence, which Annee told us was the feminine for Laurent. And we were tipsy enough to tell Madame that the nickname for a man named Laurence in America was Larry. And when she tried to say Larry, it struck all of us funny, including her. The letter *R* is where the French and Americans part company. It is as difficult for them to say an American *R* as it is for us to say a French one.

It was good to see Annee laughing. Her face was quite

pretty when she smiled, a complete transformation from her previous expression.

At one point, when Madame Morvel excused herself from the table, Annee told us that she had never seen Madame in a better mood. I was flattered, and so was Marsha, when Annee attributed the good humor to our being there. Annee herself said that she hadn't felt so good in years.

"It is a magic evening," she said, just as Madame Morvel returned to the room.

"*Oui*," Madame Morvel said.

We were all surprised that she understood, because she had had some difficulty during the evening with much of what was said in English.

"It is magic," she said, but it sounded more like, "Eat ease mahsheek."

Nobody wanted the meal to end, so we tarried a little longer, even though Annee wanted to get to the inn to supervise the cleanup after the evening meal there. We sipped at some cognac and our conversation continued, but it took a more serious turn.

"Madame," Annee said, "I expect to be arrested for Denis's death." Then she asked Madame Morvel about finding a lawyer who would handle her case.

Madame Morvel told Annee not to worry, that she would take care of getting a lawyer immediately. Then they spoke some rapid French, during which Annee's face registered complete surprise.

I assumed that Annee had not been treated so kindly by Madame before. And when they returned to the mode of conversation that we had been using all evening, Annee translated what they had been talking about, but I had a feeling it was the short version and that something had been left out.

Shortly afterward, Madame Morvel and Marsha went to the living room to manage their conversation as best they could. It had been decided earlier that Marsha would stay with Madame Morvel and, more than likely, go to bed before Annee and I got back from the inn.

As we walked through the dark, narrow streets of the village, passing houses shuttered against the night, Annee told me what she had left out of her translation of the conversation between herself and Madame Morvel.

"I didn't know," she said, "that she was giving Denis so much money every month. He never told me."

If her life hadn't been so turned around, I'm sure she wouldn't have confided in me, but I was there, and she needed someone to talk to.

"You mean you thought she was living there free, and you were treating her well because she was sending money to your son?"

"Yes, yes. I am almost ashamed, because sometimes I thought she was taking advantage. She would ask for special things from the market, and I would say to Denis that they were too expensive, and he would tell me to get whatever she wanted. I thought she was a tyrant. But you see, she was paying for this."

"You never figured out that he had more money than you thought he should have had?" This was a pushy question, but I was starting to feel as if I had to know more about her and Denis if I was going to be able to help her.

"I did not take care of money," she said.

I remembered being in a similar fix when I was married. It was so easy to let someone take over, to let someone treat you like a child.

"But she gave him so much," she said. "I had no idea. We should have been rich by now. I never spent much. The inn makes money. What did he do with it?"

"What did Madame Morvel say when you told her you didn't know?"

"I didn't tell her. I acted as if I knew, and told her that she had always been very generous. She told me that she was grateful for everything I did for her. It was so embarrassing. I don't know whether I fooled her."

I was making mental notes. I would have to have Annee go over all her financial records to see whether there was anything Denis had spent money on that could have led to his death.

"Tomorrow, you should see what you can find out about the money. Maybe Madame ought to know what Denis did so that she can help you go over the books. She must know something about money if she hasn't been working but has been handing out gobs of it for the last ten years."

"Let me think about that," Annee said. "I'm too shocked to decide tonight."

At that point we arrived at Chez le Rouquin. It was on the main street that ran through the village, and cars were parked all along the road, leaving only one lane for traffic. Like many of the buildings, the inn was built only a few feet from the road, the width of the streets being a remnant of earlier times, when horses and carriages plied the way between the buildings.

The sign out front bore a picture of a jolly man wearing an apron and a big chef's hat, with tufts of bright red hair sticking out from under it. Beneath the picture were the prices for the various menus. The menus themselves were posted next to the door.

Annee checked around in front of the inn and then glanced up the alley between the building and the wall that surrounded the property next door. Then she looked over the menu and nodded.

"I suppose everyone will wonder who made the ragout tonight." Annee laughed a bitter little laugh.

"Why's that?"

"Denis was quite famous for his ragout. People always come Thursday to eat it. And because it is still on the menu, they will be wondering if it tastes the same now that the great chef is gone."

I was getting the idea, but I asked the question anyway. "Will it taste the same?"

"Of course."

I could see a triumphant smile on her face, which was lit by the lights over the inn's sign. But such a triumph wouldn't be enough to kill for, would it?

I continued the inquiry. "And who made it?"

"I have been making it from the start, but Denis always said that the French would not accept a woman chef, so he gladly took the credit. But I must give the devil his due. He was a wonderful cook. He had taste buds that could tell you how long ago an onion had been picked. It was just that the stew caught on and made him famous. It annoyed him very much that that particular dish was the one he was known for."

"I imagine it would. But didn't it annoy you that you never got the credit?"

"Only at first. I haven't thought about it for years. Not till now."

I didn't believe that at all.

"It is crowded tonight," Annee said. "I suppose they want to have a look at me to see if they think I am a murderess."

"It's a wonder they didn't stay away. You could poison the whole village." I laughed, but Annee didn't.

"But they all know already that it was the pâté that killed him. And if I didn't put rat poison in it, well, everyone knows where he bought the pâté."

"Where?"

"At the *épicerie*, the store in the village. They make it there, and it is very good, I'm told. I never liked pâté."

"So whoever poisoned it knew that you didn't eat it, perhaps?"

"That would be an easy thing for people to know. I have been living here for many years and not eating it when we are invited to people's homes."

"What about Madame Morvel? Does she eat pâté?"

"She is rarely home on Mondays, our day off. Everyone knew that as well."

"That doesn't cut down on the list of suspects, then."

"I will tell you all about that evening later. Maybe then some suspects will occur to you. Now, we must get to work."

Annee told me that she would introduce me as her niece from the United States. "It is almost true," she said. Then she told me that she would put me to work getting drinks. "You'll need to know what we have and how to make change, but I can teach you that tomorrow morning."

"I hope I can learn it that fast."

"I'll be there if you have questions. At least, I'll be there until they arrest me."

"If you get a lawyer, maybe he can get you out on bail."

"If they think I murdered my husband, they won't let me out." Annee had a look on her face that said she was resigned to being put in jail. I was wishing she had more fight in her.

She put her hand on the door and turned back to me. "Well, here goes," she said. She stood much taller than she had since I arrived, obviously a posture of defiance, and pushed open the door.

The clatter of forks and knives hitting plates, the hum of conversation, the shifting of chairs, the clearing of throats, all the noise of people dining was replaced by a silence that fanned out into the room from the doorway.

Several dozen people, who definitely looked alien to me—whether it was their dress or their faces, or both, I don't know—stopped what they were doing, forks halfway to mouths, drinks held midway to a gulp, food swallowed unchewed. Even the candles on the tables stopped flickering, as if everyone had stopped breathing.

Annee began with "*Bonsoir*," then gave a little speech that she had obviously prepared. After a minute or so, the people were nodding sympathetically. And at the end of her talk, a small cheer went up and everyone resumed eating happily.

Annee wended her way around the room, greeting people individually and introducing me to too many for me to remember. I followed her, and eventually we found ourselves in the kitchen, where an oldish man and woman were working.

"They are Madame and Monsieur Saverne," Annee said. "They work here every day except Sunday. I'll introduce you to them later. They do not like to be interrupted."

The Savernes continued with what they were doing, casting only the briefest of glances in our direction.

"What did you say to the crowd that made them cheer?" I said.

"I told them that Denis wouldn't like them to be too sad to enjoy their meal, because food was very important to him. Then I told them that they would all get a free glass of good cognac after dinner to drink to Denis's arrival in heaven."

"Good move," I said.

Annee smiled.

Later we would have less to smile about.

Three

Annee took me out to the bar, or café, a room to the right of the dining room where a few men were seated at tables. The bar itself was not designed for anyone to sit or stand at; it was too small and laden with bottles and carafes. Behind it were the coffee machine and cups and glasses.

"I don't know where some of these guys go when they're not here," Annee said. "I won't introduce you; they won't remember anyway."

"I'm not going to remember most of the people I met tonight, either."

"But they would be meeting only one and still wouldn't remember," she said.

Annee looked over the tables and her eyes stopped at a table in the corner. "Oh, I guess I should introduce you to one of them, after all. I didn't see him at first," She started over toward his table, and I followed.

"Monsieur Foyer," she said, then continued in French until M. Foyer stood up and shook my hand.

"*Bonsoir, madame,*" he said. "It is nice to meet you."

"Nice to meet you, too," I said. But that was the end of the exchange in English.

He went on to speak with Annee, and I figured, without knowing for sure, that he was asking her about what had happened to Denis.

I stood on one foot and then the other while this conversation dragged on. He kept asking her questions and repeating what she said. Then he would shake his head and say something that I recognized: "*Quel dommage.*" ("What a shame.")

I kept getting visions of my high school French teacher, Madame Alain, who used to say, "*Quel dommage!*" when anyone got an answer wrong. As a matter of fact, I had thought about her more than once during the course of this day, and I wished I had worked harder learning French instead of mooning over a certain blue-eyed boy named Richard Kirk.

When Annee was finished talking to M. Foyer, she took me behind the bar and started talking about the various drinks that I would be called on to dispense. After a minute or two, though, she stopped and said quietly, "I don't know how much he understands, so I'll tell you later what he said."

The other men in the room—there were four of them besides M. Foyer—were so far in their cups that they hardly noticed anything going on except for when their glasses were nearly empty. Then they would knock their glasses on the table or swing them in the air in time to the music coming from an old juke box whose tunes seemed as old as the juke box itself.

Annee told me to just keep on filling their glasses until eleven o'clock. "Then tell them the bar is closed. Just say, '*Fermé,*' " she said. "Most of the time, they get up and go by midnight. If they don't, call M. Saverne. He'll be waiting to close up anyway." Then she told me that the old stews drank red table wine, so the next time one of them hammered his glass on the table, I went to fill it.

He—this one's name was Albert—looked up at me like a dog who is being given his dinner by a stranger. I smiled at him, not knowing whether those bloodshot eyes of washed-out brown were capable of focusing. Then I gave him an extra little drop in his glass.

His mouth opened into a rotten-toothed expression that I took for a smile, and he said, "*Bon.*" At least, I think that's what he said. His tongue was so thick with drink, I doubted that he could form any discernible words.

When another of the four drinkers called out, "*Encore, s'il vous plaît,*" Annee told me that she would like me to keep an eye on him. His name, she had already told me, was Robert. He was drinking a special red table wine that was kept in another decanter behind the bar.

When I poured his wine, he watched me greedily, as Albert had done before, making sure I gave him the right amount. He, too, received an extra drop or two over the amount that Annee had told me was normal. He smiled at me, and I could see that he was not nearly so clouded with drink as the others. He said something to me, but I didn't understand.

"*Je ne parle pas français*," I said, and smiled at him apologetically.

"Ah," he said, "*américaine*?"

"*Oui*," I said, and was delighted that I had had this mini-conversation with a French person. But that was as far as I got, because he then said something that I couldn't understand or answer. I shrugged and smiled again and went back to the bar, invoking once more the memory of Madame Alain and her "*Quel dommage*."

Annee wanted to know what Robert had said to me, and I told her. It was so insignificant that I didn't expect the long, pensive silence that followed.

"Robert Arnaut," she said, "has been an enemy of Denis since they were children. If anyone hated him enough to kill him, it is Arnaut."

"If he hated Denis so much, why does he drink here?"

"Because sometimes Denis would have to wait on him, and he would always complain, when Denis poured his drink, that Denis was being cheap."

"Makes a lot of sense," I said.

"Maybe not to you. You are sane. Robert Arnaut is not."

"What did he say to me that you had to think about, then?" I said.

"I was wondering whether he already knew you were American or whether he guessed from your accent."

"It's a small village," I said.

"Yes," she said. "Everything that happens is talked about. It probably didn't take long for the news to get around that you had arrived." Annee looked annoyed and then sad. "Will nothing be normal again?"

"Probably, but it will be a new kind of normal."

Annee laughed. "A new kind of normal. Of course.

'There goes Madame Rien. She's the one who poisoned her husband's pâté.' ''

Besides the Savernes who worked in the kitchen, two young women were waiting on tables in the dining room. I got to meet them when they came to the bar for drinks for their customers. One was named Odette and the other, Clarisse. Annee told me that Odette was the daughter of Jacques Toute, the police inspector.

It was about ten-thirty (the French call it twenty-two-thirty, not ten-thirty) when my eyes started to get heavy-lidded. My clock had been set ahead six hours and I hadn't slept much on the plane.

I guess I yawned, or did something that indicated I was weary, because Annee immediately suggested that I return to the house and go to bed.

"Maybe that would be a good idea," I said, "but I don't know whether I remember how I got here." We had made several turns and the streets were so narrow and all looked alike, especially in the dark.

"Wait just a few minutes, then," she said. "I'll take you there."

"Do you have to come back here?"

"Yes. There are some things that must be done."

"I'll stay, then. Maybe if I had a cup of coffee . . ."

"Of course. Please feel free to have anything you want."

I went to the machine that made the coffee—I had already used it to make cups of coffee for people in the dining room—and brewed a cup for myself. I made it the way Annee had shown me to make it, with milk, café au lait. It was strong and delicious.

It wasn't long afterward that I was feeling awake again. But I wondered whether, when I finally did get to bed, I'd be able to sleep.

The next time Odette came in for coffee for one of the tables, M. Foyer called her over to his table. She talked to him, smiling all the while until he grabbed hold of her sleeve and held it. At that point the smile left her face, and she yanked her arm away and left his table.

Annee, too, had seen what had happened and spoke to Odette when she came back to the bar to pick up her coffee. I assumed that Annee was asking whether M. Foyer had been offensive. After Odette had gone into the dining room with the coffee, Annee laughingly told me what had happened.

"He was flirting with her. M. Foyer flirts with all the women and young girls. If anyone ever took him up on his suggestions, he would run away in the other direction."

"Why did Odette get so upset, then, if he flirts with everybody?"

"She is young. And her father, Jacques, is very strict. Perhaps she was afraid. After all, M. Foyer is pretty drunk right now. He might have been worse than usual."

But that was not the worst thing that happened that evening. Shortly before closing time, when all the drinkers had left except M. Foyer and M. Arnaut, those two got into a shouting match.

I was in the kitchen talking to Annee when Odette came in gasping. "*Venez vite, vite!*" ("Come quickly, quickly!")

M. Saverne ran, followed by Annee and me, to the bar, where a noisy brawl was going at full tilt.

They weren't doing too much damage to the bar, but they were shoving and punching each other in between long strings of angry words, complete with expletives that I had learned in high school French class, but not from Madame Alain. They shouted from about six inches apart, saliva flying.

Despite the fact that M. Saverne was at least sixty, older than either of the combatants, when he arrived on the scene, they quieted down. Apparently at his bidding, M. Arnaut paid his bill and left. M. Foyer sat at his table and was given a cup of coffee.

Annee told me a few minutes later that M. Saverne was going to see that M. Foyer got home safely. "I told you, Arnaut is crazy and not to be trusted when he drinks," she said.

"If he's that crazy and hates Denis besides, why isn't he a suspect?"

"He was not in Vaudoy that day," Annee said. "He had to go to Melun on an errand." Melun is a city about twenty-five miles from Vaudoy en Brie.

"Who told you that?" I was wondering whether the friend Jacques, the police inspector, had also told Annee about the questioning of Arnaut, and what else he might have told her.

"A number of people told me. Odette, for one; M. Saverne, for another," Annee said.

"Odette could have found out from her father," I said, "and she could have told M. Saverne."

Annee laughed. "I don't even try to find out who told who what in this village."

Odette and Clarisse had just about finished tidying up the dining room and setting up the tables for the next day's lunch when a car pulled up right in front of the inn. The engine sounded like it belonged to a big car.

Annee heard it and said, "That will be Jacques. He has come for Odette."

When I looked at Odette, she was untying her apron. "*Bonsoir, madame*," she said. "*À demain.*" ("See you tomorrow.") She headed for the door.

"*Bonsoir*, Odette," Annee said. "*Dors bien.*" ("Sleep well.")

When people spoke in short bursts, I had time to digest the words, turn them over in my mind, and scan them for any meaning that I could remember. Most of the time I wasn't successful, but I did keep trying.

Odette had just gone out when a tall, sandy-haired man, who was well dressed and well groomed, entered the inn. He walked right up to Annee and the two of them went through the chicken-pecking routine. By this time I had figured out that the better you knew someone, the more pecks you exchanged.

"Jacques," Annee said, "I would like you to meet Fran Kirk. She was married to my nephew."

"How do you do, madame," he said. His English was rendered with an English accent, and his voice was deep and melodic. "Annee told us you were coming. Sorry it had to be under such difficult circumstances. I hope you like our little village. If there is anything I can do to make your stay more pleasant, please feel free to tell me what it is."

"Thank you, that's very nice of you," I said, knowing that what I had said was no match for his gallantry. Of course, I didn't believe for a minute that he would do much of anything to make my stay more pleasant, but it was great to hear someone say that, especially in that wonderful voice.

And he was handsome besides, with green eyes and strong bones in his face. His well-made suit jacket hung from broad shoulders and was tapered to a narrow waist and trim hips. Even his feet were exciting, shod as they were in soft leather. His hands, although strong-looking, were small and manicured, not the hands of a manual laborer.

"And how is Odette behaving herself?" he asked Annee.

Odette, who had reentered the inn, looked toward her father when she heard her name. I got the idea that the girl did not speak English as well as her father did.

Annee, who seemed to keep tuned in to a lot of people all at once, smiled at Odette and then at Jacques. "You know I think she is a wonderful girl," she said, and then said something in French, maybe a translation of the same compliment, because Odette smiled back.

"But is she doing her work?" He looked from Annee to Odette. He was definitely making his point.

"She is a good worker. I am quite satisfied." Annee nodded as she spoke, but did not smile this time. I guess she was trying to show that she was taking his inquiry seriously, yet it made Odette squirm. And this time she didn't translate. There was something uncanny about this man's power, I thought.

I was also struck by the girl's resemblance to her father, but the strong facial bones, although they were attractive and dramatic on the father, were less so on his offspring. Not that she wasn't a pretty girl. She was, but not in the same league with her father. Not at all. He was beautiful.

At that point Jacques Toute turned to me and said, "And now, if you will excuse us for just a minute, madame, I have to speak with Annee on an important matter."

"Just have a seat, Fran. I know you're tired," Annee said. "We'll be right back." At that she and Jacques went back into the bar, which was closed by now, and through the glass in the door I could see that she was getting him a drink, which he probably didn't have to ask for. He probably didn't have to tell her what he wanted to drink, either.

They sat down at one of the tables in the bar, and I sat down at one of the dining room tables. In a few seconds Odette joined me.

"Do you mind if I speak English?" she said slowly. "I don't get a chance to practice."

"I don't mind at all," I said, trying to speak clearly. "But surely you can practice speaking with your father. He speaks English very well."

"Yes, he does, but he is not home so much. He is in Paris often because he is working there."

"I see. Well, you speak English better than I speak French. I took it in school for three years, but I wasn't a good student," I said.

She looked confused for a second and then nodded and smiled. "I must be a good student," she said, and rolled her eyes and jerked her head in the direction of the bar. "If not . . ." At this point she ran her index finger crosswise across her throat.

"Your father is strict?"

"Strict?" she said, then, "Oh, yes, *rigoureux*."

"Yes," I said. "Rigorous."

We were both happy that we had managed that exchange.

"Very rigorous," she said. She didn't act as if the strictness made her unhappy; she was just stating it as a fact.

"Have you been working here long?" I said.

She looked up in the air, as if she were searching for the words. I knew the feeling. "Since one year," she said. "I work only at night, not *pour déjeuner*."

"Not for lunch," I said.

"Not for lunch," she repeated. "I go to school in the mornings."

"What do you study?"

"Dance," she said. "I love to dance." Her face took on an angelic expression when she said she loved to dance. At that moment she was as beautiful as her father.

We struggled on, exchanging basic information about ourselves, until her father came back into the dining room, at which point Odette got to her feet.

"*Bonsoir*, Fran," she said. "Good night."

"Good night, Odette. *À demain*," I said.

When all the good-nights had been said and the door to

the inn had been locked behind us, Annee and I walked through the darkened streets toward her house. There were few lights on in the homes that we passed and the street-lights were few and far between. Annee said nothing for quite a while, and I was too tired to start a conversation.

The only sound we heard other than our footsteps was that of the occasional dog, which thought we were tres-passing on its territory as we passed the shuttered windows of its home.

We were nearly to the house when Annee said, ''I have a reprieve, sort of. The gendarmes will not be arresting me right away. There is something more important going on at the laboratory where they are testing the poison.''

''That's a strange reason to put off a test in a murder case,'' I said. ''Not that I'm not happy for the delay.''

''It's not strange in France. This is the country that in-vented red tape. They revel in it.'' She sounded annoyed and a little bitter.

I was exhausted and expected to fall into my bed without further conversation about anything, and I believe Annee was on her last legs, too. But there would be no rest that night.

Four

"The shutters are all open," Annee said. "Usually Madame closes them before she goes to bed." She quickened her pace and started muttering. "Something is wrong. Something is wrong."

I was right behind her when she opened the door and ran into the living room, then the dining room, then the kitchen. That was where we found Madame Morvel, lying in vomit and blood on the kitchen floor. The room reeked. Her mountainous body was twisted and one shoe was hanging off her foot. Annee almost dropped beside her. I grabbed her elbow to steady her.

"Is she dead?" Annee said, her face pale, her teeth digging into her bottom lip.

I grabbed Madame Morvel's wrist and felt for a pulse with one hand and ran my other hand along the side of her jaw that wasn't in the vomit to detect a heartbeat.

"She's alive," I said. "There's a pulse, but it's weak. She seems to be having trouble breathing."

"Thank God," Annee said. "I'll call the ambulance."

We put a blanket over her and tried to talk to her while we waited for the ambulance. She groaned, but said nothing.

It seemed only minutes later that the house was overrun with men. Men in uniforms, men in white coats, and men in street clothes.

I sat on a chair in the living room, stunned and tired. Marsha had been roused from her bed by the noise and had come downstairs wide-eyed.

Some of the gendarmes tried to talk to me, but I kept saying, "*Je ne parle pas français.*"

Marsha's answer, when they tried to talk to her, was, "*Je suis américaine.*"

Annee was little help in translating, since she had collapsed when the medical team arrived. I didn't know who was doing what or who was supposed to do what.

The medical people finally hauled out Madame Morvel on a stretcher to which some medical equipment had been attached. It took four men to carry it. I was glad to see that Mme. Morvel had regained consciousness. However, she still looked pretty sick.

Annee had been given something or other and was passed out on the couch. One of the medical people had put a blanket over her, and from somewhere a nurse had appeared and was sitting next to her.

A gendarme came up to me and started talking. I said the same thing I had been saying. This time, though, he did not go away. He handed me a paper, written in French, and took hold of my arm and pulled me.

"What are you doing?" I yelled. "Stop that."

At that moment Marsha, too, was yelling. "Fran, he's hurting me."

I tried to get away from the hand that was holding my arm, but the policeman tightened his grip. He was talking to me again. This time I recognized what he was saying, because he was speaking English with a thick accent. "Come wiz me," was what he was saying.

"Why? What have I done? I'm an American. I want you to call the consulate. Leave me alone."

Marsha was protesting nonstop and including threats to call not only the American embassy but the White House as well.

Nothing we could do or say would dissuade them, and Marsha didn't even get a chance to put her clothes on. She was still wearing a nightgown with a robe over it. Her robe wasn't so different from a housedress, though, so it wasn't as if she walked into the street in something fancy and full of lace. Her robe was red plaid, zipped up the front, and fell just below the knees. Even her slippers could pass as daywear, since they were black leather scuffs.

We were put into a police car and taken to the gendarmerie—police station. I was so mad I could hardly keep civil. But even though I felt like letting loose a string of English curses, I decided I'd better be cautious. One never knew who might understand. And I had heard somewhere that in France you weren't innocent until proven guilty. The country was losing its charm.

At the gendarmerie, we again were moved, herding-style, which was half being nudged and half being directed by hand signs, from the car into the building. Most of the time I don't like people to touch me during conversation, and I was getting much too big a dose of being handled by the gendarmes. I was entertaining the fantasy of being some big macho dude with a ton of firepower, mowing down the entire corps of gendarmes. But then I cooled off enough to register the thought that they hadn't cuffed us, and that soothed me.

After Marsha and I were sat down together in a little room, we discovered that we both had been given pieces of paper that bore the legend *Mandat d'amener*. We guessed that it was some kind of arrest warrant.

After ten minutes or so, we were brought coffee and rolls. The sight of the rolls immediately made me hungry, which I attributed to being so tired that I needed food to keep me going. Marsha, too, decided that eating was a good idea. So the two of us sat there eating and saying very little.

I wondered whether Marsha felt like apologizing for bringing me on this trip, or whether she was sorry she had come herself. Then I wondered whether Annee would wake up and come and get us. Would they let us make a phone call? What did they want from us? Were they going to deport us?

They left us alone for so long and I was so numb with fatigue that I started to get punchy and muse about a place to lie down and go to sleep. Any place that was long and flat started to look good. There was a wooden bench along one side of the room, there was the table with the rolls and coffee on it, and there was a wide windowsill. The sill looked like it would do in a pinch if I had to let Marsha take the bench. The table was too small; my feet would definitely hang off the end. Of course, it was wide enough to curl up on, so maybe it would do after all. The chairs were too rickety to form a bed, and there were only three of them. The floor was too full of grit to be inviting, but I didn't rule out the floor altogether, because on second look, the windowsill was slanted too much. I'd just get to sleep and start rolling off it.

I had just about decided to head for the bench when the door opened. Marsha, who had been sleeping sitting in her chair, startled awake.

Jacques Toute, somewhat tousled and dressed now in an Adidas jacket and pants and running shoes, came frowning into the room. "What kind of trouble have you ladies got yourselves into?" he said.

I started talking immediately, thankful to have, at last, a listener who would understand. "Something happened to Madame Morvel," I began, intending to give him the rundown on everything, including our treatment at the hands of the gendarmes.

But Marsha was talking, too, and the two of us, I'm afraid, sounded like a couple of hysterical women. I'm not sure we didn't have a right to be, at that point, but nobody listens when women sound like that. So I shut up and let Marsha have her say, which wasn't so different from what I would have said.

Jacques sat down and helped himself to one of the rolls, which were still on the table. Then he got up again and pushed a small button by the door, which I had not noticed before.

He sat down again and started to question us about what had happened. Someone appeared at the door and he said something in French, one word of which I understood— "*café*." So I guessed he had asked for some coffee.

When he had finished asking us questions, he said, "Madame Morvel will be all right. I believe she had some sort of an attack or a stroke, but it wasn't serious. She should be out of hospital in a few days."

"That will be a relief to Annee," I said. "She was very worried."

"Annee is a good woman," he said. "This has been very hard on her." The look on his face was soft and affectionate.

"Yes," I said, and wondered what his feelings were toward Annee, and what their relationship was.

I knew I had been hired by Annee to help her clear herself, but it wouldn't be the first time a guilty party did that, nor would it be the first time that lovers got rid of a spouse. Which thought got me to wondering about Jacques's wife. Hadn't Annee said her name was Niki?

I was brought back to the conversation when I heard Jacques say, "You ladies can go home now. I can drop you off."

Sure, I thought, and you can check on Annee. "Thanks," I said, "that would be very nice. But can you tell me why they brought us here?"

"They got overexcited. You must remember that someone died in the house in suspicious circumstances. Any stranger in the house is, therefore, regarded as a threat."

"Maybe that makes sense to you," I said. I was getting tired of his superior attitude. As if he were explaining things to the village idiot. "It's not the way they do things in America."

He stiffened, catching my annoyance. He liked to be obeyed and catered to, that was clear. "But you are in France, madame," he said imperiously.

"*Quel dommage*," I said.

His eyes popped open and then he smiled. "Perhaps," he said, backing off. "Perhaps you will learn to like some things about France while you are here." And he was all charm again.

I made a mental note right then not to take any lip from him, concluding from his behavior that he was a bully who would back off if given resistance.

Before we left the police station, we were given a lengthy apology in English by one of the manhandlers who had escorted us to the place, the one who spoke with the thick accent. I understood only some of the English he spoke during his little speech.

When he was done, he put out his hand to shake ours. I really didn't want to touch him, but I gave him a few limp fingers to grab hold of. Marsha shook his hand enthusiastically, so glad was she to have the incident concluded.

Jacques's car was large, dark, and very slick-looking, and

when he started it up, it sounded as if there was horsepower to spare.

There was little conversation on the way back to Annee's house, and when we got there, I again had visions of getting to bed and getting some sleep. It was 3 A.M. and I was running on fumes.

Jacques came into the house with us without being invited. We were met in the hall by the nurse who had been attending to Annee.

"*Madame s'est réveillée*," she said, and I realized that she was telling us that Annee was awake. Then the nurse said something else that seemed to mean that she would be leaving. But she didn't leave; she stood in the hall. It wasn't until some minutes later that I realized she was waiting for someone to come and pick her up.

We had left her in the hall and gone into the living room, where Annee was lying on the couch drinking a cup of something hot. Her dark hair was matted and snarled and her skin was drained of color. Even the blue of her eyes was grayed.

Jacques started to speak to her in French, but then stopped and proceeded in English. "You have heard that Madame Morvel will be all right?"

"Yes, just this moment. When the nurse called for her ride, they told her. I'm so relieved. But did you hear what the trouble was?"

"A little attack or stroke, that is all. She will be fine. That is what they told me."

"Maybe she should lose weight and not eat fatty foods," I said. "Maybe her arteries are clogged."

They looked at me as if I had said, "Maybe she has eaten too many pygmies," or something equally strange.

"She is too old to change her ways," Jacques said.

"Excuse me for mentioning America again," I said, "but in America, people her age lose huge amounts of weight, and go on special low-fat diets and actually reverse hardening of the arteries."

"That is very interesting," Jacques said. And then with a twinkle in his eye, he said, "Perhaps you should mention that to Madame Morvel. She might be interested to learn about that."

I burst out laughing. We all did. It was a good tonic, that little laugh. I didn't know how badly Jacques needed it, but it was just what the doctor should have ordered for Annee and Marsha and me.

Again, while Annee was laughing, her face lit up and became so lovely. I could see that Jacques had noticed it, too. His face softened with what looked like longing.

Annee offered us all a drink, which sounded like a great idea to me. Jacques seemed to know his way around the house; he went to the liquor cabinet and brought out the decanter of cognac and poured the liquor into four glasses.

He lifted his glass in a toast. "Here's wishing for a pleasant stay in France for our American friends," he said.

"I'll drink to that," I said.

We didn't tarry long over our drinks. We were all too exhausted. Even Jacques started to look a little worn around the edges.

I managed to be pleasant and thank him for everything, even though there was something about him that irked me.

Once he was gone, we wasted no time in getting to bed. Any questions that I wanted to ask Annee would have to wait until tomorrow. And if I didn't remember them by tomorrow, well, *quel dommage.*

I hardly remember hitting the pillow. The next thing I knew, I was awake and rolled in the quilt and still wearing the clothes I'd had on the night before. I had no idea what time it was. I didn't know how the shutters in the room had gotten closed, but they were closed and the room was dark. I knew that it was day outside, because little slits of light were visible between the shutters.

I went to the window to open up the shutters, but couldn't figure out how it was done. I made a second and successful attempt after I came back from the toilet. My watch, which was still on American time, said six o'clock. If it was 6 A.M. in America, that meant it was noon here.

Noon! Suddenly I remembered that I was supposed to help Annee at the inn for the lunch crowd. Since I hadn't seen Annee yet, I had no idea what condition she was in that day.

Well, lunch or no lunch, I thought, I need a shower. The shower consisted of a dreadful little hand-held contraption that was connected to the faucets in the bathtub. It took twice as long to get a shower when you had to switch the hose from one hand to the other to wash and you had to guard against splashing the water on the floor as you rinsed.

By the time I was dressed, I felt pretty good, almost completely over the jet lag, I thought. But I didn't know then that jet lag comes and goes for a few days.

When I went downstairs, Marsha was in the kitchen washing dishes, which I assumed were the ones she had used for breakfast, but there were a lot of them for just one breakfast.

"Ah, sleeping beauty," she said, with the superior air of someone who is a slightly earlier bird.

I didn't bother to remind her that she had managed to get a couple of hours' sleep before all hell had broken loose the night before. "I needed it," I said. "I was exhausted."

"Annee left us a note," she said, handing me a piece of paper. The writing on it was neat and not at all American-looking.

Dear Fran and Marsha,

I have gone to the inn. Fran, if you get up before lunch is over, please go there, too. Marsha, if you can spare some time this afternoon, would you visit Madame Morvel at the hospital? I have left the keys to the car and a map showing the way to the hospital. Just ask for Madame Morvel.

Breakfast is on the table, and lunch is in the refrigerator.

Affectionately,
Annee

Sure enough, Annee had left some bread, rolls, and pastries on the kitchen table, along with some fruit. There was juice in the fridge and hot coffee in the little machine on the kitchen counter.

While I ate, Marsha stayed in the kitchen, and we talked about how different the kitchen was from our own.

"Did you use all those dishes for breakfast?" I said, indicating the dish rack full of the draining dishes.

"No, some were here from last night. Laurence must have gotten up after we went to bed and come down to eat."

"I guess she has to eat a lot to maintain her weight," I said.

Most Americans would feel deprived in a kitchen with as little counter space as Annee had in her kitchen. Even my little house in Cheektowaga had much more, and I was always trying to think of ways to expand what I had.

The kitchen was a big room, equipped with a big black stove, a small white refrigerator, three free-standing cupboards, a huge wooden table with decorative blue-and-white tiles inset in the middle, and six strong-looking but very old, very plain chairs.

The stove seemed to have six different kinds of burners. But when I examined it more closely, there were little knobs for only four of them. Marsha and I both were curious about it and finally figured out that two of the burners were electric, two were gas, and the two without knobs were heated by burning wood or coal in the firebox beneath them.

We came to this conclusion by taking the stove apart a little. It was in those minutes while Marsha and I were poking around in the stove, both intent on finding out how it worked, that I realized there were areas in which we could get along unconscious of the strains that had been built up between us. I didn't know how that would translate when we got back to the States, if at all, but it was instructive.

As we were just putting the last piece of the stove back in place, Annee came in.

"I thought I'd better check on you two," she said. "Did you find enough to eat?"

"I'm just finishing up," I said, and gulped the last of my coffee. "I'll be right with you."

"No hurry," Annee said. "I got some extra help this morning, so everything got done despite the mess last night."

"Anything new on Madame Morvel?" I said, just to be polite, and not expecting the answer I got.

"They changed the diagnosis," Annee said.

"To what?" I said.

"Poison," Annee said. She bit her lip and looked as if she wanted to say something else. But she said nothing. She shrugged her shoulders and lifted her hands, palms up.

I was thinking that I had just eaten in this house where two people had been poisoned, and grabbed my stomach.

I wasn't thinking about what effect that gesture might have on Annee. Why should I have thought about her at all? I had known her for less than twenty-four hours, and so far as I knew, she could have been a murderer. And then tried to kill Madame Morvel, too. Or even tried to kill Marsha or me. How did I know when Madame Morvel got hold of the poison? It could have been in something we ate the night before at dinner.

Annee took one look at me clutching my stomach and passed out.

Five

Marsha looked at me and then at Annee and started whining. "Why did you have to do that?"

"Do what?" I said.

"Grab your stomach like that. See what you did to Annee?"

I thought of plenty of answers for Marsha, not the least of which had something to do with coming to France in the first place, but I didn't say a thing.

I just looked at Marsha and frowned, because I didn't like the playing field or the rules she was using for the game. The game, I figured, was called Blame Somebody. And the rules included blaming anyone but yourself.

I bent over Annee to see whether she had a pulse. If she wasn't the poisoner, she was closely related to the folks who had been ingesting the stuff, and maybe it was her turn.

Her pulse was strong and she started to come to almost immediately.

"Don't let her get up," I said. "I'm going to get her some water."

I came back in a minute with a glass of water and a cold cloth. Marsha took the water and helped her drink. I put the cloth on her forehead.

"Maybe we'd better call the doctor," I said.

"No need," Annee said. "I know what's wrong, and there's nothing I can do about it."

There she goes again—being passive, I thought. "What is it that you can't do anything about?" I asked.

"Being pregnant," she replied.

"What?" Marsha said.

"Pregnant?" I said. Didn't this woman have enough going on in her life without having another life to worry about?

Although in the annals of crime I'm sure there have been pregnant women who were murderers, I was betting that there were very few, so my sympathies again shifted toward Annee.

"Who knows about this?" Marsha said. It was the same question I was about to ask.

"No one. I haven't told anyone. You are the first besides the doctor."

"How far are you?" Marsha said.

"Five months."

"Why, you don't look pregnant at all," Marsha said. "When I was pregnant with Richard, I was bulging out when I was three months along. You're sure?"

Sometimes it was awkward for me to be in Marsha's company. Her life had been wrapped up in her one and only child for many years, and her memories of him were shrouded in an aura of adoration. My memories of that same person were tainted and bitter. Whenever she brought up his name, I got this taste of bile in my mouth.

"Maybe it's more than five months," Annee said. "You see, I had been getting doses of hormones, and things were not regular, so I thought I was changing. The doctor says that many women have little surprises like this at my age."

"And you hadn't told Denis?" I said.

"I was going to on Monday. And then suddenly he was writhing on the floor!" Annee broke down in tears. Maybe it was because she had finally blurted out her secret that she was able to cry. And cry she did. Like a waterfall.

While she let it all out, Marsha and I just looked at each other, wide-eyed.

How much more trying can a person's life get? I thought.

"Please," Annee said as her crying jag subsided, "please don't say anything to anyone yet." Annee was a little rocky when she stood up, I thought. But she carried on as if she were just fine, brushing her skirt off and tucking in her blouse. "I really should get back to the inn," she said. "Do you feel recovered enough to come along?''

She was asking me whether I had recovered, while she was the one who needed recuperation, it seemed to me.

Marsha went over one more time with Annee the instructions for getting to the hospital to visit Madame Morvel. As Annee and I headed toward the inn, Annee told me that her son, Vincent, would be coming home that evening.

''Denis will be buried tomorrow,'' she said. ''They do not need the body to do the tests. They have taken what they need to find out what they want to find out.''

''And what about Madame Morvel? What kind of poison did she swallow?''

''They pumped her stomach last night but didn't tell anyone. That is why Jacques didn't know what had happened to her. This morning he told me they had found poison in Madame's stomach.''

''Marsha said she must have gotten up after she went to bed and come down to eat.''

Annee frowned. ''We had a big dinner,'' was all she said.

''Yes,'' I said. ''Was there any pâté in the house? Did Jacques say what the poison was in?''

''No. He didn't tell me, or he doesn't know. Maybe they couldn't tell.''

''Have they questioned you about Madame Morvel yet?''

''No; they will talk to me between lunch and dinner.''

''They're being pretty considerate, aren't they?''

''Yes. I guess so. I don't know. I don't know what to think.''

''I wish I could help,'' I said. ''I feel helpless because I can't talk to anyone, so I'm limited in what I can find out. Are you sure you want to hire a detective who can't speak the language?''

''Don't worry. I know you will be able to help. But I must give you Jacques's telephone numbers and tell you how the phones work. That's what I must do first. Then if you need help and I am not here, Jacques can help you or find someone who can.''

The thought of calling up Jacques when I needed help didn't thrill me, but I didn't say anything to Annee about my aversion to him. From the way he looked at her, it was

possible that they were lovers. I had not seen that look in
Annee's eyes, though, so I didn't draw any conclusions.

"Maybe it's more trouble than it's worth to have us here
right now," I said. "You really don't need anybody else
to take care of."

"No, no. It has already been wonderful to have you here.
And I know you will be helpful at the inn. You already
were last night. And it won't take you long at all to learn
enough to make the drinks. I could see last night that you
learn fast."

I'm as susceptible to flattery as the next one, so I didn't
protest. I merely said, "Well, the first time you feel like
getting rid of us, we'll be out of here."

When we got to the inn, only a few diners were lingering
over coffee and dessert. Clarisse was cleaning off the tables,
and another young woman, who resembled Jacques's
daughter Odette, was helping her. Clarisse seemed to be
giving the other young woman instructions.

The Savernes were working silently in the kitchen, and
in the bar was a young man who also resembled Odette. I
began to think that there was a lot of inbreeding in the
town. But before long, Annee explained. The fellow in the
bar was Odette's brother Yves, and the young woman in
the dining room was their sister, Bernadette.

"Jacques had the children come and help," Annee said.
"He knew that I'd need help today. He's been very kind.
I did not expect him to be so, so generous."

I bit my tongue, and didn't say that I thought he had a
crush on her. "Maybe you have more friends than you
knew," I said.

"That's true about Jacques," she said.

"And maybe you're so competent that people don't usually offer to help you. But now it's obvious that you need
help," I said, but I didn't add, "And they don't know
you're pregnant besides."

Clarisse came to talk to Annee then, and I couldn't pick
out even one word that I recognized when Clarisse spoke.
She spoke fast and made a lot of faces when she talked.
As the conversation proceeded, I realized that Annee was
frequently asking her to repeat what she had said. Then I
didn't feel so bad about not understanding her.

When Clarisse went back to her work, Annee told me that Clarisse had been complaining about Bernadette not being as good a worker as Odette. "She said that Bernadette mixed up the orders and forgot to take things like bread to the tables." Annee smiled. "Clarisse herself used to do the same things. Now that she is experienced, she can't put up with the same faults that were hers."

"We're all like that, though, aren't we?"

"Of course," she said. "But Clarisse doesn't realize this yet."

"So what did you tell her?"

"I told her to be patient, and that I wouldn't expect her to do everything herself and get finished right on time since she had inexperienced help."

When Annee and I went to check up on the bar, I saw three men who had been absorbing booze the night before. The man named Albert and one named Georges, looking slightly less bleary than they did at night, were poised before glasses of red wine and were alert enough to be involved in a discussion with one named Remi, whose red face hung over a glass of colorless liquid.

Robert Arnaut wasn't there, and I mentioned this to Annee.

"Don't worry," she said. "He'll be here as soon as he wakes up. He sleeps most of the day."

"Doesn't he work?"

"No; he was left money by his uncle. He doesn't need to work and doesn't want to work."

Annee, who seemed never to stop working, spoke of Robert Arnaut and his slothfulness in a matter-of-fact way. I would have expected at least a trace of a sneer, but there was none.

I went back to work in the bar, and Yves went to help the women in the dining room finish cleaning up. When the dining room was done, they all went into the kitchen to help the Savernes finish putting things away and get ready for the evening meal.

Annee had to make the special for dinner, and she left me alone in the bar to contend with the desires of the sots, who continued to imbibe at a regular rate. I wasn't as popular as I had been the night before, though, because I gave them exactly the amount that Annee had told me to give them and not a drop more.

When a young fellow who looked familiar came into the bar around three-thirty, I was at a loss. I didn't understand him when he spoke, but I did hear him mention the name Madame Rien. It took me a second to remember that that was Annee's name. Then I blurted out, "I'll go get her," because I found myself sometimes saying things in English despite the fact that no one would understand.

As I turned to head for the kitchen, he said, "Are you Fran?"

"Yes," I said, turning back.

"I'm Vincent," he said, smiling. "Annee's son." He spoke good English with a heavier French accent than Annee had. The reason he looked familiar was that he took after Annee, thin, with dark hair. But his eyes must have been inherited from his father, because there was no blue blaze under his eyebrows.

At that moment Annee looked out from the kitchen and let out a delighted yelp.

"Vincent, Vincent, how good to see you," she said, rushing toward him. She bussed him back and forth from one cheek to the other so many times I lost count.

"How are you holding up, Mom?" he said.

"So you know what has happened?" Annee said.

"Yes," he said. Then he lowered his head. "I heard."

"Well, things have been hectic. The police have questioned me many times." Annee continued to speak to him in English, which was starting to look to me as if it was their regular practice, telling him about her being suspected of killing Denis and then about Madame Morvel.

"How can that be? Why would they suspect you? I will talk to them. I will tell them."

"I am sure they will want to talk to you anyhow. They might even treat you as if you are a suspect, but don't get disturbed by it. They have been treating everyone like that. Even Madame Toute, because she was working at the épicerie on the day your father bought the pâté."

What? Madame Toute had been serving up the pâté? And now her husband was being so solicitous of Annee? Was there a connection? Some kind of plot? Why hadn't Annee told me this before? How was I supposed to help her if she didn't give me the information I would need?

I was about to corner Annee and see what I could pump out of her when in walked a couple of gendarmes. When I saw the papers they were holding, I got nervous. I knew that someone was going to be arrested.

"*Madame,*" one said. And then continued in the rapid French that I usually understood none of. But this time I picked out the words "*maintenant*" ("now") and "gendarmerie," and figured out that they wanted her to come to the police station with them right away.

Vincent started hollering at them, and then a lot of shouting ensued. The gendarmes got very rough with Vincent and then began to push both Annee and Vincent toward the door.

I tried to say something to them, tried to find out if either one spoke any English, and tried to speak to Annee, but I was moved roughly aside and given a threatening look. They hustled Annee and Vincent out the door and into a van.

The activity roused the three drinkers only slightly, and as the last gendarme left, Remi lifted his glass and said something that made the other two laugh.

All of which left me there in the inn with my few words of French and with a certain amount of responsibility for running the inn. The first thing I must do, I thought, is call Jacques Toute. Despite Annee's intentions, she hadn't given me Jacques's phone number, nor had she given me instructions on how to use the phone.

I had to find someone who spoke enough English so I could tell him to call Jacques, and I hoped that one of the Toute children could help. I ought to be able to convey to one of them that I want to call their father, I thought.

In the dining room, Bernadette was nervously setting a table under Clarisse's watchful eye. They seemed to be unaware of what had transpired in the bar. They shrugged their shoulders when I spoke to them with my hands waving in the air.

When I went into the kitchen, everyone there was hard at work. They, too, acted as if nothing had happened.

"Do you speak any English?" I said breathlessly to

Yves, who at that instant was pressing on a brick that was set in the top of a dish.

"Yes, madame," he said. "But I do not speak well."

I was relieved that he had understood. "The police just took Annee and Vincent to the gendarmerie," I said.

"Yes, I know. We were watching what happened."

"Then why is everybody acting as if nothing happened?" I said.

"Because Annee is telling us that you are the boss if she is not here."

I laughed at the notion that they were trying to impress me with their industry. "We must call your father," I said, "and tell him that they have taken Annee."

"Call my father?" he said incredulously. "But he is in Paris. He is working."

"But Annee told me to call him if I needed help. And right now, Annee needs help."

"But we never call him," he said.

"You call him and then give me the phone," I said rather forcefully, which I perceived would be the way to get the Toute children to obey.

I was rewarded with a "*Oui, madame.*" Yves went right to the phone, which was in a small alcove between the dining room and the kitchen, and made the call.

Jacques was polite but seemed off-put about having been called. But he grew gradually more concerned as I told him what had happened.

When I had finished, he said, "Don't worry. I will call and find out what they intend to do. They probably took Vincent because they had to question him anyway."

It hadn't looked that congenial to me, and that was what I told Jacques.

"The gendarmes do not like to be given resistance," he said.

And I was thinking, No Shinola, Sherlock.

When I hung up, Yves wanted to know whether his father was angry that I had called.

"No," I said. "He is going to find out what is happening to Annee and Vincent."

"Vincent should not have interfered," he said.

"He was trying to protect his mother," I snapped. But

Yves wasn't the one I was mad at. It was Jacques and his bossy stance that were annoying me, not to mention the way the police had behaved when they took Annee away.

Yves slunk back into the kitchen without another word. I resolved to thank him for making the call, but later. I was too miffed and too worried just then.

By the time I got back to the bar, the drunks were all thirsty. So I filled their glasses and cleaned up the bar while I waited for Jacques to call me back.

A few minutes later M. Saverne and Yves entered the bar.

"Monsieur Saverne wants to know what he should do about the specialty this evening," Yves said. "Madame Rien was going to make it."

"Tell Monsieur Saverne that I have every confidence that he will be able to cook a special dish for tonight."

When Yves translated this to M. Saverne, the old man's face shed twenty years and bloomed into a big smile. He said, "*Merci*," any number of times and then said some more things that Yves was to translate.

"He is very happy and grateful to have the chance to do this, he says, and he wants to know if he can spend a few francs to get an ingredient or two. He says it won't be expensive and he won't take a long time making it and he won't make extra mess in the kitchen."

"Sounds like he thought of everything," I said. Then I looked at M. Saverne and said, "*D'accord*," which was an expression I had been hearing, and which I had retrieved from my old French lessons and knew meant "okay."

The old man practically sprang toward the kitchen, from which I heard his excited voice. I assumed he was telling his wife about his chance to cook the special. She sounded just as excited when she answered him.

I had forgotten to ask M. Saverne what the dish was called or what he would put on the menu for the evening, but I thought I would let him take care of that, too. I prayed that I hadn't created a monster.

It was while M. Saverne was busy in the kitchen, creating his masterpiece and singing all the while, that Jacques called back.

"Annee will be released in a little while," he told me.

"When she gets there, ask her to telephone me. Something has been discovered that will upset her."

"She doesn't need anything else to upset her," I said, thinking out loud instead of keeping my mouth shut.

"She is a strong woman, but I am afraid this latest piece of news will be hard for her."

"Do you want to tell me, or do you want Annee to tell me?"

"I will tell you, but I also want to tell her. But I may not be able to, because I may be called out of the office at any moment. And this is something she should know before the information is made known."

"What? What is it?"

"First, have her call me. Is that agreed?"

"Yes," I said, and wished he would stop with his parade of qualifications.

"Then, if she cannot get me, take her to a quiet place and tell her. Okay?"

The way he said, "Okay," there was only one answer I could give.

"Okay," I said.

"And tell her I will do all I can to help her, and tell her to call me this evening, or, if I can, I will call her as soon as I am free."

With all this buildup, I was ready for something really calamitous. But after he told me, I thought that no amount of buildup would get Annee ready to hear it.

Six

"It is Vincent," Jacques said. "They are holding him."

"He tried to keep the gendarmes from taking his mother to the police station."

"It is more serious than that. They are charging him with Denis's death."

"Why? He wasn't even here when Denis was killed."

"But he was. He has been in Vaudoy since Sunday."

"Oh, God. Annee didn't know he was in town. Why didn't he call her?"

"That remains to be seen." Jacques's voice was cold and hard. "He was hiding somewhere in the woods by Chemin de Faremoutiers. Someone saw him arrive on Sunday, late in the evening."

The weight of his revelation was getting to me. "I hope you don't get called out of your office," I said. "It would be better if you told her."

"Yes," he said, "that is what I thought."

The man could be so irritating. Always strutting. "Yes," I said, "that is what you said." I'm sure I had just a trace of pissed-offedness in my voice. But I tried to keep as civil as I could. After all, he was doing a lot for Annee.

Then my mind ran down the other possibilities. Maybe he was staying close to the case because he was afraid that his wife had something to do with Denis's death. Wasn't she the one who had sold him the pâté that killed him?

After Jacques hung up, I stewed and fretted, wishing that Annee would arrive and hoping that Jacques wouldn't get called away from his office. What would Annee say? What would she do? Everybody who had been closest to her had been wrenched away from her in some way, and she was pregnant with an unplanned child. I couldn't imagine having that many troubles all at once.

Somehow, the things that needed to get done at the inn got done. I chalked that up to Annee having given them good instructions and hiring good help.

Odette arrived for the dinner shift and Bernadette went home. Yves stayed on, working in the kitchen with the Savernes and coming out to the bar at regular intervals to see if I needed help. The few times that I needed translating, Odette was nearby and told me what kind of drink was being ordered and where it was.

By 9 P.M., or *vingt et un heures* (twenty-one hours), I was feeling pretty confident about handling my meager responsibilities, and I had almost forgotten Annee's plight. Then she walked into the bar, looking beat.

After taking one look at her, I couldn't imagine telling her what Jacques had told me. She'd surely pass out again, I thought. Her lips were pale and her mouth hung open; her eyebrows were drawn together, creating a crease between them; and her shoulders were rounded, as if she were defeated.

"Jacques wants you to call him," I said.

"I've already spoken to him," Annee replied in a low voice that was just barely controlled. "He said he told you about Vincent."

"Yes." I didn't know what to say to her. I had no idea what would give her comfort.

"I don't know why he would come to the village and not come home. It looks bad. So bad."

"Have you been able to talk to him?"

"No. They wouldn't let me. They were probably afraid we would get together and make up a story. And they are not wrong. I would lie for Vincent if I thought it would save him."

"Do you mind if I mention a lawyer again? You really need some legal help."

"No, of course I don't mind. Jacques has found someone who specializes in criminal cases. Jacques says he is so good that all the police hate him." A small smile briefly lifted the corners of her mouth.

Jacques again. I hoped he was better than no friend at all. I didn't know what to think about him, and I didn't know how to bring up my misgivings about him, some of which had to do with his manner and could be classified as personal.

When I had talked to Annee the day before about getting a lawyer, Madame Morvel was going to help her. Now I didn't know where Madame Morvel stood. Did she think Annee had tried to poison her?

"Have you heard anything new about Madame Morvel?" I said.

"Yes; I went to see her. She was looking very healthy and she wanted me to tell her everything. She kept questioning me. I wasn't going to tell her about the baby, but I ended up telling her that, too. She was very good. And she wants to help Vincent, too. She is sure that there is an explanation, and she told me not to worry, that Vincent is a good boy." Annee looked sad and wistful.

"Have you been to the kitchen yet? I may have done something you might not like."

"No. What is it? I'm sure it couldn't be serious." Annee's smile was broader now.

I told her about M. Saverne making the special, and said that I hoped he wasn't a lousy cook. Even if he was, I thought, in the range of events that had occurred that day, it wouldn't rank as a major misfortune.

"Why, I never thought to ask him to cook something of his own. I'm sure M. Saverne has come up with something wonderful." She seemed buoyed and went immediately to the kitchen.

I stayed in the bar and filled glasses. By then, Robert Arnaut had come in and started to work on catching up with the others, who were several hours ahead of him in the buzz department. He had downed three glasses in quick succession before M. Foyer came in, and I was hoping that they wouldn't pick up where they had left off the night before. But they drank in silence, as if a cross word had never been breathed.

M. Foyer ordered a bottle of Bordeaux and a plate of

cheese and drank happily in the corner. Odette greeted him politely, as did Clarisse, when each came to the bar to fetch drinks. Later, Yves also said hello to him. I remembered getting the impression from Annee that M. Foyer was a person of some influence in the village.

Annee didn't come back from the kitchen for some time, and I worried that she was trying to undo the harm I had done by letting M. Saverne have a free rein. I glanced kitchenward a number of times, waiting for a grim-faced Annee to emerge.

When she finally did come out, though, she was smiling and carrying a plate with a big helping of something on it. "You must have this for your supper, Fran. It is a marvel. M. Saverne's Crêpe Symphonie, I have christened it."

"You liked what he cooked?" Thank heaven, I thought.

"I have arranged for M. Saverne to make it every Friday night. He is very happy, and so am I."

I looked over at the plate and could plainly see that there were layers of crêpes and other things and that it all was sitting in a sauce. "What's in it besides crêpes?" I said.

"Well, you don't expect him to reveal all the ingredients, do you?" Annee was clearly enjoying M. Saverne's debut.

When I lifted the fork to my mouth and got a whiff of the aroma rising from the new creation, I remembered that I was in France. My mouth was watering in anticipation.

As the first flavors hit my taste buds, I let out an involuntary "Mmm," at which Annie smiled. I could detect the fact that there was some kind of meat in the layers between the crêpes, and I also knew there was cheese. But to say there was meat and cheese in it would be like reducing Hamlet's soliloquy to a single sentence. The sauce had a flavor all its own but blended in with the other flavors. The crêpes, too, had a unique flavor, mild, and in perfect harmony with the others.

"Isn't it like a symphony, Fran? So many melodies all blending together?"

"Yes," I said. "A perfect name for a perfect dish." At that moment I saw M. Saverne's head and shoulders hanging out of the kitchen doorway. He was grinning that grin that tore the years off his face.

Annee was so excited about the new dish, she went over

to tell M. Foyer about it and to offer him a taste.

M. Foyer acted delighted to be asked to sample it, and when he had, his reaction was enthusiastic.

Shortly thereafter, M. Arnaut started complaining that he hadn't been asked to sample the dish, and continued to make a big fuss about it until Annee brought out a plate of it and served it to all the rummies.

M. Foyer looked at him with disgust while Arnaut was delivering his complaints, but he said nothing.

Annee whispered something to me about it being a waste to serve such good food to a bunch of drunks who had long ago pickled their taste buds, but she said a plate of food was a small price to pay to keep M. Arnaut quiet. Tiptoeing around the moody and incendiary M. Arnaut might be a village pastime, I thought.

Annee stayed in the dining room and spoke to the diners about the new special. On her brief stops in the bar, she reported that Saverne's Symphonie was a sensation.

When the evening was over and we were walking back home, she said, "It is peculiar, isn't it, that Monsieur Saverne should have one of the triumphs of his life as a by-product of the tragedies of mine?"

"I'm glad it turned out that he's a good cook. I had no idea it would be such a big deal for him. As soon as Yves told him that he could do the special and I saw his face light up, I began to get nervous."

"Yes. It was a big deal," Annee said. She walked a few steps in silence. "And now I go back to the horrors."

"What's next?" I said.

"A lawyer for Vincent. Getting Madame Morvel back on her feet. I wish Vincent had not come home the way he did."

"Why would he do that?"

"It might be Odette again. He used to go out with her, but for a year now, he has been living with another girl in Paris. But a few weeks ago, he said that they were not getting along."

"Why would he not come home if he were going out with Odette?"

Annee sighed. "Jacques does not permit his daughters to go out with young men. They may visit on Sunday nights and sit in the living room with the family and have drinks, but that is all. And for young people, that is not enough."

"So if Vincent wanted to see her, he would have to pretend not to be in town so that Jacques wouldn't get suspicious?"

"That is what I am guessing. I'm not sure. I will have to wait to talk to Vincent."

"What about talking to Odette?"

"She surely won't say anything. Her father is already suspicious that that was the case."

"Why is he so strict?"

"His children are all very artistic and talented. He has told them that if they want to be artists, they must work harder than anyone else, must be disciplined, and must not be distracted by the lure of the other gender."

"Do they mostly obey?"

"Mostly. But before Vincent went to live in Paris to study, Jacques caught Odette with him. Nobody saw Odette for weeks afterward."

"What did he do, put her under house arrest?" I was joking, but when Annee answered, she wasn't.

"Something like that. Vincent told me that she had been confined to her room, and was let out only to bathe and use the toilet."

Jacques was not gaining in stature in my book. "Tyrant" was the word for him, plain and simple.

"Are the children such great artists that all this vigilance is worth it?" I said.

"Yves is a poet, and I have read a few of his works, which I find difficult to read, but several have been published. His brother, Clement, is a sculptor, and I am not sure about his raw talent. His technique is very polished, though, and that is rare in one who is only seventeen."

"What about the girls?" I said. "Are they as talented?"

"More so, I think. Odette dances like a feather, and Bernadette plays the flute like an angel. If you want to see something that you never will forget, you must watch them perform together."

"That good?"

"Better. You'll see. Tomorrow, I'll show you where they practice. Many people go to watch them."

"With Odette's schedule—school, practice, and working at the inn—when did she get time to see Vincent?"

"I don't know, Fran. I don't know." Annee looked tired. I didn't know whether I felt more sorry for her before, when she was the chief suspect in her husband's death, or now that her son was charged.

"Is there any reason that Vincent would be a suspect, beside the fact that he was in Vaudoy? Did he and Denis get along?"

"That was the reason he went away. Vincent almost killed his father the last time they fought. Everyone knew about it."

"What did they fight about?"

"Denis wanted Vincent to work at the inn. He wanted to pass on the tradition that his father had passed to him. Vincent wanted to go to Paris and study. He is very smart." She stopped for a minute and I thought she was going to cry. "But what he did was stupid."

When we got to Annee's house, Marsha was waiting up for us. "At last you're home," she said. "I have a surprise for you." Marsha looked bright and happy.

"What is it?" Annee said. "I could use a nice surprise."

"Laurence. I brought her home. She was much better, so they let me bring her home."

"Good. Good," Annee said. "Where is she now?"

"In bed. I made her some supper and we ate together. She said it was the best meal she ever had in her life." Marsha laughed.

I was thinking that Laurence was probably starved on the meager fare dished out by the hospital and was glad to get home, where she could stuff herself as usual, but I didn't say it.

"What did you make her?" Annee said. And then, to me, she added, "Two chefs discovered in one day."

Then we told Marsha about M. Saverne's triumph in the kitchen. Marsha told us that she really hadn't made anything so special, but Annee wouldn't let it go at that. She insisted that Marsha tell her everything she made and how she made it.

I was impressed with what Marsha had turned out, which

included a salmon mousse, some of which was left over, and which Annee and I tasted.

Annee, who apparently was in the mood for trying new things at the inn, asked Marsha if she could prepare enough for thirty people.

"Why don't I just give you the recipe and you can make it for thirty people?

"Don't you want your moment of victory, like the one M. Saverne had?"

"No. You can tell people it was my recipe, though."

"It's a deal," Annee said.

I tuned out on the conversation and dozed off. Suddenly I heard Annee saying, "Fran, I'm sorry to keep you up. I forget that other people sleep more than I do."

"It's a good thing you don't need much sleep," I said. "You'd never finish all you have to do." I had been in France less than two days, but it felt like a month.

The next day was Saturday and Denis was to be buried. I was guessing that I would see many of the townspeople.

"The service is in the morning," Annee said as I walked up the stairs, "and we are not opening the inn until six o'clock tomorrow."

"Wake me up when I need to get ready," I said. "I'm so tired, they're liable to throw dirt on me." Ugh, I thought, what a tasteless joke. I turned around to apologize to Annee, but she was smiling.

"I like having you around, Fran," she said with disarming warmth.

I smiled back at her and fumbled for something to say. I did like her, admired her, but I was uneasy when confronted with affection. "Thanks," I said. "I like you, too." What a jerky thing to say, I thought. But I couldn't think of anything else, so I retreated as fast as I could.

I didn't fall asleep with my clothes on that night. But I didn't spend much time looking at the ceiling, either.

Seven

The next day was a perfect day for a funeral: gray and rainy. Perfect, that is, in terms of the mood, but not perfect for those of us who had to stand around the grave in the rain while the prayers were said and the mud ran over our shoes.

Raincoats were the order of the day, and I had not packed one. I borrowed one (*un imperméable*) from Madame Morvel that hung in many folds around my legs. It did have the saving grace of being longer than the one that Annee had offered. Madame Morvel was shorter than Annee, but she wore her clothes practically to the floor.

Marsha had packed her own, and had given me the surprised look of a mother being disappointed with a child when she realized I hadn't brought one along. I swore at her inwardly and remembered again some of the things I didn't like about her.

I will say this for Marsha, though. She didn't use her recent bout with cancer as an excuse for anything, nor did she seek sympathy or special treatment from anyone. She had had a lump removed from her breast and had undergone chemotherapy, but she said not one word about it until I asked her. I had gotten many of the details on the plane. I didn't know how much she had told Annee, but I figured that since they wrote to each other regularly, she had pretty much told her the whole story.

When I was standing there by the graveside, I wondered what was going through Marsha's mind. Such a serious illness, I thought, would make anybody have grim thoughts at a funeral.

A few minutes into the service, the rain got heavier and the big black umbrellas went up, making the scene even more somber. One of the things I wanted to do at the funeral was to get a good look at the people in the town. Since I was standing near Annee and the crowd was behind us, I was thwarted in that effort until the service was over and people came over to speak to Annee, who was holding up well, considering the strain she'd been under.

I had seen her shoulders shaking once or twice during the ceremony, and I knew she had more than one handkerchief stashed in her dress, which, I had noticed before we left the house, was a bit snug across the middle. I wouldn't have said she looked pregnant, though, if I didn't already know she was. She just looked a little, well, dumpy.

The mourners formed a line to say whatever comforting things they say at funerals. And at that point they got invited to come to the inn for a snack. It was in the line that I saw for the first time Jacques Toute's family all together, and the first time I had ever seen the younger boy, Clement, and the mother, Jacques's wife, Niki.

Nobody had told me what a beauty she was. I couldn't take my eyes off her. Neither of her daughters had her stunning good looks. I thought how strange it was that two such gloriously handsome people should have children who, though they were handsome enough, were not nearly so knock-'em-dead good-looking.

Niki was tall, five foot eight, very tall for a French woman, with blond hair that she wore in a long braid. Her eyes were gray with a black ring around the iris, and her nose and mouth were small and well shaped. Her skin was smooth and unlined, making her look as young as her daughters, except for the knowing look in her eyes.

She spoke less English than her children, but when Jacques indicated that the family was to speak English to me, that was what she did. And she put up with the corrections from her husband and children with good humor.

Standing alongside Niki were an older couple, whom she introduced as her father and mother, Henri and Jeanne Bouchegrande. They spoke no English, but nodded pleasantly at me and said, "*Bonjour, madame.*" Annee told me later that they owned the *épicerie* where Denis had bought the pâté.

An enormous buffet had been set up at the inn. I supposed that Annee had arranged it, but I hadn't heard a word about it.

The Savernes seemed to be in charge, and there were several boys of twelve or thirteen—at first I didn't know how many, because they all looked alike and wore black trousers and white shirts—who were directed by the Savernes to fetch and carry whatever needed to be moved.

I wasn't the only one who couldn't keep the boys straight. It was one of the pastimes of the lunch, figuring out who was who. Eventually I realized that there were five of them.

The rest of the information about the five young waiters was related to me by the youngest Toute, Clement, after he had had a glass of wine and was acting just a little silly. He told me that they were the Saverne grandsons, sons of their two sons, who had married women who were sisters. The sisters were second cousins to the Saverne sons, he said. "And that's why they all look alike. Besides, they were all born within two years of one another." Clement was sitting next to me at one of the big tables that had been set up in the dining room of the inn. "They breed like the Toutes." He giggled and gave a little hiccup and immediately looked to see where his father was.

But Jacques wasn't looking at Clement. He was in earnest conversation with Annee. Probably about Vincent, I thought. Meanwhile, Jacques's wife was getting little attentions from every man in the room who could tear himself away from his own wife. She accepted these attentions with the manner of a queen who is obliged to let the unwashed kiss the hem of her gown.

M. and Mme. Saverne kept calling the five boys by their names, which added to the confusion, because all the names ended with a syllable that sounded like "bear." Clement took great delight in giving me all the names: Albert, Hubert, Dagobert, Delbert, and Gilbert. And Clement laughed when I pronounced the *t*'s at the ends of the names after he spelled them for me.

Annee didn't take any part in serving the food, and when she was done talking to Jacques, she spoke to the various people of the village. I recognized the old drunks from the bar, Albert, Georges, and Remi, who were polished up, combed, less bleary-eyed than usual, and sitting next to women, all of whom seemed to wear the same stolid expression.

Robert Arnaut was there, too, but alone, sitting at the end of one of the tables and not speaking to anyone.

Annee introduced me to M. Foyer's wife, Monique, and she charged right in with her broken English, wanting to try it out. She said, "Guy is meeting you at the inn?"

It was the lilt at the end of her sentence that told me it was a question. "Yes," I said. "I met him the first night I was here, Thursday." Had I been here only two days?

"Guy is going there after dinner, most often."

"It's a good place to go for wine and cheese," I said, remembering that that was what M. Foyer had ordered the night before. I hadn't the slightest idea whether it was a good place to go for wine and cheese or not.

She looked at me intently when I spoke, studying every word. And that gave me a glimpse of what I must have looked like when I was trying to understand French.

"Yes," she said, acting delighted. I guessed she had understood. "A good place," she repeated.

Guy Foyer steered his wife away from the English lesson and to a table, where they were greeted fondly by the Toutes, the Bouchegrandes, a man who, I was told, was the mayor of Vaudoy, and his wife. The kissing showed no sign of letting up.

The Savernes set up each course as a buffet, and the guests lined up to have their plates filled by Mme. Saverne, who worked behind the buffet table.

After each course, the food was taken away and a new course was set up. Nobody seemed to be in a particular hurry, and the Savernes were not exactly speedy when shifting from one course to the next. After the aperitif, there were crudités—raw vegetables in various types of vinaigrette—and several selections of cold fish with Sancerre wine. The bread baskets were constantly being filled with chunks of baguettes.

In between courses, sauces were cleaned from the plates with the bread. Sometimes the bread and sauce were eaten, and sometimes not.

The main course was roast pig, which was displayed on the buffet table, complete with its apple. M. Saverne stood behind the table and carved, while Mme. Saverne served warm vegetables and potatoes at one end of the table. The wine was a Côtes du Rhône.

By the time everyone had finished the main course, we had been at it for two hours. Annee, even though she had a lot to do in the hostess department, did keep an eye out for me and made sure I was introduced. Some of the people I had met the first night at the inn, but, of course, had no memory of whatsoever.

I met most of the people in my trips to the buffet table, including a man who, Annee said, was another longtime rival of Denis, and sometimes an unfriendly one. His name was Pierre Bouton, and he, too, ran an inn, which was called Bouton de Rose (Rosebud) and was in the neighboring town of Rozay en Brie.

M. Bouton was with his wife, who didn't say a word, and four adorable little girls, the oldest of whom looked no older than four. Two of them were in diapers, and Mme. Bouton looked like she was carrying another little Bouton.

While the Savernes were putting away the main course and getting out the cheeses, a noisy, but blessedly short, argument arose between M. Bouton and M. Saverne. The last word was delivered by M. Saverne, who had the same look on his face that he had worn the night M. Arnaut and M. Foyer were arguing in the bar. M. Bouton backed off and sat down.

I found out later that Bouton had offered Saverne a job and wanted him to bring his new creation to Bouton de Rose. I marveled at the way news seemed to spread like wildfire in the town. It had been less than twenty-four hours since I had told M. Saverne to take care of the evening's specialty.

Annee, without making a big show, found out what had happened and took M. Bouton aside to speak to him. He was looking anything but comfortable when he returned to his table, and when the cheese course was over, he made his apologies, saying that the children were tired and that he had a lot of work to do at his own restaurant, and left before dessert.

As discreet as Annee was, though, everyone knew what had happened before the dessert was served.

In addition to fresh fruits with crème fraîche, a cross between sweet and sour cream, the Savernes served three flavors of mousse with Chantilly (whipped cream). When the coffee was served, it came with *gallettes* (cookies) and small cakes.

At each course, my helpings grew increasingly smaller, but still, when the lunch was over, I felt like waddling out.

We had traveled to the cemetery and back to the inn in Annee's old Renault, in deference to Madame Morvel's condition. But Annee asked Marsha to drive Laurence, which was what Marsha was calling her now, back to the house when the lunch was over.

"Fran and I have some things to get ready for tonight," she said. "We'll be along in an hour or so."

I didn't much feel like doing anything except lying down to digest the monster meal I had just put away.

Annee talked briefly with the Savernes, and then she led the way into the bar, which was closed, and poured me a cognac.

Over the warm liquor, I finally got to ask Annee some of the questions that had been bothering me. Some had to do with Denis's death, and some just had to do with her life in France in general and with Denis in particular.

Annie loosened up and told me things about her life that, I knew, hurt her to tell. But when she was done, I knew she hadn't killed Denis, but I also knew she had had reason to.

Eight

"Denis was not a good husband," Annee said.

"You mean because he didn't tell you about the money he got from Madame Morvel?"

"More than that. He was with other women. I don't know how many."

"How long have you known about this?"

"Since the beginning. I used to think he would change. That if I did this right or that right, he wouldn't wander. But he never changed."

"So the money he got from Madame Morvel was spent on other women. Is that what you think?"

"Probably. It's like waking from a dream, to look back and see what I put up with. I can't believe this is me. When I first came from America, I wasn't like this."

"Being in love makes you think everything will be okay," I said. That was a subject I knew something about.

"Love is blind," she said. "Isn't that what they say?"

"Is that why the police suspected you? They thought you were jealous?"

"Yes," she said. "One of the officers who questioned me talked about Denis's affairs. He even mentioned some names. But I didn't know who the women were that he mentioned."

I still didn't think I had the whole story. What was it she was holding back? "Had he been having an affair recently?"

She blinked and swallowed. "Yes, he was."

"Do you know who the woman was?"

"Yes." Annee sat very still, as if she were hoping the question would go away. I waited. "I didn't want it to be true," she said.

"Didn't want what to be true?"

"Who it was."

"And was it true? Who was it?"

"Yes. It was Niki."

"Jacques's wife? Does Jacques know?"

"I don't know. I haven't told him what I . . ." She looked miserable.

"Do you know this for a fact? Or do you just suspect?"

"I'm quite sure," she said.

"And Niki sold him the pâté. Do you suspect that she poisoned it?"

"I can't let myself think that of Niki. I've known her for so long."

"But she did have an affair with your husband. If her morals slip one way, they could slip another."

Annee let out a little gasp and buried her face in her hands, but she didn't sob. It was as if she were trying to hide from the truth. She stayed there, hunched over, for several minutes. I didn't know what to say to get her to go on.

Finally she stood up and said she would be right back, and would I get her a cup of coffee.

I made the coffee and then sat by the cup, watching it cool. Finally I got up and went to the bathroom (or W.C., as they call it) and found Annee standing in the hallway, her face as white as ash and wet with tears.

"What's the matter?"

"I'm . . . I think I'm losing the baby. Would you call the ambulance?"

"Where are the Savernes?" I asked. "I don't know how to use the phone."

"They have gone home." Annee looked wobbly.

"Tell me what to say, how to use the phone. Don't pass out on me." I was panicking, but I told myself to take a few deep breaths and do one thing at a time.

I led Annee to the little alcove where the phone was and had her lie down on a bench. I could see that blood was dripping from her, and I almost passed out myself.

I tried not to think about her bleeding to death and made her tell me what to say and what to do to get the ambulance there.

"Dial eighteen," Annee said.

"Eighteen," I said, pushing the buttons. "What do I say when somebody answers?"

"*Venez vite*," she said. ("Come quickly.")

When I heard a voice on the other end of the line, I repeated what Annee had said, not knowing at the time what it was I was saying.

Then Annee slowly told me what to say next, giving me the words a few at a time. I repeated them into the phone. The words were: "*Il y a une femme enceinte qui saigne beaucoup.*" ("There is a pregnant woman who is bleeding a lot.")

Then Annee did pass out, and I realized I hadn't told them where she was. "She's at Chez le Rouquin," I said. "Annee Rien. Madame Rien." By that time I was screaming into the phone, not listening at all to what the person on the other end was saying, since I knew I wouldn't understand.

Finally I dropped the phone and ran to the front door of the inn. Maybe there is someone who lives nearby who would come and help, I thought. I don't know whether the ambulance people understood me. I can't just let her lie there and bleed.

When I looked out the front door, I didn't see a soul on the street. There were some shuttered windows nearby, but I didn't know whether anyone lived behind them. How do I call for help? I thought. Just then I heard the wailing of a siren, and I crossed my fingers that they were on the way.

I ran back to check on Annee, and she was awake, but very weak. "I think they're coming," I said. "Hold on."

When I went back to the door, not only was the ambulance out front, but the street was full of people. Where had they come from? I wondered.

I rode in the ambulance with Annee to the hospital, after I had given instructions to M. Saverne, who also had appeared when the ambulance arrived. I was able to communicate with him because he knew more English than he had appeared at first to know. He seemed to be trying very hard to understand me, too, probably because I was the instrument of his big success.

I told him that Madame Rien wouldn't be at the inn that night, and that he should try to make the Saturday special as much like it was usually made as possible. The mousses at the lunch, I told him, were wonderful, and if he wanted to add them to the dessert list that night, he could.

He nodded and said a few words that indicated he understood.

At the hospital, I was shown to a room with a few chairs and some plants and some magazines. A few of the nurses tried to ask me questions, but I was no help to them.

After I had waited for an hour or so, I called Annee's house and Marsha answered. Marsha said something in French.

"What did you say?" I said.

"Laurence told me to say it. It's just telling the caller to wait a minute until Madame Morvel can get to the phone. We were wondering what was taking you so long. Where are you?"

I told Marsha what had happened, leaving out what Annee had told me about Denis.

Marsha said, "How bad is she?"

I told her that I was very worried, that I thought Annee had lost a lot of blood.

"Oh, God," Marsha said. "Poor Annee. Should I come to the hospital?"

"You don't need to. I'll call you as soon as I know anything."

"Have you called Jacques?" she said.

"No, but give me the number and I'll call him next." I had thought about calling him, but I actually didn't want to talk to him, because I didn't want to tell him what had happened to Annee, and I didn't know how to act with him now that Annee had told me about Niki and Denis.

Another hour passed, and I was still steeling myself to dial the number of the Toute house when a nurse came out and walked toward me. "*Madame Kirk*?" she said. The French say "Kirk" in a really funny way, with the *i* sounding like an *e* and that *r* they say in the back of their throats.

"Yes," I said.

She signaled for me to follow her. I remember thinking, as I walked behind her down the pale green corridor, that her shoulders were incredibly narrow.

I was surprised when she took me to a room where someone was lying in a bed. At first I didn't realize it was Annee. Her hair was plastered to her head—by sweat or water, I didn't know which—and her face was deadly white and looked so gaunt she reminded me of a skeleton. It wasn't until she opened her eyes that I could shake that notion.

Even then she didn't look at me or seem to focus on anything in particular. Her eyes seemed to have the expression of a very young baby who doesn't recognize anything she sees.

The nurse had managed a few words before she left, to tell me that I could sit with Annee and that I should ring for her if Annee got sick to her stomach. The doctor would be coming in to talk to me, too, the nurse had said. At least, that was the meaning I gleaned from the words she spoke to me in English. She also said a lot of words in French, and I suppose the meaning was clear, but I understood only a word or two.

Annee's clothes had been taken off and replaced by a white hospital gown. As she tossed in the bed and the gown twisted and the sleeve rode up, I saw bruises and red gashes on her arm. Then I saw the same kind of marks on her other arm. Was it a rash or some kind of disease? I wondered.

As I sat there looking at the strange marks, I recalled that Annee wore long sleeves every day, no matter what she was doing, even when it was quite warm. Had she been hiding the marks?

My thoughts were interrupted when I heard Annee say, "Fran, is that you?"

She was looking right at me and asking me that.

"Yes," I said. "How do you feel?"

"I don't know. Tired, I think, but distant, as if I'm far away."

"Well, you're right here. I've called Marsha, and I'll call her again to tell her you're awake."

"What happened?" she asked, suddenly alert. "Did they tell you anything?"

"Nobody's told me anything except to call them if you started throwing up."

"Ring the bell," she said. She was getting agitated. "I want to know what happened. I feel different, empty." Her mouth was quivering.

I rang the bell, and the nurse came running.

Annee was halfway out of bed by the time the nurse got there. I don't know where she thought she was going, but she certainly seemed determined to get there.

"*Non, madame,*" the nurse said, among other things, as she struggled to get Annee back in bed.

That was when I saw more of those marks, on Annee's legs. It was only then that I remembered that she kept her legs covered all the time, too, with thick stockings.

"The baby," Annee said, and then, "*L'enfant.*"

The nurse said something, finally, that quieted Annee and got her to get back into bed.

"The doctor is coming," Annee said. She was twisting the sheet—unconsciously, I was sure. "The baby is gone," she said, rubbing her stomach.

The doctor was a small, tidy man with close-cut steel-gray hair; thick glasses magnified his yellowish eyes. "Madame Rien," he said. "How do you feel?" His English was almost without an accent.

"Tired," she said. "I want to know what happened."

"Of course," he said. "The child is alive but small, two kilos."

"Alive?" she said.

"I would guess," he said, "that she was two months early."

"She? A girl? Will she live? Is she going to be all right?"

"She must stay here until she is bigger."

Annee's face was a mixture of confusion and delight. "I thought it was only the fifth month," she said.

"No," the doctor said. "If it had been that early, she wouldn't have survived. Especially since you were in such distress." Then he went on to explain to Annee that the placenta had been delivered first and that that was very dangerous to mother and child.

By the time the doctor left, he had extracted a promise

from Annee that she would stay in bed, and he told her that a nurse would be along to take her to see the child.

I sat there listening to all this, wondering how on earth Annee was going to take on this new facet of her life. But Annee was looking so pleased that I had the feeling that this was one area in her life where she would enjoy all the toil.

They brought a wheelchair and a blanket and helped Annee out of bed. I was told to follow. I was going to be able to see the baby, too.

Before we entered the nursery, Annee and I were told to wash our hands and were fitted with sterile gowns and masks.

The baby was in an incubator, and some kind of monitor was attached to her chest. She was wearing an incredibly small diaper and her tiny fists were moving in little jerks. Her eyes were barely open, her mouth was moving, and she was making little squeaks.

"Oh," Annee said, "she is so little, my *fillette*—little girl. Oh, see her hair."

It looked to me as if the baby had a little fuzz on her head, nothing I would call hair.

"Look," Annee said after the nurse detached the monitor and took the baby out of the incubator and gave her to Annee, whose face was a picture of ecstasy. "Just look at her hair. It's going to be red like Denis's."

I looked closer, and maybe I saw a tinge of red on the fuzz, but I wasn't at all sure.

After she had held the baby close to her face and kissed her and whispered to her and counted her fingers and toes, she said, "Fran, would you like to hold her?"

I have been afraid of many things so far in my life, but never the way I was afraid to hold that baby.

"She's too little. I'm afraid," I said, backing away.

"Babies are sturdier than you think," she said. "Just make a little cradle, like this, and be sure to hold her head."

My skin was crawling and I began to sweat as I got closer to Annee with my arms in the cradle posture that she had shown me. "Don't let go of her," I said. "I'll just help you hold her."

"All right," Annee said, laughing. "I won't let go. But

stop looking so terrified. She won't bite you." Annee's face clouded over for a second and then it resumed the smile, but something had passed through her mind that made her uncomfortable.

She put the baby in my arms and I felt something weird in my chest toward this helpless little creature.

"Do you feel comfortable?" Annee said. "Do you want me to let go of her?"

The baby seemed to fit right into the crook of my arm, and I pulled her closer to me as Annee let go.

"You should see your face," Annee said.

"I wonder if it is anything like yours was," I said. "A strange power these little things have over us."

"Yes," Annee said. "Wonderful and terrifying. They are so helpless and so demanding."

"This wasn't exactly the way we had planned the afternoon," I said, feeling more comfortable holding Annee's baby. But the baby wasn't comfortable; she started fussing and I got afraid again. "She's wiggling," I said with some alarm, because I was afraid she would wiggle right out of my arms.

Annee took the baby and started fussing over her again, and the baby stopped wiggling.

"She knows who her mother is," I said.

"Maybe," Annee said. "I never thought that I would have this baby. I kept thinking I would miscarry, and when I started with the pains today, I thought, Now it is happening."

"Well, if you thought you were busy before," I said, "just think of how busy you're going to be now."

"I've been thinking about that, thinking about who could do what at the inn, thinking about whether I could leave the inn in M. Saverne's hands most days. Now that I know he is such a good cook, thanks to you, I feel that I could leave him in charge."

"Surely you must have known he was a good cook. I got the impression he had been working at the inn for years."

"Mostly he worked with Denis, and Denis never talked about the Savernes in any other way except as helpers."

"But you worked in the kitchen with them."

"Ah, I was just another helper, too. Even when I made the ragout. But I know now how competent M. Saverne is, and I know I can trust him to run the kitchen. He is very grateful to you, Fran. You don't know what you did for that man. If he had it in his power, he would name a city in your honor. Maybe he will tack your name on the crêpe dish that made him famous."

I was laughing at the idea of the crêpe dish being named after me, when Annee suddenly looked at the clock on the nursery wall. "You missed them," she said.

"Missed who?"

"Odette and Bernadette. I was going to take you to see them practice."

"Well, it's not as if you were wasting your time."

"Tomorrow," she said, "I will give you instructions on how to get to the place where they practice. When you get close you will know, because there will be others there."

"Speaking of others," I said, "I have to tell Marsha and Madame Morvel the good news."

"Wait, let me tell them," she said.

"Sure," I said. "The nurse let you come this far, she ought to let you go use the phone." I thought this was as good a time as any to tell her whom I hadn't called. "I didn't tell Jacques that you were in the hospital," I said.

Annee nodded. "There's no hurry. Maybe I'll call him later."

The nurse came back to take the baby from a reluctant Annee, and we made the arrangements for Annee to use the phone. Annee spoke first to Marsha, and I could tell from the end of the conversation that I heard that Marsha was gushing. When Annee started speaking French, I knew that Laurence had wrested the phone from Marsha to do the Gallic version of the gush.

Annee seemed to be regaining her health by the minute, and by the time Laurence and Marsha had finished oohing and aahing, she was positively glowing.

In the back of my mind, though, there was a huge and very wet blanket that dissolved all the joy. And I knew it wouldn't be long before some of that dampness permeated Annee's consciousness. I tried not to let the gloom show in my face so that Annee could hold onto the magic a little longer.

But, of course, all the troubles came back to her in a flood when she hung up the phone and realized that the next call she had to make was to Jacques.

Nine

Annee could not reach Jacques at his home, because he had gone to his office in Paris immediately after the lunch at Chez le Rouquin. Her conversation was short and polite, with no mention of the baby, and I surmised that Niki was the one who had answered the phone.

I had asked Annee if she wanted me to wait somewhere else besides next to her wheelchair.

"No need," she had said. "I would just as soon you hear everything now."

I wondered what that "now" meant. Was it because she would need me more than ever now that she would be busy with the baby, or because she would tell me what she had been holding back?

Annee reached Jacques at his office, and the smile that she had on her face and in her voice disappeared before she got to tell Jacques her news.

A gasp caught in her throat, and she said, "What happened? . . . When? . . . Where? . . . Poison, again?"

I stood there stunned, knowing what had happened but not who had died this time. When she hung up, she told me.

"Monsieur Foyer was found dead this afternoon. Poison. The gendarmes are closing the inn so that they can examine all the food there."

"Was anyone else poisoned? There were a lot of people at the inn. If he was the only one, they should be asking what else he ate. They should—"

"We don't tell the police how to do their work. They

wouldn't listen anyway, and maybe they would arrest you for interfering.'' Her voice was bitter, and I thought surely she was thinking about her son trying to keep the gendarmes from arresting her the day before.

''Do you have any theories about the poisonings?'' I said. After all, at one time Annee was supposed to have been a good detective. ''Can you think of a connection between Denis, Laurence, and Monsieur Foyer?''

''I think that the poisoning of Laurence was accidental,'' she said. ''I have been trying to remember what food there was left over in the refrigerator after Monday. I thought the gendarmes had taken everything, but maybe there was something that they missed and it got into something that Laurence likes to eat.''

''What about Monsieur Foyer? What's the connection?''

Annee sighed. ''Well, he drank at the inn often, and he was very kind to Vincent when Denis and Vincent weren't getting along. But Monsieur Foyer was kind to all the children.''

''What kind of work did he do?''

''He worked with the schools and the villages, planning things for the children—the summer programs for swimming and sports, dances, picnics, fairs. He was busy all the time.''

''And he didn't have enemies?''

''The only time I saw him have words with anyone was that night at the inn when he and Arnaut almost came to blows.''

''What was that about anyway? Did you hear?''

''Monsieur Saverne said that Arnaut accused M. Foyer of fondling Odette.''

''You did tell me he was a flirt,'' I said.

''But no one took him seriously.''

''But Odette complained about him.''

''Yes, she did. But I can't think that Monsieur Foyer would have done anything serious.''

''But Odette is young. Maybe she didn't know how to take his flirting.''

''Maybe.'' Annee was starting to look tired, so I quickly got her back to her room and into bed. She lay back on the pillow and closed her eyes. ''I am tired,'' she said. Then her eyes popped open. "You know, I'm glad Vincent is in jail right now."

"Why?" I said. But I knew the answer before she told me. If word got out about the Arnaut-Foyer fight and that it was about Foyer flirting with Odette, the police would probably be suspecting Vincent of that, too.

Annee fell asleep before I could talk to her about the one suspect, Jacques Toute, who had motives to kill both Denis and M. Foyer. I wondered whether he had been questioned at all, since his wife had sold the suspected pâté to Denis. I was wondering, too, how much Annee had told the gendarmes about Jacques. Had she told them that Denis was having an affair with Jacques's wife? Or was she afraid to give the police information about someone who was powerful within the law enforcement community?

The nurse interrupted my thoughts. "Ah, *Madame Rien dort* [Madame Rien is sleeping]. *C'est bon*," she said. "*Et Madame Kirk vous attend* [And Madame Kirk is waiting for you]."

I didn't understand, but I heard the words "Madame Kirk," and I already knew that Annee had arranged to have Marsha come and pick me up.

Marsha kept asking me questions about the baby as she drove back to Annee's, yanking my thoughts away from the subject on which my mind was ruminating. I tried to get in the spirit of happy welcome for the new citizen, and I decided I would wait a while and tell Marsha and Laurence at the same time about M. Foyer.

In the car, as we drove back to Annee's from Coulommiers, where the hospital was, I gave Marsha a detailed account of what had happened to Annee, right down to the call for the ambulance and Annee's shock when she was told that there was a live baby whom she had been carrying a couple of months longer than she had suspected. I neglected, however, to mention the marks on her arms and legs.

I figured that I would let Marsha repeat the story to Laurence while I went back to my ruminating. Then, after they had digested the good news, I would tell them about M. Foyer.

But that wasn't to be, because when Marsha and I got

back to the house, the gendarmes were crawling over the place again, looking for poisons, I assumed. So I blurted out the news to Marsha as we approached the house and she was wondering out loud why the gendarmes were there again.

While Marsha and Laurence fluttered around the house, trying to stay out of the way of the policemen, I decided to try to get a feel of what was going on in this murderous little village. On the pretense of telling Odette not to come to work that evening, I called the Toute house.

Niki answered, but quickly relinquished the phone to Yves because he spoke "better the English," she said.

"Odette knows that the inn is not open tonight," Yves said. "M. Saverne has told her, but, of course, our father had told us before."

"Of course," I said, not trying to hide the sarcasm.

But Yves didn't notice. "Papa called us when the body was found," Yves said, sometimes halting as if searching for the next word, "this afternoon."

"Did he say who found the body?"

"Madame Foyer found him. She was going to meet him to watch Odette and Bernadette practice."

"Weren't there other people going to watch as well?"

"Yes, but Monsieur and Madame Foyer had a special place."

"You mean a place that was reserved for them?"

"Mmm, yes, I guess that is right."

"Was he found before or after the practice?"

"Before. There was no practice, of course."

"I've never been to watch the girls; where do they practice?"

He described the place, and told me how to get there from Annee's place. I thought I would be able to find it. The spot where M. Foyer was found would, no doubt, still be roped off.

The gendarmes had no problem with my leaving the house, and Marsha and Laurence were in such a dither that they didn't ask me where I was going.

Yves had told me that the hillside was next to the field of sunflowers, and I had noticed that field several times as I walked to the inn. A few trees and a hedgerow separated the sunflowers from the open pastureland next to it. On the other end of the sunflower field were woods.

There was no one around now, and I assumed that most folks were home having dinner. The shadows were lengthening, but darkness was still several hours away. As I got closer to the field, I could see the path worn down in the wild grasses. The path led up a rise and over the top and into a valley that nature had made into a miniature amphitheater. A few steps down into the bowl and suddenly the town was out of sight, except for two towers, one the steeple of the ancient church and the other holding the village water supply.

Even the highway noise, which I had noticed was an ever-present background sound in this little village between two main roads that led to other, bigger places, was silenced in this little world away from the world. Perhaps the quiet was what had originally attracted the girls to this place, a place where the notes of a flute would not be warped by the sounds of civilization.

A movement on the ridge at the other side of the valley caught my eye and startled me. I kept looking at the spot where I had seen the movement, but nothing came into focus, and nothing moved except the grass and the leaves in the evening breeze that was just picking up.

I was uneasy and was wishing that I had my .38 with me, but that was home in the closet in Cheektowaga, New York, the suburb of Buffalo where I lived. I hadn't even thought to try to get the gun through airport security—legally, of course.

I didn't see any place that had been roped off, and was beginning to think that the police had finished their work out here when I saw that movement on the ridge again and realized that there was something tied to a bush up there that was waving in the breeze.

In the event that someone was lurking in the area, I decided to climb up out of the valley and walk around the perimeter on the high ground. That way I would be able to see the town, and better yet, I would be visible to anyone from the town who happened to be looking in this direction.

I was visible, all right. Before I got halfway around, I had company in the person of a gendarme. He was just below the ridge, and possibly his hat had been visible before. Perhaps I had seen his hat as well as the piece of plastic, which I could now see was just a piece of a shopping bag caught on a bush. He waved me away and said something loud and bossy to me.

I used my favorite line: *"Je ne comprends pas."* ("I don't understand.") I was getting pretty good at saying that, even my accent, I thought.

He waved me away as if I were an annoying gnat, and I started down from the ridge. I didn't want to have to be rescued from the gendarmerie by Jacques again.

As I descended, I followed a path that was worn more deeply in the grass. This one headed toward the other end of town, where the Toute family lived.

There was something strange and rather wonderful about two young women creating such beauty that the people in the town quietly came to watch them. I was hoping that the terrible events of the past week wouldn't spoil it for the girls or for the townspeople.

Then I thought of the girls' father, and all the suspicions and uneasiness I harbored toward him were awakened again.

The gendarmes had roped off a spot next to the woods, which I could see now but couldn't see before, because the trees were below the line of the ridge and on the opposite side from which I had approached. I squinted toward the woods and could see two other men in uniform, and two in plainclothes, who were within the perimeter of the trees and almost lost in the shadows.

I kept a respectful distance from the cops at work, but I circled close enough to watch what they were doing. I thought it was strange that they were going over the ground so thoroughly, since it was a poisoning and clues to such a crime did not usually present themselves in the dirt. Maybe he had written a message in the soil while he was in his death throes.

While I was in a snooping mode, I took a detour to scout the Toute place, which I thought I would recognize from what Annee had told me about it. It was one of the biggest in the village, she had said, and the front of it, unlike the rest of the cement houses whose doors opened directly onto the garden path or, in some cases, the street, had a porch complete with pillars.

I spotted it from two hundred yards away, and probably if there had been a longer open space between the corner I turned and the house, I still would have been sure which house it was. A small French version of an American Federal style, sort of like Monticello, or Tara in *Gone With the Wind,* complete with its own little rise from which the inhabitants could survey the rest of humanity.

My intention was to walk past the house, just to get a look at it, but as I reached the corner of the yard, which was also huge by the standards of Vaudoy, Jacques pulled up in his Renault, a model that most of the French only envy, a Safrane. He stopped and got out and stood by the car.

"Wait for minute, please, Madame Kirk. I would like to speak with you."

I didn't particularly want to speak to him, but I couldn't very well tell him what I was thinking: that he was a tyrannical son of a bee and I would rather sit in an anthill than sit in a room with him.

He turned the car into the driveway and stopped in front of a metal gate in the concrete wall that surrounded the property. As if on cue, the front door opened and Bernadette ran out to open the gate.

I could hear Marsha in my mind saying, "It's a pleasure to see such well-behaved children." She said things like that, even though her one and only child had never been a model of deportment.

And then I got a wave of nostalgia for my high school days and the cutting up that her son and I had done whenever we were out of sight of a responsible adult. It's a wonder we survived. We hitchhiked with anyone who had a vehicle that moved, regardless of how seedy or disreputable the person looked. We had eyes for each other and no one else mattered. We were immortal, impervious to harm. And so happy.

I sighed and willed myself to the present. Bernadette moved like a kid in the middle of a growth spurt, gangly, thumping, clumsy, not knowing what to do with a new length of arm or leg. Although the sisters' faces were similar, Odette was small, well proportioned, and graceful, while the younger girl looked like a puppy who had not yet grown into its feet. I was reminded then of Clarisse, the other waitress, and her complaints about Bernadette. Perhaps the clumsiness had made Clarisse ill at ease, fearing a dropped pile of plates at any moment. Bernadette had that way about her. She was someone who would strike terror in the heart of the owner of a china shop.

Jacques drove his car through the gateway and parked on a concrete apron next to the garage. The yard was awash in color. Roses climbed the wall; pansies grew in little clumps next to the path, along with some sort of carnation in pinks and reds; and climbing a trellis on one side of the porch was a monster wisteria with its purple flowers drooping from the porch roof.

Bernadette closed one side of the gate and then stood by the second side looking at me with that impatient look that teenagers get when they're unsure of what they're supposed to do. Her father ended her uncertainty by shouting something at her in French.

Bernadette immediately said, "Please come in, madame."

Jacques waited for me to walk up the drive and we took the path to the front door several yards behind the retreating Bernadette.

"Please come in and join us for an aperitif," he said. "The officers are still busy at the Rien house. I will send Yves to get your mother-in-law and Madame Morvel to join us also."

Even though I knew it was a considerate thing for him to do, I still couldn't shake the idea that he was taking over and telling people what to do.

Before we got to the door, Niki appeared, wearing an apron and flashing a smile that could have made her rich if she had tried to market it.

Jacques rattled off some instructions to Niki and then walked past her and into the back of the house. I could hear more of his imperious tones when he found someone who would obey his instructions.

"Good evening," Niki said, pronouncing "evening" with three syllables. "Come into the parlor," she said, and

I wondered who had taught her English, and tried to remember the last time I had heard anyone call a living room a parlor.

"I am afraid that I don't speak English very well," she said.

I felt sorry for her, struggling as she was with every word. But I knew she spoke English better than I spoke French, so I decided to give her a sample of Madame Alain's teaching.

"*Je ne parle pas français très bien aussi*," I said, pronouncing syllables that the French usually slur over, and speaking in an accent that was not only American but also bore the stamp of western New York and probably had errors in grammar or syntax.

"*Pardon*?" she said.

I knew what that meant, but I was darned if I was going to go through the torture of repeating myself. Well, it's the thought that counts. "Your English is better than my French," I said.

She smiled again, and it was worth something to see that face light up. I don't usually get excited about a good-looking face. There are a lot of them around, even in France. But Niki's was a gem, an idealized version of what a pretty face should be, and there it was in the flesh, and beautiful flesh, too.

The Toutes parked me in the "parlor" and took turns coming in to sit with me while I drank something called Martini, which wasn't at all like a martini, thank heaven, but was like vermouth. It had been served with exactly one ice cube, and I noticed that each of the others also had but one ice cube.

When I served drinks at the inn on the first night, Annee had told me not to put too much ice in the glasses because the French were not used to it. But serving a drink with only one ice cube was carrying the consideration for French sensibilities too far.

Another thing I noticed was that Clement was given a drink about the size of one that a careful parent might give to a ten-year-old for a taste of what the grown-ups were drinking. And I remembered how silly he had been at the lunch after the funeral. I was betting that he had sneaked a few sips that his dad didn't know about.

Jacques had excused himself because he had to make some urgent phone calls, and Niki was busy in the kitchen, but she did take her turn entertaining the guest. The children came in two at a time usually, although Yves had gone to fetch Marsha and Laurence, and the others had duties in the kitchen. Although I offered to help, they insisted that no help was needed.

No one mentioned M. Foyer, and I didn't bring it up. Nor did anyone say anything about Annee. We spent the entire hour, from my arrival until the arrival of Marsha and Laurence, talking about the weather—it had been unseasonably hot so far this summer—and about food—if the heat continued, the wheat would be early and it would be an exceptionally fine year for the grapes and that meant good wine.

"We will be looking forward to the Beaujolais Nouveau in November," Clement said. Whenever it was his turn to come in and talk, he took great delight in teaching me French words and giggling at the way I pronounced them. When Bernadette was with him, she went along with the game, but Odette gave him a dirty look when he giggled, and so did Niki. I didn't mind his giggling, because he was taking the time to give me some French lessons, and because I found Clement to be the most charming of the Toute children, probably because I thought he was the most irreverent and, I was betting, the one who wiggled out from under his father's thumb the most.

When Marsha and Laurence arrived, the parlor filled up. Jacques had finished his phone calls and Niki had finished in the kitchen and all the children were in attendance at once, looking more spiffed up than they had been when I arrived. Perhaps all the spiffing had been taking place in between their turns in the parlor, but I didn't notice it until they were all together, all combed, all wearing tidy clothes that were tucked in. "Tucking in" was something young people weren't doing, not even in France. But no fad or peer pressure, I theorized, could overcome the pressure those kids got from Jacques.

Marsha and Laurence acted as if they were thrilled to be

invited to the Toutes'. Marsha spent some time salivating over the house and Laurence made a fuss over the Toute children.

But then the conversational floodgates opened wide, because Laurence truly loved children, and she couldn't wait to start talking about Annee's new baby, her grandniece. I wasn't surprised that everyone had heard about it. The surprising thing in Vaudoy was when somebody hadn't heard the latest bit of news.

During the part of the conversation in which the female hormones were discussed, I saw Jacques squirm in his chair. That was not an area where he felt comfortable, but he couldn't very well shut up his guests, and it was definitely a reasonable part of the discussion. I might even have prolonged that part of the conversation just a little so that he could wriggle around helpless for a change.

Odette, Bernadette, Niki, and Clement all pressed us to ask Annee when they could see the baby. Yves was a little more restrained, possibly trying on his father's mantle.

The next order of business was to think up names for the baby. That degenerated after a while into hilarity, with Clement suggesting names of American rock groups he liked to listen to.

It seemed that the whole family enjoyed Clement. He apparently was the least disciplined, as the babies of families often are. Even Jacques smiled as Clement came up with one outrageous name after another.

We had been chatting and sipping for at least an hour, and that made two hours of chatting and sipping for me, when Jacques was called to the phone.

When he came back, he said, "The officers are finished at your house, but please do not think about going right home. Niki has prepared enough dinner for us all, and we would love to have you join us."

At that he looked around at his family, and, right on cue, they said, "Oh, yes, do join us," and, "We're having so much fun," and, "Mother is such a wonderful cook; we're having coquilles Saint-Jacques, which was named after Father." The last was from the wag, Clement, and got everyone, including Jacques, laughing.

It had to be nine-thirty at least, and we were just sitting

down to dinner. My body was telling me to go to bed, but I was about to stuff it with strange and wonderful French food.

And it was wonderful. We all told Niki so. Jacques told us that Niki had been cooking all her life, since her parents owned the *épicerie* and she had been weaned on delicacies that most people eat but seldom. "She has discerning taste buds and an educated palate," he said proudly.

Niki sat all ablush, basking in the praise, while my bad angel kept talking to me about Niki having had an affair with Denis. I tried to remember if Niki had reacted at all to the conversation about Annee, the baby, or the hormones. I didn't recall that she had said much of anything. But with everyone else talking, it would have been easy to sit back and say nothing.

Despite all the jolly family goings-on, I was uneasy about eating what Niki Toute had prepared. I ate what everyone else ate, and paid close attention to how I felt as each mouthful went down. Hardly a relaxing meal. But I didn't refuse anything except the pâté. Even though everyone was enjoying it, I couldn't bring myself to taste it.

It was over dessert, a fruit *tarte* with Chantilly, that we finally got around to talking about poor M. Foyer.

Ten

It was Laurence who brought up the subject. And I think she was sorry she had the moment the words were out of her mouth. A stiffness seemed to descend upon the room, and there was much wriggling in chairs. To give the devil his due, it was Jacques who smoothed over the difficulty by explaining to us, the outsiders, what the rest of the family already knew.

"We have been trying not to think about this, madame," he said, "because the girls were very upset. They were on their way to the little field where they play when they met Madame Foyer, who had just found him."

Odette and Bernadette sat with horrified looks on their faces, as if reliving the events of the afternoon.

Laurence said something in French that sounded as if she were commiserating with the girls and apologizing for reminding them.

Odette pulled herself together and said, "It was quite terrible, madame. Please do not feel badly. We will have to talk about it with other people besides the gendarmes."

"We told Maman first," Bernadette said, her voice high and tight. "We ran to the shop and told her."

"I was in the shop when they came," Clement said. "They looked like wild animals. It made me afraid, seeing them. There were grasses stuck in their hair and their clothes from running through the woods."

Odette held up a piece of her hair on one side. "Maman had to cut out, what was that called, Papa, that was stuck in my hairs?"

"A bramble," he said, "or a thistle. One of those plants that catches in anything that brushes it."

"Burdock," Marsha said. "We have plants that do that. We call them burdocks."

Irrepressible Clement piped up at that moment with the word "Buttocks?" which was a word that you'd expect a seventeen-year-old to acquire when he was learning a new language.

The giggle that usually followed Clement's jokes was short-lived this time. Jacques, apparently, was not amused.

"Niki called me immediately at work," Jacques said, "and I called the gendarmes. The girls spent some time with the police this afternoon and they found it very trying."

"Was Monsieur Foyer on the way to watch the girls practice?" I said.

"That's what Madame Foyer said," Jacques said. "They often went to that little grove and had a picnic and then went to the practice."

"And how is Madame Foyer?" Laurence said. "The poor woman."

"After she was questioned, the doctor gave her a sedative," Jacques said.

"I will call her tomorrow," Laurence said, and clucked and shook her head.

"When will you practice again?" I said, looking first at Odette and then at Bernadette.

"*Jamais* [never]," Bernadette said. "I will not go there *encore*."

Niki stood up and put her hands on Bernadette's shoulders. "*Viens* [come]," she said, taking the girl's hand and pulling her.

Odette's eyes filled with tears. "Baba," she said, and followed her sister and mother from the room.

Clement, ever the caretaker of good humor, changed the subject adroitly. "Odette calls Bernadette Baba, and Bernadette calls Odette Dodo."

Yves decided that that was as good a subject as any to smooth over the gap. "They've been doing that since they were babies. Well, since we were all babies," he said with a look at his father, "at the same time, practically. I'm less than three years older than Clement."

Jacques chose to ignore the disparaging insinuation in Yves's reference to the rapid multiplication of the Toutes. "Niki was quite busy for a while," he said. "Now she is glad that she had the babies all at once so that they could grow up together."

I wanted to get back to the subject of M. Foyer, and I couldn't think of any graceful way to do it. So I did it clumsily. "Monsieur Foyer had so many friends, Annee told me. Who would want to kill him?"

"I would not want to kill him," Yves said. "But I was not his friend."

I looked at Jacques, expecting him to put the lid on this confession by one of his brood. But Jacques sat quietly, with only a slight narrowing of his eyes to show his displeasure.

"What didn't you like about him?" I said.

"He was always flirting with the girls." Yves was leaning forward in his chair, his indignation driving a mist of spittle from his lips. "Clarisse was in tears one day when he said something to her."

Jacques sat forward, obviously catching the notion that Yves's affection for Clarisse had exceeded the bounds he had set for his children's attachments.

And I was getting the idea that M. Foyer was not so harmless as Annee had indicated. He had upset both Yves and Odette with his flirting.

Jacques looked at his son and, with a cruel glint in his eyes, said, "Clarisse is a little trollop. Monsieur Foyer was probably taking his cue from those clothes she wears that make her look like a tramp."

Yves held onto the edge of the table, his knuckles whitening. Even Clement said nothing. It was obvious to everyone left at the table that Yves was barely in control of his temper.

Jacques sat back and waited while Yves struggled with the tides that were running strongly in his life. Tears of rage were gathering in Yves's eyes.

I was getting ready to take flight if the dam broke, the tension was so high in the room. I don't know what would have happened if Niki had not returned at that moment.

"Jacques," she said, "I'm sorry to interrupt." Then she said something in French, and I understood something about a pharmacy.

"I must excuse myself," Jacques said, "to go to the pharmacist for a sedative for the girls. Yves, you take the other car and drive the ladies home."

It was close to midnight before we got home, and then we were confronted with the disorder left by the gendarmes in their search for poison.

It wasn't that the cops had just thrown things around, but they had moved everything and then piled it. The piles were neat, but they were piles. Books, papers, clothes, anything that would stack was stacked. Most mothers would have been thankful to see a teenager's room that neat. But neatness doesn't mean things are in order.

Another mess the gendarmes left was the floors. They had been going in and out all afternoon and evening. That part of their mess they didn't try to clean. Gendarmes don't sweep floors.

Laurence was too fragile to have the energy to help clean up at that hour, and after about forty-five minutes of wading through the disorder, Marsha was ready to give it up.

"Fran," she said, "I can't go on any longer. I'll pitch in again in the morning. Why don't you go to bed, too?"

"I will," I said. "But I want to get the kitchen straightened out. Then, at least, we'll be able to have breakfast."

Marsha almost staggered up the stairs, and I went back to work. I wasn't tired at all, and I thought that it was because of all the tension at the Toutes'. That tight lid that Jacques was keeping on his kids had steam escaping all around it.

M. Foyer's reputation altered according to who was talking about him. And then there was Denis's reputation. The truth, whatever that was, seemed to lie with whoever spoke his or her version of it last.

I made a mental list of the people who spoke a little English who might be willing to talk to me. M. Saverne was high on it.

I worked for another hour, and it was close to 2 A.M. when I decided to call it quits. I had the kitchen in shape and I had closed the shutters. There was a mound of garbage, which I bagged up and wanted to get out of the house so that we wouldn't have to look at it in the morning.

I remembered that Annee put the garbage in a shed behind the house because, she said, the dogs that ran loose in the village were fond of ripping up the plastic bags and tipping over the garbage cans (*poubelles*) if they were left out.

The light at the back door was bright enough to show the way to the shed and keep me from stumbling on the rocks that made up the path.

There were four bags, and I put them all outside the door before I started carrying them back to the shed, which I had to unlock with a key that was kept near the back door to the kitchen. The bags were heavy, but I managed to carry two at a time, and they were sturdy enough so that I didn't worry about their breaking.

There were no other lights nearby, but down the road I could see a streetlight, one of the few streetlights in the village. All the other houses were shuttered and had no outside lights burning.

The first two bags had been deposited in the shed and I was returning with the other two when I heard a rustling sound, which seemed to be coming from the shed.

I stopped and listened. If an animal were near, it would probably do the same, stop and listen. I was wishing that I had a flashlight, and I couldn't remember just then whether I had seen one in the house. I quietly moved closer, but I heard nothing more. Then I decided that if it was an animal, maybe a little rustling would flush it out.

I shook the bags and made enough noise for any animal to get its bearings on where I was. No response. Then I put the bags just inside the door to the shed and tried to see inside. If there was an animal in there, I wanted to chase it out. But I didn't want the thing to spring out at me.

That was when I heard the breath, a quick intake of air. Then something hit me on the side of the head.

When I opened my eyes, I was trembling with cold, lying on the ground, covered with dew. Where I was, I hadn't the slightest notion. Nothing looked at all familiar. Of course, I was looking for things that were familiar in

Cheektowaga, not Vaudoy en Brie. A thundering ache had taken possession of my head, and I put my hand to the spot where it hurt the most. It was sticky. Then I remembered being hit.

The shed door was open; the back light was still on. Then I began to worry about whether whoever had hit me was still nearby. I tried to lift my head, but the pain knocked me back. This is serious, I told myself. You've got to get yourself some help.

I turned over onto my stomach and lifted myself onto my hands and knees. That action alone started me retching. I was really worried about myself, and everyone was asleep. I tried hollering, but that hurt, too.

I threw up and that gave me a few seconds' relief, during which I started crawling toward the kitchen. As I crawled, blood dropped on the backs of my hands. I knew that I was scratching my knees on the rocks, but I couldn't feel the pain in my legs because the hurt in my head kept my attention.

I had no thoughts whatsoever about who had done this to me; my whole focus was on getting someone to help me before I passed out, before I died. That was what I thought was happening to me. I was dying.

I didn't get to the kitchen. I was about halfway there when, instead of the rocks of the garden path, I saw in front of me two big black shoes.

With what was left of my strength, I screamed. Then I passed out.

Eleven

My eyes weren't focusing when next I opened them. People were looking at me, but their faces were warped, as if I were looking through a fun-house glass. Sounds weren't coming in too clearly, either. Voices had echoes that tumbled over one another, so that no words were distinct.

I moved my mouth and it felt like a cotton wad. "Water," I tried to say. But the sound I heard was something like, "Wawa," but not that clear.

Then I remembered that I had been whacked on the head, and I lifted my hand with the intention of feeling my head. But my arm felt like it was made of lead, and it never made it all the way to that thing sitting on my shoulders.

Somebody grabbed my hand and it scared me so that I pulled back and yelped. Then there were a lot of voices, how many I couldn't be sure because of the new sound system that had been installed in my head.

One thing I realized rather quickly was that my head was no longer aching. I wondered whether some important linkage in my nervous system had been short-circuited. Perhaps that was why my arm wouldn't work. Or maybe I was drugged. I pushed to the back of my mind the possibility that the damage was permanent.

I tried again to tell them, whoever they were, that I wanted water, with better results this time. "Warger," I think is what I managed. And within a minute, someone was lifting my shoulders and putting a cold glass to my lips.

I tried to gulp it, but the hand would let me take only one lunge at it before it was pulled away, spilling some on my chest.

"Not so fast," I heard quite clearly, and I nearly cried with gratitude. Maybe the cloud was lifting, I thought.

"Okay," I said, almost correctly. Consonants weren't my strong point just then. After that I politely sipped the water until the glass was empty. And by that time the glass started to come into focus, and then the hand, and then the face behind it, which belonged to a nurse who looked familiar, but I didn't know where I had seen her before.

Oh, I thought. I'm in a hospital. I don't know where I thought I was, but I do know that the realization came as a surprise.

"How do you feel?" the nurse said.

"Drugged," I said, but that was a hard one to say, and I don't know how to spell the sound that came out.

"Is your head hurting?"

"No, but I'm dopey," I said, but that was not exactly what came out. The nurse had a heavy French accent and I'm not sure her English was good enough so that she would have understood me even if I had spoken clearly.

I wondered what had happened to all the other people who had been in the room when I woke up, but then understood that it had been only the nurse and that I had been supplying the extra visions and echoes.

Just about the time when I was wishing for someone who could speak English to come in and help interpret my garbled sounds, Annee walked in.

"Annee," I said. ("Ahyee.")

She frowned. "You don't have to talk, Fran, if it's hard for you."

It wasn't hard for me to talk, but hard for everybody to listen, dammit. "I want to talk," I said. ("Ah wanh ha daw.")

Annee sighed. "I'm sorry, Fran, I can't understand. Do you want me to talk, and you can shake your head yes or no?"

I tried nodding slightly, and that seemed to work without hurting anything. Next time, I thought, I'll leave out the words.

"Let's see, what shall I tell you? How you were found?"
I nodded again.

"Monsieur Saverne found you in the backyard. He had come over to make sure everything was all right at the house. He knew I was in the hospital and he was going to ask you if you needed help. I guess you did."

I nodded, but I didn't know what she was talking about, or whom.

"The police say you didn't fall and hit your head, they think you were hit. The doctors say you could have been killed."

"Hit," I said, and it sounded pretty clear to me, except for the *t*.

"You were hit?" Annee said. "You remember being hit?"

I rocked my head up and down again.

"Oh, Fran, I'm so sorry you got involved in this. I can't think of who will be attacked next. Why would whoever it was attack you?"

I couldn't answer her, not only because I couldn't talk right, but because I couldn't remember much about before I was hit. What was the "this" that I had gotten involved in?

I remembered arriving at Annee's house and having dinner with Madame Morvel. I remembered a policeman named Jacques and some men fighting at a restaurant. I knew there was more, but I didn't know how much more. What had I done in the few days I was in France to make someone want to bean me?

I couldn't recall the places I'd been or most of the people I'd met. I tried to tell Annee about my state of mind, but I said, "Ah no memah," which was Franlish for "I don't remember."

I think she understood, because huge tears washed over her lids and down her cheeks. And because I was in a pitiable state and feeling sorry for myself, I joined her in a good cry. Why it is called a "good" cry, I can't figure.

The next person who came into the room looked very familiar and he made me feel uneasy. Was he the one who had hit me? Was I afraid of him? I couldn't identify the feeling he aroused.

When Anne called him Jacques, I remembered he was a policeman.

"It's hard for her to talk," Annee told Jacques. "She remembers she was hit, but I'm not sure what else she remembers."

Jacques came closer to my bed and I pulled the covers over my face. Nothing about the man made me feel right.

"Fran," he said, "I'd like to ask you some questions. I'll ask them so you can answer yes or no."

I stayed behind the sheet.

"Jacques is trying to help," Annee said.

I lowered the sheet just enough to see over it.

"Can you answer a few questions?" Jacques said.

"No," I said. It probably sounded more like "*Non*," but I was in France, and there was no mistaking my meaning.

"I'll come back later," he said. "Annee, will you be able to come back when I do? She seems to respond better to you."

He was talking about me as if I were some kind of lump. And then it occurred to me that I *was* some kind of lump. There were big pieces of me missing and I wanted them back.

The first thing I would have to do was try to talk right. And when Annee left, I practiced talking. I started with the letters of the alphabet, which took me a few minutes to bring to mind.

All that day and the next, I practiced talking. And when the nurse came to give me medicine, I refused to take it until the doctor came in and told me what each dose was and what it was for. When he got to the painkillers, I shook my head.

"But your head will hurt," the doctor said.

Slowly I formed the words to answer him. "Can't talk. Can't think."

"Ah," the doctor said. "Let me find something else for you. Something that will take away the pain but won't make you so sleepy."

"No. Maybe night."

"You want me to give you something at night but not during the day?"

I was about to say the word that I had been embarrassed

by but I had been practicing. "Yesh," I said. Well, it was better than "Yef." When my tongue got a little thinner, I would be able to get it right.

My efforts were so concentrated on learning to talk again that I didn't count the days. And I didn't know how long I had been unconscious, either. I was in my own little world, doing my own rehab. Nobody bothered me, and nobody came to see me. The nurse told me several times each day that Annee had called the hospital and asked whether she could come, but each time I told her no.

And one morning they let me take a bath, and I was lying in a huge tub of warm water, feeling layers of skin peel off. Suddenly I remembered the feel of my body, the way it had felt before I got clobbered, and then I remembered everything. My mind was clear and I was sure that when I opened my mouth to speak, the words would all come out right.

The first thing I wanted to know was what day it was, something it had not occurred to me to ask all the while I was numb.

"Nurse," I called. "I'm better. I remember. Call Annee. I want to talk to her."

Once I started talking, they couldn't stop me, but being medical people, they didn't want to stop me. The nurses were all chattering and smiling and they called the doctor.

By the time I was back in my room, they had a woman there who spoke English and carried a notebook. She was small and trim-looking, with dark hair pulled back at the nape of her neck. Her eyes were round and were rimmed with long, dark lashes. The irises were a gold color speckled with brown. She wore a white coat that was long and shapeless, but she had enough shape underneath it to make it look fetching.

She asked me questions and wrote down my answers. She was interested to know when my memory had returned, and how it had returned, and what my thoughts had been during the days when I wouldn't see anyone.

I told her how I had suddenly remembered, and I tried to recapture the feeling of knowing everything all at once. I was so happy to be talking.

After I had talked for it seemed like hours, I asked her

who she was. She introduced herself as Dr. Berenger, a psychoanalyst. She said she thought I was an interesting person, and I got a nice, warm feeling. Then she told me that she would like to continue to talk to me while I was in France.

How could I refuse?

"What day is it?" I said. "How long have I been in the hospital?"

"Two weeks," she said. "You arrived Sunday, the tenth of July, and today is Sunday, July twenty-fourth."

"Two weeks?" I shrieked. "What's been happening in those two weeks?"

Dr. Berenger smiled in an impish sort of way and said, "Well, there was Bastille Day on the fourteenth."

I calmed down a little in response to her injecting a bit of normality into the conversation. But then my mind started racing. I thought about my arrival in France, my first visit to Europe, which was supposed to last a week. My return ticket was nonrefundable. Annee had had a baby. M. Foyer had been killed.

What had happened since someone had hit me on the head? And who had hit me? And why? Was I still in danger? Was I in more danger now that I had my memory back? And what was it that I could remember that would put me in danger?

All I wanted to do was get out of the hospital and back to my life. I had to call my office in Buffalo and tell Natasha and Delia, who shared my office, where I was and what had happened. I had to call Ted, my significant other, too.

Marsha. What had happened to Marsha? Was she still in France? Her ticket was nonrefundable, too. I felt buried in loose ends. I started to tell Dr. Berenger, but there was too much to tell. I stopped and asked her when I could leave the hospital.

She said that now that I had regained my memory I could leave soon. She said my head was healing nicely but that I would have to be careful of certain activities. The doctor would give me a list of things to avoid and medicine to take whenever I felt pain or dizziness.

No sooner had Dr. Berenger left than Annee arrived. She

walked in wearing a big grin. "They told me," she said. "Thank goodness you're better. I was so worried about you."

"But what's been happening to you? Have they caught the murderer? Have they found out who hit me? How is Laurence? Where is Marsha?"

"Wait, wait. I'll tell you. One thing at a time.

"Laurence is fine. Marsha has got her taking a walk every day."

"Marsha is still here?"

"Yes. She called the airline and they make exceptions for people when there are drastic circumstances. And yours was surely a drastic circumstance."

"She didn't by any chance call Buffalo to tell the people in my office what happened? And my dog, Horace. Who's taking care of him?" Usually when I go away, the paperboy, Wally Klune, and his family take care of Horace. They even took him camping with them once. But they don't usually have the dog stay in their house. Wally walks Horace and feeds him and takes him on his paper route. I had told Wally I would be gone a week. I had visions of Horace starving to death or dying of dehydration, not to mention what kinds of messes he would have made before he passed away.

"Marsha called your office and a woman there said she would take care of everything and you shouldn't worry. There are several cards and letters for you that have arrived from the States. What was the name of the woman in your office?"

"Natasha," I said.

"That's the name," Annee said. "Natasha. Lovely name. I've been thinking of lots of names lately." Annee smiled, almost a smirk.

"The baby," I said, remembering the little creature I had held in my arms briefly. "How is she?"

"Little Frances is fine," she said, beaming at me.

It took a few seconds before I realized what she had said. "Frances? You named her Frances?"

"Yes. And now you must stay for her christening. I would like you to be her godmother."

It was hard for me to identify the feelings that were

erupting in me at that moment. An obligation was being thrust upon me, but it was a delightful obligation. The combination was new to me.

"I would like that," I said. "I've never been anyone's godmother."

"Good," she said. "Frances will be getting out of the hospital soon. I'll have the christening a day or so after she comes home."

Home, I thought; it had a nice ring to it. But it was the place where Denis had been murdered and I had almost been murdered.

"Is there anything new on the murders?" I said.

"Yes, yes. They have let Vincent out. He mustn't go back to Paris, because they are not finished questioning him, but they have dropped the charges against him."

"Why? Have they found out something new?"

"Yes. Oh, there is so much to tell you. Where do I start?"

"What have they found out to make them drop the charges against Vincent?"

"One thing they found was that the poison that killed Denis and Monsieur Foyer was the same poison, but it was not rat poison. The laboratory found it was a poisonous mushroom."

"Do they think the poison was administered purposely or do they think it was an accident?" I said.

"If you had not been hit on the head, they might have leaned toward the accident theory. But since you were hit, and since with this mushroom one would have to eat a lot of it for it to cause death, they are still talking about murder."

"Is there a theory as to why I was hit on the head?"

"I haven't heard one, but I have my own idea."

"I have one, too. You go first."

"I think maybe someone was in the shed trying to plant evidence that would incriminate me or Vincent."

"Is there someone who would want to kill Denis and Monsieur Foyer and also have a grudge against you or Vincent?"

"There is Robert Arnaut, of course. And the officers have been talking to him."

"What about the guy who runs the other restaurant? Bouton. That was his name, wasn't it?"

"Pierre Bouton, yes," she said, nodding. "He didn't like Denis, and I think at one time there was some argument he had with Monsieur Foyer."

"Let me guess," I said. "Was the argument about Foyer flirting with Bouton's wife?"

Annee looked surprised. "How did you know?"

"How could I not know the man was a flirt? Everybody knew it."

"But he didn't mean anything by it."

"Everyone didn't think he was so harmless as you think he was."

I could almost see the wheels turning in Annee's head. I hoped she would get to the conclusion I had drawn before I had to tell her.

"So both Denis and Monsieur Foyer were known as flirts, and someone could have wanted them both dead for that reason?"

"I don't know," I said. "But we were looking for some link between them." Then I told her how irritated Yves had become when he spoke about M. Foyer flirting with Clarisse.

"I was wondering whether he and Clarisse were seeing one another," she said. "Jacques will be furious."

Then I told her what Jacques had said about Clarisse, how he had called her a trollop and said she dressed like a tramp.

"Jacques is a difficult man," she said.

"I think he's in love with you." I didn't get subtle. I just barged in.

Annee raised her eyebrows and opened her mouth. "So he says," she said.

"So he has brought up the subject with you?"

"Many times," she said.

"How long has this been going on?"

She sighed. "On and off since I came to France. Since Denis's death, the subject has come up frequently."

"But what about his wife and his family?"

"I don't think anyone knows," she said. "Nothing has ever happened between us. Not even one kiss."

"But if I could detect his affection in the way he looks at you, other people could."

"You are more observant, Fran. You must know that."

"I may be observant, but I'm not the only observant person on the planet. What about Niki? Or Denis? Could that be the reason they got together? Because they could read Jacques's glances at you?"

"No, no, nothing like that. Why, if Denis had had the slightest suspicion, he would have screamed it at me. And he would have . . ."

A picture flashed through my head at that moment, a picture of Annee's arms and legs when she was in the hospital just after the baby was born. Those marks. Those weird marks. "What did he do to your arms and legs?" I said. "What were those marks?"

Annee covered her face with her hands for a brief minute. "I hate to think about that. It makes me nauseated, makes me ashamed, makes me furious, makes me glad he's dead." Annee was twisting her hands, shaking her head, making low moaning sounds, and gritting her teeth.

I didn't push her any further. I didn't know what the marks were, but I knew now that Denis had made them, and if I thought about it a while, I probably could figure out how. But thinking about it gave me the creeps.

"When did it start?" I said after a minute or two had gone by.

She was biting her lip so hard that it started to bleed. When I told her that her lip was bleeding, she laughed, a deep, guttural sound that was unpleasant, almost nasty. "He's done digging his teeth into me," she said, not to me, but to some presence that she was in contact with. "So now I bite into myself."

Then, in a split second, she was herself again, but she continued with the conversation as if she hadn't gone into another world. "It was exciting at first," she said, "and didn't leave such marks. But he got more and more vicious. Every Monday, on our day off. He used to say it was our feast day." She laughed her nasty laugh again, but this time I interpreted it as a way to put distance between herself and the subject.

I didn't know what to say. I was embarrassed, grossed

out, disappointed, maybe, that she had let it happen to her. And that feeling wasn't new to me. Every time another woman would come to the battered women's group and tell her story, I would get that same disappointed feeling.

It wasn't about the women, I finally realized. It was my own disappointment with myself. How had I let myself get into the relationship I had with Dick Kirk? How had I let him take over my life? How did I get to the point where I couldn't figure out what other options I had?

Well, I had come a long way, and I guessed that Annee had her own path to choose. "Those marks," I said, "had you seen them on other women?"

She nodded.

"How could you be sure?" I wasn't comfortable with the subject, but I forged on, thinking that there might be something important about it.

"I knew those marks," she said. "And no one else could have made them." Annee's face had gone hard. "His front teeth were crooked. The marks were distinctive." She rolled up her sleeve and revealed a scar that clearly showed the outlines of crooked teeth.

The picture that rolled through my mind was of Annee looking at other women's arms and legs, inspecting them for the imprint of her husband's crooked teeth. How much of this did the gendarmes know? I wondered.

When the subject was motive, Annee still looked like a suspect in her husband's death, but not in M. Foyer's, at least from what I had found out so far.

Annee was reading my face, and possibly my mind. "I may have had a motive to kill Denis, but I didn't," she said. "And I didn't have the opportunity, and I certainly don't know anything about mushrooms."

"What do you mean you didn't have the opportunity? I thought you were having supper with him when he died."

"I had just come home. He had done the shopping for our supper. He always did the shopping on Mondays. He would go to the *épicerie*, the one owned by the Bouche-grandes, Niki's parents. It's supposed to be our day off, but often I work with the Savernes during the day. That Monday, Monsieur Saverne and I were at the inn very late because Madame Saverne was not there. The police know all this. They checked my story with the Savernes.''

''I don't know what I can do to help you,'' I said. ''So far, I haven't found out anything useful, I can't talk to half of the people who might be able to tell me something, and I've managed to almost get myself killed.''

I was starting to feel sorry for myself, and I didn't realize it, but I was tuckered out from all the talking I had done.

When the nurse came in and shooed Annee out, I fell asleep almost immediately.

The next day I would go home, the nurse said. ''You'll have plenty of time to talk then.''

Twelve

That night I dreamed about mushrooms, giant ones, as big as atom-bomb clouds, but they had teeth marks in them and under them were piles of bodies. Annee was walking among them, and she was putting up tables so that she could serve her customers. I was supposed to help her get the bodies out of the way so that she could open the inn for lunch. I suppose that dream meant something.

But there are several theories about dreams. Some people go to great lengths to interpret them and have a lexicon of dream symbols. Other theorists say that dreaming is just a way to toss out the mental garbage. I was leaning toward the latter theory the next day when the memory of the dream popped into my mind as I was eating breakfast from the tray.

The food was fancy for hospital fare—ham omelet, bread and strawberry jam, coffee that wasn't half bad, and orange juice that tasted as if it were freshly squeezed. I was ravenous and ate every crumb. When the nurse came in to take the tray, she looked at me and then at the clean dishes and said she would get me more coffee and bread. I didn't refuse.

I was finishing the seconds when Annee came in.

"You're here early," I said.

"I come early every morning to feed Fanny." Her smile was beautiful, almost saintly. How could anyone think she had killed her husband? And then I remembered her strange laugh from the day before and wondered what other chameleon acts she had in her repertoire.

101

I was getting a jolt out of the fact that that little person was wearing my name. And I was glad that no one had decided to hang the nickname Fanny on me.

"How many times a day have you been doing that?" I said.

"I come three times and I deliver milk for the in-between feedings."

It took me a minute to figure out what she was talking about. My first reaction was that she was playing milkman. I don't know much about babies, and it's not a subject that I have ever warmed to. Maybe it's because my mother always told me what a big job children were. Heck, she had only one, and I was it. I always assumed that I wore her out.

"Just what you need," I said, "more work."

"The work for Fanny is a pleasure. And Vincent is a big help. He is so different now that Denis is gone." Her face took on a puzzled expression, but it was fleeting. "How soon can you be ready?" she said. "I can take you home now or I can come back and get you around noon."

"Now," I said. I got up and went to the closet, where I had seen my street clothes hanging. But when I pulled them out, they were stained and dirty, and I remembered that I had spent some hours lying on the ground in them. "Oh," I said, "my clothes."

"I brought some," she said, holding up a bag.

I didn't move as fast as I thought I would. Hanging around a hospital doesn't do wonders for one's stamina. I hadn't jogged in weeks, I had been recovering from a nasty injury, and I'd been spending a lot of time in bed. I felt like a klutz. Even putting on my clothes seemed hard to do, a foreign set of movements.

"You don't have to hurry so much," Annee said. "I don't have to be anywhere soon."

"But I do," I said. "I want to put this place behind me."

"Ah," she said, "and I like to come here. It's where I got the nicest surprise of my life."

I was almost dressed and I realized that Annee had brought an outfit that I had worn one day to work at the inn. She had seen me wear the shirt (black-and-green cotton paisley) and slacks (black cotton) together, so I guess she thought I liked the outfit, but really, I had chosen it because it wouldn't show spots if I got dirty at the inn.

I packed up the dirty clothes in the bag that Annee had brought, and I was ready to make tracks when the nurse came in with another bag.

"Medicine," she said. "Instructions in the sack." She smiled.

"Thanks," I said.

"Also," the nurse said, "you must come for Dr. Berenger." She pointed to the bag. "In the sack."

I assumed that my appointment with the doctor was written on something inside the bag.

When I got home—I was calling it home even though I had spent more time in the hospital than I had spent at Annee's house—I got another surprise. Marsha was speaking some French. And she could understand some of what was said when people spoke French. I actually felt jealous.

"Laurence has been teaching me to speak right," Marsha said, "and I have been helping her with her English."

"Lucky you," I said. "I just spent a couple of weeks trying to speak English." I didn't mean it to sound as cranky as it did.

"Poor Fran," Marsha said. "I'm feeling so guilty about pestering you to come with me."

That was the first inkling I had that she knew she had been a pest, and it made me madder at her than I had been. It's one thing to be a pest and be unconscious of it, but quite another to be a pest and know darn well you're being a pest and be a pest anyway. I was sure she had fessed up to feeling guilty so that I would say something to ease her guilt, but I wasn't feeling like being kind to her. "I'm not feeling so good myself," I said, and started up the stairs to my room.

"We'll call you when lunch is ready," Marsha said to my back. "If you don't feel well enough to come down for lunch, we'll bring it up."

"Marsha and I have been cooking good things," Laurence said.

At that I turned around. "Thanks," I said. "I'll look forward to it. And I'm sure I'll feel well enough to come down."

I spent a few minutes sorting out my clothes and then lay down on the bed to rest for a minute. The next thing I knew, Marsha was standing by the bed asking me whether I wanted lunch brought up after all.

Lunch with Marsha and Laurence was grilled slices of duck with a cherry sauce, followed by a mixture (they called it a mélange) of vegetables in a butter-and-wine sauce, followed by salad, followed by cheeses—including a Pont l'Évêque that had so many tastes that my mouth was tingling—followed by a pear tart with chocolate sauce.

There was a red wine from the Loire Valley that Laurence told us she buys a couple of cases of every year and keeps them for several more years before she drinks them. But before I drank the one glass that I would let them pour for me, I checked the instructions in my bag of medicines, instructions notable for their lack of syntax and wonderful mixture of French and English. "Two *par jour* [per day]" and "not *avec du lait* [with milk]" were clear enough, but "leaving various *jours sans* distress" I couldn't figure out. When Annee had read it, she thought it meant I could take it or not, as I pleased.

While we were running the wine over our tongues with appreciation, Marsha informed me that there was a wine cellar in the basement, called a *cave*, where Denis and Annee and Laurence had a huge store of wine.

"Denis had a very good nose," Laurence said with a sigh. "But it sometimes was where it shouldn't be."

My eyebrows went up at that comment, because I wondered what Laurence knew about Denis's wanderings. I didn't think Annee had ever spoken to Laurence about the subject, and I was trying to think of a way to keep her talking about Denis's nose and where it shouldn't have been. But Marsha spoke up first.

"I've been hearing things since Denis died," Marsha said. "Of course, I've told Annee about them."

"What things?" I said.

Laurence wiped her mouth on her *serviette* and stopped chewing.

"Shocking things. Right, Laurence?"

"*Vraiment* [indeed]," Laurence said.

"Tell me," I said. I felt like a kid being teased by an older child.

"Well," Marsha said, milking the suspense, "I was working at the inn and I heard Clarisse tell Odette that Denis had raped one of her friends."

"Rape? You heard her say this in French and you understood?"

"I pretend not to know as much French as I do," Marsha said. "I hear a lot that way."

My estimation of Marsha grew exponentially. I had never figured her for that much guile.

"What else did you hear? Did you get the name of Clarisse's friend?" I said.

"No," Marsha said. "And I don't think there was a friend."

"What do you mean?"

Marsha and Laurence exchanged conspiratorial looks. "Laurence and I talked about it," Marsha said.

Laurence nodded.

"You know how sometimes people want to tell you about themselves," Marsha continued, "but they can't own up to whatever it is they want to tell you about, so they manufacture a friend who had this misfortune. And Clarisse wouldn't say anything about something like that, because she needs the job."

"Her parents are very poor," Laurence said.

"So you and Laurence think that Clarisse was raped by Denis?"

"We think it's possible," Marsha said. "But we do know that Clarisse says he raped somebody, even if she won't say she was the one."

I got a picture in my head just then of Yves Toute's face when he had spoken of Clarisse being in tears because of some remarks that M. Foyer had made. What would Yves have done if he had known Denis had raped Clarisse?

"You didn't question her about it?" I said.

"No," Marsha said. "I don't want her to know that I understand French. I'm doing some undercover work for Annee."

Laurence laughed. "And she's very good at it."

"What's going on?" I said. "What's been happening since I went to the hospital?"

"Well," Marsha said, and if she gave me one more damn "well," I was going to bop her, "where should I start?"

"Annee already told me about the poisonous mushrooms and that Vincent was let out of jail." I thought I could hurry her if she didn't have to repeat what I already knew.

"Well, Vincent has been working at the inn, and he started to go over the books."

"Vincent is very good with figures," Laurence said. She beamed when she spoke his name, and I hoped the kid was worthy of her affection. Obviously his father hadn't been.

"And he found out that there was money missing," Marsha said.

"But wasn't Denis cooking the books?" I said.

"This was since Denis has been gone," Marsha said. "And Annee thought that someone might say something in front of me that they wouldn't say in front of her or Vincent."

"What else have you heard?"

"Well, nothing that would help Annee find out what's happening to the money. And mostly I get to hear Odette and Clarisse, because Annee has me helping in the dining room. We've been very busy lately. Monsieur Saverne is doing a wonderful job running the place."

We were finishing dessert by this time and I sat back to listen to Marsha tell about some of the conversations she had overheard between Odette and Clarisse. Marsha was quite funny imitating the young girls and their exaggerated ways of saying things.

Apparently Odette and Bernadette had sufficiently overcome their discomfort about the place where they practiced, because they had started their rehearsing in the little hollow again, Marsha said.

"And Yves comes up in the conversation quite a lot," Marsha said.

"I'm not surprised," I said. "Are Yves and Clarisse seeing one another?"

"Yes, and Odette helps them arrange their meetings. She tells her father that Yves is taking her to school and she gets a ride with someone else, and Yves goes to see Clarisse in the morning. You should see the looks they give each other while they are working at the inn,'' Marsha said. "Love is wonderful.''

"*Vive l'amour*,'' Laurence said.

As long as it isn't lethal, I thought.

"Speaking of Jacques,'' Marsha said, "he wants to talk to you about what happened the night you were hit. He said you wouldn't talk to him in the hospital.''

"Oh,'' I said, recalling his visit before my memory had come back. "I can remember being afraid of him.''

"That's what he said. But you're not afraid of him now, are you?'' Marsha said.

"No, but I don't feel exactly easy with him, either.'' I didn't say that I thought he had a strong motive for killing Denis—make that two strong motives. I couldn't figure out the mushroom angle, though. And I didn't know what his motive would be for killing M. Foyer.

"I understand,'' Laurence said. "I am also not comfortable about him.''

"I think he's a lovely man,'' Marsha said. "And he is so good to Annee.''

Laurence gave me a look at that moment that told me she had noticed Jacques's affection for Annee. And I wondered whether she thought Annee returned that affection. I wanted to blurt out what Annee had told me about Jacques, but I settled for, "If the poison is killing men who flirt, maybe Jacques is on the list, too.''

"But not me,'' Laurence said with a sarcastic smile.

"I forgot about you,'' I said. "Of course not you. But you didn't get a big dose of it. Did you figure out how you got hold of the poison? The police took all the food, didn't they, after Denis died? What did you eat the night you got sick?''

"From the kitchen. Annee always prepares—'' Laurence stopped in mid-sentence.

"You couldn't think that Annee did that?'' Marsha said, an edge to her voice.

"I was thinking of the pâté,'' Laurence said. "I thought Annee had left it for me.''

"What pâté?'' Marsha and I said together.

Laurence was agitated and her English got spotty. Marsha and she talked in their mixture of English and French, and Marsha translated when I couldn't catch the drift of the conversation.

What Laurence remembered was that the night she got ill, she had come downstairs after she and Marsha had gone up to bed. The pâté was on the kitchen table. She tasted it, and it was delicious, but she couldn't eat much of it because of the big dinner we had all had earlier that night.

I remembered the huge dinner. Madame Morvel was a champion eater, to have gotten even a little hungry again that night.

"What happened to the pâté?" I asked. "I don't remember seeing one when Annee and I found you."

"*Mais je ne sais pas* [But I don't know]," Laurence said.

"Does that mean someone was in the house to deliver the pâté, and in the house again after you ate it?" I shivered, thinking that someone was watching the house for his chance to get in and out.

"And you haven't told the police this yet?"

"*Non, non.*" Laurence started speaking rapidly in French.

"And you thought they would think that Annee had made it?" Marsha said.

"And they were looking for something that Annee had brought you," I said, thinking that at that point the gendarmes had made up their minds about Annee.

"Of course," Marsha said.

"And whoever came into the house that night might have been hiding in the shed that Saturday night when I was putting out the garbage. And it wasn't the first time he had been prowling around out there."

"The shed is locked," Laurence said. "Denis wanted it to be locked."

I was trying to remember whether I had had to unlock it that night to put the trash in it. Yes, I had. But what had I done with the key? "The key to the shed," I said. "I used it that night."

"Gone," Marsha said. "Annee put a new lock on it."

I didn't know whether it was important, but I wanted to remember where I had put the key. I told Marsha and Laurence that I wanted to jog my memory and went out in the

backyard. Even though it was daylight, waves of fear broke
over me when I looked toward the shed.

I took the path to the shed, inspecting the ground that I
had walked on that night. The person who hit me probably
had been watching me. After I had taken the first two garbage bags to the shed, perhaps he thought I was finished
and had forgotten to relock the shed. So he had gone into
the shed to look around, and when I came back with the
other two bags, he banged me on the head. Maybe he had
worried that he would get locked in.

I retraced my steps to the kitchen and went to the hook
where the key was kept. There was a bright new key. I took
it and went out to the shed and unlocked it. Then I put the
key in my pocket, and it was such an automatic gesture that
I thought surely that was what I'd done the last time.

I locked up the shed, returned the key to its hook, and
went to my room to find the clothes I had worn that night.
I pulled them out of the laundry hamper, where I'd put
them earlier, and examined the pocket of the jeans I'd worn.
I don't know what I hoped to find, a fingerprint, a dirty
smudge, a tear, but there was nothing I could identify as a
mark made by someone looking in my pocket for a key.

Of course, the person who had hit me didn't need the
key once I was knocked out. Unless he wanted to come
back again. But where was the key? I guessed it could have
fallen out of my pocket when they took off my clothes at
the hospital.

And then I felt embarrassed at the thought of people
undressing me while I was out cold. And the thoughts of
all the other invasions of one's privacy that happen in a
hospital crowded in on me and I felt really rotten and vi-
olated.

By the time I got back downstairs, Marsha and Laurence
had finished the dishes. I was surprised to see Laurence
working in the kitchen, because I had gotten the impression
that she was waited on most of the time. Another surprise
was the way Laurence was moving. She no longer had that
slow, painful waddle of the very obese.

I didn't know whether she would be insulted if I told her
I thought she had lost weight. Obviously there were some
cultural differences that I knew nothing about. In America

everybody liked being told they had lost weight, but in France it might be insulting. "You're looking healthy," I said, and immediately wondered whether she would infer from that that I thought she hadn't looked healthy before.

"I am getting very healthy." She smiled and looked at Marsha.

"We walk every day after lunch. Do you want to join us? We walk to the place where the Toute girls practice. Did Annee tell you they are practicing there again?"

"Yes," I said. "But they practice later in the day, don't they?"

"Now they practice after lunch. About two," Marsha said. "Niki comes with them while the *épicerie* is closed in the afternoon."

"I'll put on walking shoes," I said. "I'd like to see the girls perform. I'm told it is a wonderful sight."

"Ah, yes," Laurence said. "Very beautiful."

But it was not all beauty at the little hollow in the fields.

Thirteen

We took a different route to the field from the one I had taken when I had been given directions by Yves, who no doubt never gave it a thought that people couldn't walk through fields and paths made up of uneven terrain. Laurence, although she was considerably more mobile than before, was still not up to the route to which Yves had directed me.

Consequently, we went on streets that I hadn't been on, and I got to see a different part of the village. We went past an ancient fountain, which, Laurence told us, was where women used to come to do the washing before there was such a thing as running water in houses. There was a large rectangular stone tub to which water flowed from the fountain and from which the water flowed into a stream. Now the tub had too many cracks in the stone to hold water, and the dam of the sluiceway was always open.

Near the fountain, at the corner of two of the town's main roads, was a memorial to those who had died in the world wars. It was apparently built after World War One and said: *À LA MEMOIRE GLORIEUSE DES ENFANTS DE VAUDOY MORTS POUR LA FRANCE* 1914–1918. Below that inscription was a marble plaque that had been added after World War Two that read: 1939-1945, and then listed six names. On the sides of the monument were plaques listing the names of the men who had been lost in World War One; there were twenty-two of them.

Laurence told us that such memorials were common all

over France. "Every *ville* has such a memorial," she said. "France lost so many in the first war."

I got to thinking what it would be like to have a war fought right where you were used to living. I couldn't imagine house-to-house combat in Cheektowaga or tanks rolling down the Thruway or bombs dropping on factories and bridges and houses.

There was plenty of time for thinking on the walk, because Marsha and Laurence were not breaking any speed records. If I hadn't just got out of the hospital, I would have been chafing at the bit to go faster. As it was, in my infirm condition, I was wishing for more haste.

There was one more landmark, the church, which Laurence told us about, but I wasn't listening very attentively. I just knew that it was old and in poor condition. Birds were nesting in the holes between the ancient stones, and the windows were covered with chicken wire to protect them from getting broken.

Laurence was saying something about Mass being said there once every three weeks, because there was only one priest who traveled around to the various churches. As we passed the front entrance, which was barred by a locked gate, we could see a light fixture hanging over the stone arch with one wire that went down the wall to an outlet that was crudely attached to the wall. On a bulletin board there was a notice from "*Le Curé de la Paroisse*"—the parish priest.

I couldn't have walked anyone through any part of Cheektowaga and given the history of a church or a fountain or a memorial. I thought that maybe I'd take a look around my town when I got back and find out more about its history.

We finally got to the path I had taken when I left the field last time. That was the smoother path, and the one that most people used, apparently. Other people were on the path, all of whom greeted and were greeted by Laurence, and some by Marsha, who had made herself at home while I was lost in some netherworld.

A couple of families had laid blankets on the grass and looked like they were finishing up picnics. A few comfort lovers had brought their own chairs. Most of the people, however, stood or found some stump or rock or congenial patch of grass to sit on. The Toute girls were nowhere in sight, but I was assured by Laurence and Marsha that they would be there any minute.

I saw people I recognized from the lunch after the funeral and from the inn, Mme. Saverne among them. Yves Toute was there, hovering near the path. Was he waiting for his sisters or for Clarisse? I wondered.

I saw Robert Arnaut there, too, but he wasn't standing with the rest of us. Instead he was lurking in the bushes near where M. Foyer's body had been found. He seemed to have something on his mind other than watching the girls perform. He was looking along the ground for something one minute, glancing over his shoulder the next, and then watching the paths to see who was approaching.

Suddenly there was a flutter and everyone sat down, even the children, who had been running around and carrying on in ways that children, even French ones, do. Laurence had some sort of cane that opened up into a chair. I sat, too, because there were folks behind me saying, "*A bas*" [down] and "*Asseyez-vous* [Sit down]." I didn't understand the words, but I got the idea.

Odette and Bernadette were walking together and talking as if no one else were there. When they got to the center of the bowl-shaped area, Bernadette sat cross-legged and started to run scales on her flute. While she did that, Odette, dressed in pale pink leotards and a short white skirt that flowed nicely when she moved, did warm-up exercises. Both of them wore their blond hair long and flowing.

I was struck by the competent air about them. It was as if, in this setting, they were ten years more mature. I didn't know whether the events had done it to them or if they had always seemed older when they were in their own element.

Everyone was watching them, and the conversations had stopped. There must have been forty adults and half as many children gathered on the grass. Robert Arnaut was still lurking in the bushes, though, and not watching the girls.

In a few minutes Bernadette stopped playing scales and held her flute down in front of her chest. Odette stood with her right foot in front and perpendicular to her left—I think it is called the third position. She held her arms out at her sides and her hands were arched at the wrists, her fingers slightly apart.

And then they started.

I don't know much about ballet and have never seen ballet dancers except on television, so I didn't know what to expect. But I did realize that those two girls created something magical there in that little valley. There in the grass among the wildflowers, with bees and butterflies going about their business, unheeding the dance, Odette moved to the strains of the flute and Bernadette played to the movement of her sister.

The music was not anything I recognized, which isn't surprising, because I'm not someone who turns on the stereo for company, and if I did, I would be playing rock and roll or country and western, nothing classical. But you'd have had to be made of stone not to feel something when Bernadette played. And when Odette danced to it, well, I think my knees turned to jelly. Odette, truly, seemed to be a creature of the air, as if she might float away on the next breeze.

Even Arnaut, who had been wrapped up in his own concerns earlier, had stopped and was leaning against a rock, watching. I wondered how something so beautiful could be kept from the larger world. It seemed that it would be only a matter of time before someone asked the girls to perform in a bigger arena.

When the sisters were done, they stood together and curtsied to the audience, which responded with clapping and shouts. The girls smiled, but showed no inclination to do an encore. They left as suddenly as they had come, yet did not exit by the path but through the woods, at the edge of which Arnaut had been standing. Arnaut now was nowhere in sight.

I felt a momentary shiver, wondering whether he was still in the woods or whether he meant them any harm.

While the crowd was filing down the path, I made an excuse to Marsha, Laurence being occupied in a conversation with someone, and took off after the girls.

I tried not to make it too obvious where I was going and went around the edge of the woods for a ways before I

actually got on the trail. I thought I could hear the girls
chattering in the distance, but I couldn't be sure, because
there were other people chattering not too far away. I knew
the woods weren't very large, since I had been driven
around the village and I knew it was surrounded by fields.

However, once under the canopy of the trees, the woods
seemed dense, and I remembered someone saying that wild
boars lived in the French woods. I didn't think that my
body in its present frail condition could take an encounter
with a wild boar.

I was following a rough trail that wound through the
trees without going in any one direction in particular. In
not many minutes I knew I was lost, and I hoped that I
would either meet someone or see the edge of the woods.
I wondered whether it was true that people who were lost
in the woods traveled in circles.

Just as I was worrying about where I was, I found something more frightening to worry about. Ahead of me on the
path I saw Arnaut.

I stopped and ducked behind a tree, hoping he hadn't
heard me. But as I peeked around the tree, I knew he had
heard, for he turned and was looking right in my direction.

I didn't move, because I knew that movement was what
could be seen in the camouflage of leaves and branches. As
I stood there doing my imitation of a stone, I felt something
crawling on my neck and willed myself to stay still.

I knew that the spiders were large in France, having seen
a couple of doozies in the corners at Annee's. I was sure
that a large, hairy one had fallen off a tree, and I hoped
that it wouldn't take a nip out of me. All this spider fear
was making me nauseated.

It seemed like forever before Arnaut turned back to the
path and started walking. I waited for him to take several
steps before I brushed whatever it was from my neck.

But the thing that fell from my neck to my arm was a
large ant. One more brush and it was back among the
leaves.

Arnaut was still ahead of me, but he wasn't walking like
someone who had some place to go: he was walking like
someone who was following someone, sort of the way I
was walking.

Then I heard the voices of the girls and realized they were just ahead of Arnaut. He kept walking and caught up to them. I watched the girls' faces when they saw him, and they looked frightened.

I don't know what he was saying to them, but they looked alarmed. Then he grabbed Odette by the arm. Odette tried to pull away, and Bernadette was pulling on Odette. Arnaut was grinning and holding on.

I decided to make my presence known. Even in my condition, I figured, I would be of some assistance in fighting off Arnaut.

"Leave her alone," I said, which meant nothing to him, but he would understand the tone, I thought.

He stood his ground, but I kept coming closer, shouting at him. I don't know what would have happened if the cavalry, in the form of the girls' brother Yves, had not arrived. He, too, was shouting.

Arnaut took off into the brush like a frightened deer.

"I'm glad you showed up," I said to Yves. "I saw him in the woods and wondered if the girls were safe, so I followed them."

"I saw him and I saw you," Yves said. "So I followed, too."

"Are you all right?" I said to Odette and Bernadette.

"Of course," Odette said. "Arnaut is nothing, a clown, a madman." Although she tried to sound as if she were above such concerns as her safety, the tremble in her voice said otherwise.

"Madmen can be dangerous," I said.

"Yes," Yves said to his sisters. "You must be more careful. Especially with what has happened."

Bernadette was less haughty and her face was quivering as her poise fell apart and she burst into tears. She rattled off something that sounded like a recrimination against her sister.

"What did Arnaut want?" I said.

"I don't know," Odette said. "I did not listen."

I looked at Bernadette, whose face was telling a different story. She said, "I think he wants Odette to dance once more." But I wasn't convinced that that was what Arnaut had said. Maybe Arnaut would show up at the inn tonight, I thought. Maybe I could ask him.

Yves spoke to his sisters briefly in French and then turned to me. "I told them not to come here to the woods without someone to protect them," he said.

"But," Odette said, "we love these woods."

"Yes," he said. "Maybe they will be safe again."

Odette and Bernadette turned toward home without further argument. I didn't know which way they were turning until we got to the edge of the woods and I saw where we were.

"I guess they know their way around those trees," I said to Yves as the girls walked on ahead to the Toute house.

"I think they are knowing every tree," he said, smiling. "Mother was all the time busy when we were growing up. We were playing often in the woods. It was a good place to play."

"But a little dangerous," I ventured.

Yves paused, I think for dramatic effect. "Not so dangerous as a highway. More dangerous than one's bed." He had a way of sounding like his father, a sort of imperious tone directed toward lower life forms.

Then, because I am snotty sometimes, especially when a little ticked off, I said, "Did Clarisse come to the rehearsal today?"

He answered before he thought. "No, she is at her home. Her mother is not well today." It was kind of cute to see him struggle with the "th" sound.

He knew immediately that he had revealed the fact that he kept close tabs on Clarisse. His lips clamped together and he shrugged his shoulders. "Odette told me," he mumbled, but we both knew better.

We walked a little farther in the direction of the Toute house, and Yves, recovering his usual suave manner, said, "Can I give you a lift? I know you have come from hospital. You need rest, perhaps."

"Thanks," I said. "But I'd like to walk. I haven't had much exercise in a couple of weeks. Thanks anyway."

As Yves entered the gate, his mother was coming out.

"*Bonjour*, Fran," she said.

"*Bonjour*," I said. "I watched your daughters play the

flute and dance, and I've never seen anything so wonderful.''

"Thank you," she said.

"I didn't see you at the practice."

She looked confused for a minute, and I guessed that she was translating, or trying to. "Ah, no. I had to prepare food."

"Food for the store?"

"Store? Oh, store, *l'épicerie*. Yes, I go there now."

I didn't think we would get far with this conversation.

"I'll walk with you," I said. "I'd like to see the *épicerie*."

"Good," she said, and seemed delighted out of all proportion to the event. I wondered whether she had misunderstood me again, until she said, "It is a good store."

Then she made her biggest effort yet to speak English and tell me about the store. She told me that her parents took over the store from her mother's parents and that her mother's parents had started the store before World War Two and they had a hard time during the war because the Germans took all the good things. At least, that was what I understood her to say.

Needless to say, the transmission of information was slow. But I was wishing that I knew as much French as she did English so that I could have held up my end in the effort-making department. I found myself liking the woman despite what I knew about her. Besides being blink-twice beautiful, she was a charmer, and her enthusiasm for the *épicerie* surpassed any I had seen her display before.

"You must have been horrified when the police thought the poisoned pâté came from your store," I said, ever the diplomat.

"It is no possible," she said. "We have thirty-five to eat that pâté."

"Thirty-five people bought pâté that day?" I said.

"Yes, thirty-five."

"And no one else got sick?"

"But no, of course."

When we got to the *épicerie*, Clement was working behind the counter, cutting some cheese for a woman who looked familiar, but I couldn't place her. Clement was being his charming and witty self and the woman was smiling and acting very kittenish, even though she was at least three times Clement's age.

Niki listened to Clement's conversation and gave him a fond look, then gave her head a slight shake and smiled in my direction. I smiled back as if I were agreeing with her silent comments about this boy who obviously was the apple of her eye.

When Clement finished with his customer, he took off his apron and came over to greet me. Niki plunged into the work of the store, filling up dishes and adding things to the display.

Clement, imp that he was, said, "Would you like a piece of the deadly pâté? We make it the same way, absolutely the same, every week."

"Clement!" Niki said. "*C'est suffit* [That's enough]." Then she turned to me and said, "He is bad boy sometimes."

Clement, however, wasn't finished. "I'll get you a piece with some bread," he said. "I helped to make it today. I used a better-tasting poison."

Niki swung a wooden spoon at the back of his legs, but he leaped out of the way, nearly knocking over Robert Arnaut, who had just walked in.

When Arnaut saw me, he looked, briefly, as if he would turn around and walk out. Instead he came over to me and said, "*Bonjour, madame,*" then greeted Clement and Niki.

Niki waited on him and he had her getting one thing and then another and showing it to him and then putting it back because he didn't want it after all. This went on for several minutes and then I realized what he was doing. He was choosing things from the bottom of the glass display case and then looking down the front of Niki's dress when she bent over to retrieve the item he had chosen.

When Clement saw my face as I watched the action, he came over close to me and said, "Don't worry about it. It happens all the time. Mother is one of the attractions of the place."

It was while Niki was reaching for something that Robert Arnaut had asked for that I saw a faint mark on her arm. It was all but healed, but it was clear all the same. I wondered if Annee had seen it and then knew what Denis had been doing. I wondered if she had seen those marks on many women over the years. And Jacques, had he seen it?

Sick, I thought, this whole situation is sick. And I had a ferocious urge to get out of there. But just then Odette and Bernadette showed up, and my curiosity overcame my distaste. I wanted to see what reaction Arnaut would have to the girls, and vice versa.

Bernadette went quickly to the back of the store and started dusting shelves, while Odette narrowed her eyes at Arnaut but said nothing. Arnaut kept Niki doing the same thing until he had looked at just about everything on the bottom shelf.

I glanced over at Bernadette, whose face had turned red. She came to the front of the store and said to her mother in English, "I will help him. You have more important things to do." She sounded as if she had rehearsed the line, it came out so perfectly, almost without an accent.

Niki nodded and went to the rear and into the back room, where I assumed there was a kitchen and possibly the living quarters of her parents, the Bouchegrandes.

A snide smile crept over Arnaut's face and he said something, which I interpreted to be the name of whatever he had finally chosen to purchase. Bernadette wrapped up a slice of the something for him and he left.

He was no sooner out the door than Odette and Bernadette started yelling at their mother. I didn't know what it was about, but I could guess. So I made my exit.

But I wasn't rid of the Toutes yet, for Clement was right on my heels. "You didn't have any of the pâté," he said.

I was getting cranky. I was tired and I wanted to get back to the house and lie down. "Aren't you carrying this joke a little too far?" I said.

He looked surprised, probably by the tone as well as the content.

"I'm sorry," he said immediately.

We walked along in silence, and I was starting to feel like some kind of ogre.

"I made it. It was good," he said.

"I'm sorry, Clement. I'm tired, that's all. I'd love to taste your pâté. But I have to go home now. I'm exhausted."

"I will bring some for your dinner," he said.

"I'd like some," I said. "But leave out the poison mushrooms." I smiled at him to show him that I could be just as big a tease as he was.

He was all smiles now. He was just a kid, after all. And a nice kid at that.

I waved at him and went into the house.

Fourteen

The house was quiet and I expected that Annee and Vincent were at the inn, doing whatever needed to be done on Monday afternoons, and Marsha and Laurence were off doing something together. My intention was to get a glass of water and then go to bed for a while. My stamina had not returned, and I felt like my body was turning to mush.

It was when I was walking up the stairs with my water that I heard a strange sound coming from one of the bedrooms. It sounded sort of like a cat, and I knew there was no cat that belonged there. That noise was followed by footsteps. I turned to bolt. Whoever it was, I didn't want to see him or her. I didn't want any confrontations and I didn't want to get hit.

I ran down the stairs, spilling water helter-skelter and figuring that I would throw the glass at anyone who chased me.

"Fran, is that you?"

It was Annee's voice. I gulped and sat right down on the steps. It was then that I realized that whoever had hit me had not only messed up my body, but had also scared me. I dusted off one of my old lectures about fear and administered it with a promise to myself that I would repeat it every day until I straightened out. "Yes, I'm here," I said. "I got scared."

"Sorry," she said. "I thought you were with Laurence at the church sale."

"I didn't know there was a church sale," I said, thinking

that I probably wouldn't have wanted to go if I had known about it. "I thought you'd be at the inn."

Annee was standing looking down at me over the railing at the top of the stairs. "Come back up," she said. "I'll show you why I am home."

If I hadn't been so rattled, if I had had my head on straight, I would have known what she was talking about before I followed her into her bedroom.

In the middle of her bed was the baby, tiny and pink and making a small noise that was half gurgle and half breath.

"Oh," I said. "The baby, she's home."

"When I went to feed her today, they told me that her weight was almost two and a half kilos and she could leave the hospital."

"Great," I said, and knew it was great for Annee, but I knew, too, that she would be so distracted that I wouldn't get much help from her in trying to find out who had slugged me. And it occurred to me that if someone was hanging around this house slugging people, none of us in the house was safe.

"Yes, it is," Annee said, and I forgot for a second what she was responding to. "I have to find something for her to sleep in. I know I have a basket in the attic somewhere. Would you just sit here and watch her so she doesn't fall off the bed while I go find the basket?"

"Sure," I said, wondering how on earth this little lump who couldn't do anything was going to roll off this big bed. I sat on the edge of the bed and watched Fanny, who had stopped gurgling and was now yawning and moving her arms in a jerky way and kicking at the little blanket on her legs. Then she started a little meowing sound like the one that had scared me earlier.

She was crying, but not like her heart was really in it, just a little fussing kind of cry. I bounced the bed a little. Isn't that what people do to make babies feel better? Bounce them?

It didn't help, and Fanny kept on crying and waving her arms and sometimes getting her hand close to her mouth and then opening her mouth and sticking her fist into it. She'd get in a few sucks on her fist and then wave her arm again, and her fist would escape and her mouth would still be reaching for it.

God, she's got a lot to learn, I thought. I considered helping her get that fist back into her mouth, but I didn't want to touch her. She looked so breakable. I kept on bouncing, but I was the one who was getting sleepy.

Annee's room was furnished with the same kind of big old wooden furniture that was in my room, but there was more of it and the room was much bigger. The floor was covered with a huge Oriental rug that looked ancient. Maybe worth a bundle, I thought. The fanciest piece of furniture was an old desk whose wood was reddish and which had curved legs with carved flowers, leaves, and curlicues on them and across the top and sides.

I was taking inventory of the bedroom when I heard thumping above me, and again I was startled and felt that I ought to run and hide. I'm too jumpy, I thought. The sounds are only Annie rummaging through the attic. I didn't like feeling the way I was feeling. It wasn't like me, and I wanted my old self back.

I thought then about the doctor at the hospital, the shrink, who had said she wanted me to come back and talk to her. Maybe I would do that. Maybe she could help me deal with this nervousness I was experiencing.

A few minutes later, Annee poked her head in the door. "How's she doing?" she said.

I had all but forgotten the baby. "Huh?" I looked at Fanny. "She's asleep."

"Good. I have to clean up this basket. It's covered with dust. But I'll put the baby in a drawer so you can get some rest," Annee said. "You look exhausted."

"I do?" I was.

Annee hustled me off to my room, where I looked over the various medicines and tried to remember what they were for and when I should take them. The medicines seemed like a good idea, because my head had started to hurt and the pounding had started up again.

Damn, I thought. How long am I going to be like this? I popped a couple of the pills and let my head down gently onto the two pillows that I had stacked. The pounding subsided gradually, but I didn't feel sleepy. I worried about myself, I worried about Annee and the baby, I worried about a killer being loose in the village. I was still worrying when I woke up.

I looked at my watch and it was 2 A.M. That was about the same time I got whacked over two weeks ago. I shivered and picked up the bag that had the medicines in it. I had suddenly remembered that there were supposed to be instructions in it about the medicines and about an appointment with Dr. Berenger.

The instructions were clear, a pill for pain, a pill to sleep, a pill for relaxing. The appointment was not until Thursday, the day after tomorrow. I looked at the bottles and realized I had taken a sleeping pill and a pain pill. No wonder I slept so long.

I was hungry and trying to decide whether to go downstairs and find something to eat when I saw the tray on the table, complete with note:

Fran,

You were sleeping so soundly we couldn't wake you. If you wake up hungry, here is a snack. There's more in the fridge, of course. Clement delivered the pâté. It was delicious. Laurence and Marsha and Vincent raved so much about it, even I had some. I may have changed my mind about pâté. It's in the fridge.

Annee

There was cheese and bread and butter and a peach and a pear. There were also two small carafes, one of wine and one of water.

Propped up in bed and eating good food, I began to think that my life could get straightened out, until I heard a noise in the hall and my heart started thumping with fear again.

I put down the hunk of bread, which was the second one I had spread with butter, and got out of bed and went to the door. When I peeked out into the hall, I saw Annee carrying the baby over her shoulder and patting the baby's back. I opened the door farther and waved to Annee.

She looked startled for a second and then came into my room.

"Thanks for the snack," I said.

"You were really knocked out," she said. "I wish Fanny would go to sleep. She's been up all night. Every time I turn off the lights, she starts crying."

"Maybe she's not used to the dark. They don't turn off the lights in the hospital, do they?"

"Why didn't I think of that? Of course. I'll leave a light on. Thanks, Fran. You're a genius. Have you got everything you need? Are you all right?"

"I'm fine," I lied. "See if you can get some rest. And if you want one of these sleeping pills, help yourself."

"I wouldn't dare," she said. "If they knocked me out the way you were out, I'd never hear Fanny. Besides, the medicine might get into the milk and put Fanny to sleep like that, too."

"Isn't that what you want?" I laughed.

"I'll try your lights idea," she said.

When she left, the house seemed quieter than before. It was almost three and I wasn't feeling at all tired. I hadn't had any of the wine on the tray, but I decided I would have it with the cheese.

I moved the table and a chair over to the window and turned off the light and opened the shutter halfway. The air was cooler outside, so I put on a sweater and watched the stars and the waning moon. The windows in my room looked out the front of the house onto Rue de Faremoutiers, which was a quiet street near the outskirts of the village. I ate and drank until I felt myself getting sleepy again. I changed into my pajamas in the dark and was trying to decide whether to leave the shutter open or not when some movement in the road caught my eye.

I hid behind the shutter and strained my eyes to pick out the moving shape in the patches of moonlight. A man and a woman were walking with their arms around each other. Then they stopped and kissed. When they faced each other, I could see who they were. Yves and Clarisse. It was clear that they were enraptured. And it was clear to me that if Jacques knew of this, there would be hell to pay.

If Yves was spending his nights running around with Clarisse, it wouldn't be long before Jacques suspected something. Clarisse would be falling asleep at work: Yves would be nodding off when he was at school or working. No, it wouldn't be long, I decided.

I waited until the lovers were out of sight before I closed the shutter, which squeaked when it was moved. I heard no more noise in the house and hoped that Annee was getting some sleep.

The next morning I slept late again, but I felt great when I woke up, not groggy or tired. I was even considering taking a short jog, but when I bounded down the stairs in my running shoes and I felt the bumping in my head, I settled on a brisk walk.

The day was warm and sunny, but there were clouds that looked like they were being blown toward the village and like they were full of rain. Walking felt good. My legs were saying "Thank you" with every long step. I swung my arms and was wishing I had a set of weights to work my arms while I was walking.

I walked by the post office, where some men were working in a ditch. One of them said, "*Bonjour, madame.*" I greeted him in return and the other men laughed that laugh that I interpret as being dirty and degrading to women. Maybe it isn't; what do I know about men?

I kept walking, determined not to let some jerks, even French jerks, ruin my morning, or what was left of morning. By the time I was finished with my walk, I figured it would be lunchtime. I would skip breakfast altogether.

When I got to the *épicerie*, I could see Niki and her parents working inside. I opened the door and told Niki that Clement's pâté had made a big hit.

She came to the door to shake my hand and smiled. "He likes you," she said.

"The feeling is mutual," I said. "He's a great kid."

She looked as if she wanted to say something, and then looked over her shoulder. Her parents were working at half speed and putting the other half of their efforts into listening. That little tableau made me think that her parents understood about as much English as she did.

Niki turned back to me and straightened her already straight shoulders. "I would like to talk to you," she said, rather loudly for her parents' benefit, I thought, "about the baby—*un cadeau*—a gift." She translated for me. Then she rolled her eyes and cracked a half smile. She said some word that was close to "baptism," but not quite, and then, "Is Friday?"

I hadn't heard the date yet, but it didn't surprise me that people in town knew about it before I did. Annee could have made the arrangements this morning with the priest and by now the whole town knew. But I didn't think that Niki wanted to talk to me about the baby's gift at all. Something else was on her mind.

"I don't know what Annee needs," I said, trying to figure out how I was going to talk to Niki when her parents were working at about a quarter speed now. I finally settled on the obvious. "I'm taking a walk. Doctor's orders. Do you want to walk with me?"

Niki's face lit up. "Yes, I will walk with you," she said.

Once outside, she didn't launch right into whatever it was she wanted to say, but started with small talk about her children and Annee having the baby and what a surprise it was, all in her combo Franglais, which I was getting the hang of, but which would never help me to learn French.

When we got to a small section of road that wasn't visible to any houses, she stopped and rolled up her sleeve. She stopped rolling just above the mark I had seen and identified as Denis Rien's teeth marks. She pointed to the mark.

"You saw this?"

"Yes," I said, feeling very uncomfortable and not a little afraid. I backed away from her. She was bigger than I was and I wasn't in good shape just then.

"You know who did this?" She looked angry.

Since I wasn't feeling too brave, I shrugged my shoulders.

"Denis. He did this."

"Why are you telling me?"

Suddenly her anger turned to tears, and she blubbered out a story of being raped by Denis and then being blackmailed into more sexual encounters with him. He apparently had taken something of hers, she said, and wouldn't give it back. At least that was what I understood. And then she said that she was there the night I was hit.

"What? You were there? Did you hit me?" I said, backing away.

"No, no. I no hit. I see him." Her English was deteriorating as her voice was rising.

"Who?"

"Monsieur Saverne."

"He hit me? He was the one who found me."

"I saw him with stick."

"What were you doing there?"

"I was find *le collier*."

"You were looking for a collar? Why were you—never mind," I said. My mind was racing. I didn't know what to ask her next. And I didn't know whether I would understand her answers anyway.

"Can you find?" she said.

"You want me to find your collar?"

At that point she started giving me a description of the "collar" and talking about a blue jewel, and I realized that it was a necklace she wanted me to find.

My next shock was when she said she would pay me for finding it. She had heard I was a detective and she wanted to hire me to find her necklace. I almost laughed out loud at the idea of getting hired in France, twice.

"I'll try to find it," I said.

She was so happy, I started to feel uneasy in the event that I didn't find it. Niki was taking on an entirely new position in my pantheon of Vaudoy citizens. I felt a little sorry for her, besides envying her her astounding good looks.

She pulled a wad of bills out of her pocket and pushed them into my hand. "I will give more," she said.

I was about to protest, but figured it would take too much energy. Besides, if I was going to look for her necklace, I should get paid something. And the voice of Delia, who shares my office in Buffalo, came in loud and clear. "Get the money up front, just like a hooker. Afterward, they don't need you and don't think you're worth as much." Delia doesn't mince words.

I tucked the bills into my pocket and told Niki that I would talk to her every day or so about where I'd looked.

She told me to start looking in the garden shed. Appar-

ently Denis had stored a lot of things that were private
there. According to Niki, Annee rarely went into the shed.
At least, that was what I thought Niki was saying. I figured
it was close.

Niki turned and walked back toward the store and I continued my walk. But not far. A few steps farther and there
was Robert Arnaut, lurking in the trees. He stepped out in
front of me, lurching slightly as if he had already been
drinking. His clothes were dirty and he smelled like a barn-
yard. Sweat was pouring off his face and he was emitting
a sort of growl. He sounded drunk to me.

He lunged toward me. Headache or no, I told myself, get
your feet in gear and run.

I ran back in the direction Niki had taken and passed her
in a few seconds. "Arnaut is coming," I said. "Run." I
could hear his heavy tread behind us, getting closer as I
had decreased my speed to warn Niki.

We had no trouble outrunning him, and when we reached
the shop, Niki said something to her father, who ran into
the back of the store and came out with a huge shotgun. In
old movies, I think they called a gun like that a blunder-
buss.

But the gun wasn't necessary. Arnaut had fallen in front
of the store, and wasn't moving at all.

Fifteen

By the time the gendarmes got there, I had managed to work out our story with Niki. There was no sense in telling them what we had been talking about. Niki told them we had been walking together and talking about the baptism and that when Niki had turned to go back to the store, Arnaut had tried to grab me.

It wasn't until much later in the day that I realized that I had run, and run fast, and my head hadn't hurt at all.

Arnaut was dead. I felt guilty, thinking that he hadn't been trying to grab me at all, but had been asking for help. But then I remembered the look in his eyes and convinced myself that he hadn't looked like a man seeking assistance.

An English-speaking gendarme was giving me the French version of the fisheye when he talked to me. I had been too close to too many of the deaths in Vaudoy. While he was questioning me, I wanted to tell him that I knew who had hit me, but I couldn't do that without giving Niki away. And I wasn't ready to do that yet.

I tried to think why M. Saverne would have hit me. He was so grateful that I had given him a chance to cook. He always treated me so cheerfully. How would I go about finding out why he had clobbered me? I didn't want to give him a chance to finish the job, either.

The policeman didn't question me for too long despite the way he had been looking at me. Maybe it was because I was a victim, too.

By the time the police were through, Jacques was there, along with the rest of the Toutes and half of the village, but not the Savernes or any of the folks living at the Rien house except for me.

Mme. Foyer was there, making a terrible outcry about all the killing. I picked out a couple of words that I was getting used to hearing when tragedy struck: *meurtrier* (murderer), *tueur* (killer), *mort* (death). What a vocabulary I was acquiring. Mme. Foyer cried and yelled, and it seemed that she was berating the police for not finding the murderer.

The Toute girls went to comfort her and offered to walk her home. She accepted their offer and went quietly with them, apparently glad for the attention.

Yves was there with his eyes looking like burnt holes in a blanket. That boy needed some sleep. Clarisse wasn't there, and I assumed she was busy at the inn. I wondered whether she was suffering from lack of sleep.

The Bouchegrandes were serving coffee and *pain chocolat* (a bun with a chocolate filling) to the gendarmes and were doing a roaring business as the crowd stood outside getting hungry and thirsty before the body of Robert Arnaut was taken away. I wolfed down a bun and coffee when Madame Bouchegrande offered them to me.

When I was getting ready to leave, Niki came over and patted my arm. "Yves will drive for you."

"Thanks," I said. "I'll walk."

"You are fine?" she said.

"Yes, I am fine." I smiled at her, hoping she would flash her Hollywood smile at me. And I was rewarded. Where were the guys who made the screen tests?

I had walked only a few minutes when Jacques drove up beside me. "Get in," he said.

"Is that an official order? Am I being arrested?" I said, not without a bit of bile.

He turned off the engine. "Not at all," he said. "I want to ask you about the night you were hit. You never spoke to me about it when you were in hospital." He spoke with an English accent and left out the definite article in phrases like "in hospital."

There was something odd in the way he was talking. And I wondered why he had waited this long to question me again about that night. Then I had a flash: Suppose he knew

Niki was in the garden that night. Suppose he was there also. Suppose things went on after I was hit, and he wondered whether I had heard them. I shivered, and I was sure he saw it.

But I was making all this up. I didn't know anything about who was in the garden that night. And then I began to wonder whether I *had* heard something. Maybe that was why I lost my memory. Maybe I was blocking out something horrible. Maybe someone still wanted to kill me.

It was difficult for me, with this kind of imagining going on in my head, to bring myself to the here and now.

"What do you want?" I said. I meant to say, "What do you want to know?"

But he answered before I could correct myself. "I want to talk to you. It is not official. It would be completely voluntary on your part."

Even when he was saying it, I didn't think he believed it. He was so used to being obeyed. "So it's personal, then?" I said. I saw him wince and dug into him a little deeper. "I would be doing you a favor by talking to you?"

I could see the muscles in his jaw working, and I felt that he was in the atypical position, for him, of not being in control. I was entirely unprepared for his reaction.

"Damn it, Fran, do I have to beg?" he said, and punched his palm.

I almost laughed, but instead I smiled and said, "Probably. You have been rather bossy ever since I met you."

"Bossy?" he said, as if it never had occurred to him that he was bossy.

"Yes. You think you always know what's best for everybody." I was launched now. "Even if you're right some of the time, it doesn't mean you're right all the time. And other people have opinions and desires and even whims that they like to act on. And sometimes people have to make mistakes so that they can find out what's right." At that moment I thought of poor Yves sneaking around with a girl his father didn't approve of. And I wondered whether it was his father's disapproval that made Clarisse so attractive.

I knew I had said too much and had let him know how

he had gotten under my skin. He was not a man to let such an advantage go.

"You're right, of course," he said, his self-control and correctness back in place. "I am the boss at work and I am the boss at home." He shrugged his handsome shoulders and smiled his handsome smile.

"So what do you want to know?" I said. I knew when to give in.

"If you would get in the car, we could take a drive while we talk."

My terrors had not left me. I was afraid to get in the car with him. "I don't want to take a drive and I don't want to get in the car. What do you want to know about the night I was hit?"

He had been leaning over the passenger seat, but he finally gave up on the idea that I would get in and slid over onto the passenger seat and opened the door. "Did you see anyone before you were attacked?"

"No. I heard a noise in the garden shed and looked inside. Then I was cracked with something."

"We found a garden tool with your blood and hair on it."

The thought of my blood and hair going through tests in a lab gave me the eeriest feeling, as if I were part of a postmortem. "What kind of garden tool?" I didn't care what kind of tool; I just felt I had to say something.

"I can't think of the word. It's for digging."

"A shovel? A spade?"

"I think a shovel. We call it *une pelle*."

That was one way to learn vocabulary. Learn the names of things you get hit with. "Who do you think was in the garden that night?" I said. "And why isn't this part of the official investigation?"

"I must ask you to keep this confidential."

"You may ask," I said. "But I think that depends on how it affects me."

"Very well. I know who was in the garden that night." He hung his head. "I don't want to have to arrest my wife."

"Niki was in the garden?" I said, doing my best to seem

startled. "But how do you know she was in the garden? And do the gendarmes know this?"

He looked almost defeated. Almost. "I followed her."

"Why were you following your wife? And if you were in the garden, doesn't that make you a suspect, too?"

"Yes, but you have my word that I didn't hit you. I didn't see you get hit. I lost sight of Niki because I had to back off some distance so that neither you nor Niki would see me."

"And you're wondering whether Niki hit me. And because you saw Niki in the garden, you are obligated to tell the police that. And the longer you wait to tell them, the more culpable you are." I could see him shriveling up. I almost felt sorry for him. Almost.

"Did you smell anything just before you were hit?" he said. "Niki wears a distinctive perfume."

He didn't want her to be guilty. He wanted a reason not to have to report her. As soon as he mentioned the perfume, I remembered it. True, it was unusual. I was betting that the money she had given me had her scent on it and I was feeling glad that I hadn't gotten in the car with him. He probably would have smelled it. "No, I don't remember smelling that. I do know what you mean about her perfume." I felt like backing up; I was so conscious of the money being in my pocket. "Do you think Niki is strong enough to have hit me as hard as I was hit?"

"Niki is strong, but I have never known her to be violent. Yet she was there."

"Have you asked her?" I said.

"Um, no."

"Because you didn't want her to know you were following her?"

"Yes." He took a couple of deep breaths, as if he were making a decision.

"It's up to you," I said. "I didn't see her or smell her. I don't know who hit me. I can't help you." I was getting miffed. It seemed to me the garden had been crawling with people, and yet I had gotten bashed and almost killed. Niki hadn't told the police who hit me because she had a secret. Jacques hadn't told the police because he had been following his wife. The next thing I had to do was talk to M.

Saverne, who, according to Niki, was the one who had hit me.

Again I got a case of the terrors, and I had the strange feeling that there was something I didn't want to remember.

"I don't see how I can ask her," he said. And I imagined I got a look into Jacques's personal can of worms.

"Is there anything I can do?" I knew I shouldn't have offered.

He brightened immediately. "Could you tell her that someone has told you they saw her there? That would be true. Then watch her. She scratches her nose when she lies."

"Is that why you followed her? She said something and scratched her nose?"

"That, yes, and other things."

I began wondering whether Jacques had been trying to build a case against Niki so that he could divorce her and be free to pursue Annee.

"Why do you think she was in Annee's garden?" I said.

"I don't know. I didn't expect her to go there, but I didn't know where she would go. Then when she went to Annee's, I kept following and watching. I thought she was going to meet someone."

"Anyone in particular?" I said.

"Yes, but I don't want to say."

Well, he didn't suspect Denis, because Denis was already dead by that night. I ran down the list of men I knew, but obviously there were men I didn't know.

"Where did you think she was going when you started following her? You said you didn't expect her to go to Annee's."

"I thought she would go to the woods. She and the children love the woods. And I thought if she were going to meet someone, that would be where she would go."

The woods. Where the Toute children used to play and hide. Where Niki used to go looking for them, no doubt.

"I'll see what I can find out about Niki. If she scratches her nose, I'll let you know."

He handed me his card. "Call me any time," he said.

I walked away feeling that I had gotten myself into a pickle. Now I would have to lie to both of them.

Sixteen

When I got to Annee's, my stomach was rumbling. I hadn't eaten anything all day except some *pain chocolat* and coffee at the *épicerie*.

"Anybody home?" I called into the silence when I went into the center hall. Then I went through the house looking for someone, and found only Fanny sleeping peacefully in Annee's room. I figured Annee wouldn't be far with the baby here.

When I went back to the kitchen, I tore the end off a fresh baguette that was on the table, along with some other groceries that were still in their little plastic bags. Then I ate an apple and drank a glass of milk. My stomach was once again working peacefully.

I remembered that I had put Niki's money in my pocket, and because I was curious, I took it out and smelled it. Yes, there was the perfume, a sweet mixture of herbs and flowers. And it was distinctive, as Jacques had said. The closest I could come to describing it was vanilla and honeysuckle, but it was more complex than that.

She had given me five hundred francs, a little less than a hundred dollars, according to the currency listings in the *International Herald Tribune*, which Marsha had delivered daily by the letter carrier, who was a woman on a bicycle. That would get her a couple of hours' work, I thought. Well, no time like the present. I took the new key off the hook and went outside to the shed, thankful that this time it was daylight when I had business there.

I unlocked the door and propped it open so that there

would be light inside. I hadn't had much of a look inside before and I was surprised to find it so neat. After all, the police had searched it, hadn't they? Annee had told me that they took rat poison from the shed after Denis's death. I puzzled over the condition of the shed, then decided that the gendarmes had stopped searching once they had found the rat poison.

All of the walls but one were covered with shelves, and there were plastic boxes on some of the shelves that were labeled. Other shelves had baskets on them; some had rows of jars and small boxes. There was a row of bins along the bottom and when I opened one, I found a plastic bag, sealed shut with a rope. As long as I had gone that far, I opened the bag and found seeds inside.

There was no way I could identify the seeds. They could have been anything from grass seeds to the secret ingredient in one of Denis's dishes. I resealed the bag and closed the bin, and I began to calculate how much time it would take me to search the shed for Niki's necklace. Even a small shed could hold a lot of stuff if the space were organized as this space was.

On the wall without the shelves, the tools were hung, and I shuddered when I saw the empty hook.

The necklace would be in one of the boxes if it were in here, I thought, but I couldn't read the labels. I started at one end, taking the plastic boxes off the shelves and removing their lids. The first seven or eight boxes were filled with papers. Then I hit one that was loaded with pieces of clothing, mostly underwear, women's underwear.

I tried to keep down the urge to swear.

I was on about the tenth box when I heard someone walking outside. I closed the box and shoved it back in place, but not before I caught a glimpse of some jewelry. Damn, I thought, that could be the box. I made a note of its position.

But I didn't want to get caught looking in the boxes. Nor did I want anyone to shut the door to the shed and lock me inside. In a few feverish seconds everything was back in place and I hurried to the door.

There, looking just as surprised as I was, was M. Saverne, broad as a bull, his big hands hanging loosely at his sides, his big face red and gleaming, and wearing his dark, shapeless jacket and his black, shiny shoes. I was terrified. Hadn't Niki told me that he was the one who almost killed me?

My heart was shaking my chest like an animal in a cage. It was broad daylight. He wouldn't hit me again, would he? I knew that he did double duty as a bouncer at the inn. Hadn't I seen younger men cringe when he told them what to do?

I had to get hold of myself. Fear was not going to save me. Trying to control my voice, which I was sure would come out with a terrific vibrato, I said, "So you return to the scene of the crime." When I heard myself, my voice sounded like Joe Cocker's or Lauren Bacall's; they sound alike to me.

I stood watching him, ready to jump for a garden tool and give him a fight this time. I don't know how long we stood there, face-to-face. It was one of those minutes that I can call up perfectly whenever I think of it. I can see the house behind him with its shutters open. I can even see the open cellar door.

"Madame," he said. Then he moved his hands, and I jumped for a spade and grabbed it and held it in front of me.

He put his arms up in front of his face. "No, madame, if you please."

He was acting as if he were afraid I would hit him. I lowered the spade, but not enough to preclude my giving him a whack with it if I needed to. "What do you want?" I said.

"I have come to see you."

"I didn't know you could speak English that well."

"I learned during the war," he said. He was looking at the ground in front of his feet.

I raised the spade again. "Did you hit me?" My voice had gone up an octave and now resembled the voice of an adolescent boy, cracks and all.

"You know." he said. "I am so very sorry."

"Why? You almost killed me."

"I thought you were someone else."

"One of the Toutes?" I blurted out without thinking.

"The Toutes?" He shook his head as if a bug were biting one ear. "One of the Toute children?"

I remembered then that Yves had been in the neighborhood in the early-morning hours and wondered whether he had seen him one night, too. "Never mind," I said. "Who did you think I was when you hit me?"

"I would never try to hurt you, madame. You are a wonderful person in my life."

He was stalling. "But you did hurt me. Who were you trying to hurt?"

"Arnaut. And now he is dead. I must tell the gendarmes, but I have come to see you first. To apologize."

"What would Arnaut have been doing here?"

At that moment Annee's head rose from the cellarway. She saw us, and we must have made an odd picture standing in the doorway of the shed, me with the spade facing M. Saverne. His back was to Annee and he didn't hear her as she came closer.

"Denis, you should know, was blackmailing me. I worked for practically nothing. I don't know how Arnaut found out about the blackmail, but he told me after Denis died that he kept his file on his blackmailing in the shed. Then he said he knew what Denis was blackmailing me about and he said he had a key to the shed. For a large amount of money, he gave me the key. When you came to the shed at that hour of the morning, I thought it was Arnaut."

"And you tried to kill Arnaut? Did you also kill Denis?" Annee said. She was right behind him.

He jumped and turned with such speed that I realized I would have been no match for him. But I almost beaned him because I thought he was going to attack Annee.

Annee was startled and backed away.

"I'm sorry, Madame Rien. I didn't mean to startle you. But I myself was startled."

"What were you saying about Denis? Did you kill him?"

"No, I didn't kill Denis. And I wouldn't have killed Arnaut. But I did mean to hurt him. It would have been easy to kill in the position I was in. But I am a fighter, not a killer."

He said it with pride and with a certain tilt of his head that made me see the young M. Saverne in his prime. And he had been formidable, I was sure.

"And you were in the shed looking for what exactly?" Annee said. Which was my next question.

"Something that belonged to me. Something that Denis stole from me and then made me pay and pay not to reveal."

"What was it?" I said.

"It is old, but valuable to me. And I wouldn't want anyone to know about it."

"How are you going to go to the police if you aren't going to tell them what it is?" I said.

"I am going to lie to them about what I was looking for."

I didn't think he had thought this out. "But, Monsieur Saverne, if you tell the police that you were looking for something in the shed, and that Denis kept things in the shed that had to do with blackmail, don't you think the gendarmes will come to the shed and search it thoroughly? And don't you think they'll find what you were looking for?"

His face contorted with anger, then fear, then confusion. "What can I do?" he said.

"We'll all search the shed," Annee said. "Together."

"And you'll have to wait to go to the police," I said. "Maybe you won't have to go at all."

"Maybe you're right about that," Annee said to me, and then to M. Saverne, she said, "But we won't blackmail you."

There were tears in the eyes of this man, a man who had almost killed me, but a man who seemed to live so honorably. So honorably that other people took advantage of him. I thought I would want revenge when I found out who had hit me, but instead I felt sorry for him.

"I have to go in and feed Fanny," Annee said. "We can start our search later."

That suited M. Saverne fine, but I thought about Niki's necklace and knew I wouldn't be able to wait. Maybe I was a rat not to tell Annee that Niki had hired me to get the necklace. But I couldn't very well call Annee and Niki and

Jacques together and explain to them all the misapprehensions that they had about one another.

After Annee left, I asked M. Saverne another question that had been scratching at the inside of my temple when he talked about money. I knew that Annee hadn't mentioned it to him, but I was playing my own hunch as to his honesty. "Do you know that there has been money missing from the inn since Denis died?"

"But no. Annee, Madame Rien, never told me this."

"Who do you think could be taking it?"

"There are not many possibilities. Madame Saverne and myself, Annee and Vincent, Clarisse, Yves, and Odette."

"And your guess is?"

He didn't hesitate. "Clarisse. She is poor and has had to get money many ways in her young life."

"What do you know about how she has gotten money?"

"Many people know."

He was matter-of-fact, not outraged, not scandalized. Small wonder Jacques didn't like the idea of his son going out with her.

M. Saverne had an uncomfortable look on his face and he seemed to be squirming in the crumpled black suit he always wore. "I believe Denis gave money to Clarisse every week in addition to her salary."

"Oh," I said dumbly. Another one of Denis's escapades. The list of suspects just grows and grows in Denis's case. But what connection was there to M. Foyer? Or M. Arnaut? And what about Laurence? The idea that someone was hanging around the shed and possibly watching the house seemed more plausible than ever.

M. Saverne seemed to expect more of an answer, but what could I say? I tried. "Was he being kind because he knew her folks were so poor?"

M. Saverne made a face that seemed to be a mixture of disgust and anger. "Denis Rien was not kind."

I had heard so many rotten things about Denis that a protest burst from my mouth. "What did Annee see in such a monster?"

"Ah, Madame Annee is a fine woman, very loyal, but she doesn't want to see some things."

Doesn't want to see, of course. That was why M. Foyer,

according to Annee, was much loved, and his flirting meant nothing. The only way she could have stayed married to Denis was not to see some of things he did. What else did she refuse to see?

Were there things about Vincent that she refused to believe? Did the police have facts that she couldn't face? Did she seem impossibly gullible to the police, and therefore they didn't believe her?

"Madame," M. Saverne said, "I am at your disposal. I will go to the police and tell them my story if that is what you tell me to do. I will have to accept the consequences."

I thought he was going to salute, his bearing was so formal.

"No," I said, "don't go to the police. There is someone else we both need to find. Someone who has done a lot of killing. I suspect that Arnaut met the same fate as Denis and Monsieur Foyer. I don't know who will be next. The killer might be someone who was being blackmailed. If we start searching the shed, the killer may find out and think that we know something that's worth killing us for."

"Perhaps we should do our search secretly, perhaps late at night, with the door closed," he said. Despite the fact that there was something about him I liked, the idea of being in the closed shed with him at night made me tremble.

"Perhaps," I said. "I'll mention it to Annee."

"À bientôt [so long]," he said. "Will I see you at the inn this evening?"

"Probably," I said, and thought that I would take some time to search the shed after Annee had left for the inn.

When I went inside, Laurence was at the kitchen door, waiting for me.

"What happened out there?" she said. Her posture was that of an inquisitive hen, head poked forward and to one side, her arms held at her sides and slightly back. Her weight had definitely changed in the weeks since Marsha and I had arrived. The number of chins had been reduced and her breadth was now almost suitable for one chair, rather than the two-seat width that she used to carry. It appeared that she had been doing some serious dieting.

"A day full of discovery," I said, and suddenly didn't

want to tell her what I had discovered. But I had to tell her something after blurting out that I had new information.

"Yes?" she said.

"Where is Marsha?" I said, stalling.

"In the living room."

I remembered then that in the conversation with Annee and M. Saverne, Arnaut's death had not been mentioned. "Have you been told that M. Arnaut is dead?"

"*Mais non.*" She started to run off in French and did her version of running toward the living room, where Marsha was sitting next to Annee on the couch and both of them were cooing over Fanny.

Laurence broke the news in French and then both Annee and Marsha started asking me about what had happened.

I told them what I knew and what my part was in what had happened to M. Arnaut. I said nothing about M. Saverne and hoped that Laurence would let it drop.

But after we had been through the details of M. Arnaut's demise, Laurence returned to the subject.

"What was Monsieur Saverne doing near the shed?" she said.

Annee leaped in, as if she had been anticipating the question. "He wants to search the shed for a book that he lent to Denis. I told him I had not seen the one he described. A very ornate leather-bound book about the French Revolution," she said. I was relieved and a bit startled by Annee's adroit lie.

"Ah," Laurence said. "No, I have not seen such a book in the house, either. Did he happen to say what color the leather was?"

"Black," Annee said without missing a beat. I imagined Annee telling M. Saverne about the lie she told Laurence, just in case the two should meet and the subject come up.

"And you, Fran, what were you doing in the shed?" I was starting to get uneasy about Laurence's questions about the shed. What did she know about it?

"Is there something I should know about the shed before I go out there?" I said. "Something that I should have known before I went out there the first time?"

Laurence looked surprised and hesitated before answering. "I don't know anything about the shed. Denis always insisted that it should be locked and he did not like anyone to go into it. So naturally I am curious about it.''

The frown on my face found a mirror image in Annee's. Laurence was hiding something. Could she be the killer? She knew everyone in town. It was possible that M. Foyer and M. Arnaut had acquired the necessary doses from Laurence. It was possible that she had taken a small dose of poison herself to avoid being suspected of poisoning Denis. What was her interest in the shed? Had Denis secreted something of hers in there? Was she also a victim of his blackmailing? Was her secret worth killing for?

Again I thought it would be prudent to search the shed in secrecy and darkness. But if Laurence was keeping an eye on the building, it would be almost impossible to get to it without being seen.

And then the simplest of ploys occurred to me. After all, I thought I would need only a few minutes to check the box in which I had seen the jewelry. I reached in one pocket and then the other as if searching for something. ''Damn,'' I said.

The other women looked at me, concerned.

''What is it?'' Annee said. ''Have you lost something?''

''My notebook, the small notebook that I carry. I thought I had it with me.'' I shrugged my shoulders. ''I could have dropped it anywhere.''

''You could have dropped it when you were getting ready to do battle with Monsieur Saverne,'' Annee said, smiling. I'm sure she thought I wanted to snoop around and she was indulging me by making my excuse seem plausible. What she didn't know was that I was after Niki's necklace, and I felt guilty about deceiving her.

''Yes. Why were you holding the implement?'' Laurence was not satisfied with the explanations, nor was she sure what to call a spade.

''I heard someone coming; I panicked. I was sure someone was coming to hurt me again.''

Laurence clucked a few times sympathetically. ''If you want to look for your notebook,'' she said, ''we will keep watch. That will help you, no? You will feel better?''

''Thanks,'' I said. ''But I'll only be a minute or two. The notebook couldn't be in many places.''

I started toward the back door, but I heard Marsha say, "Don't worry, Laurence, I'll watch out for her."

The trip to the shed was even more brief than I thought it would be, for I found Niki's necklace in the box where I had seen the jewelry, and, wonder of wonders, in the same box I found a notebook, which would lend credence to my story. Besides, I thought, maybe the notebook would be just the thing to entertain a nosy person like me.

Seventeen

While I waited for Annee to get Fanny settled down, I leafed through the notebook I'd found in the shed. It was written in French and despite the neatness of the handwriting, I couldn't make out some of the letters. But there were names in the book that I recognized, Saverne and Niki among them. When Annee poked her head into my room to say she was ready to go to the inn, I tucked the notebook into my pocket where the necklace was already secreted.

Marsha had already gone to the inn to do her spying. Laurence was to baby-sit and call Annee if the baby woke up. This would be my first time at the inn since I got out of the hospital, but everything seemed different now that I knew more about the people who worked there.

I wanted to get rid of Niki's necklace as soon as possible. The thought of the necklace and the other jewelry in that box on the shelf made me uneasy. How could Annee not have known about it? Hadn't she gone through the boxes in the shed since Denis had died? Or had events taken up too much of her attention for her to be able to focus on the shed? Or was it more of the ostrich syndrome?

It did occur to me that it wasn't right to give the necklace back to Niki. If blackmail played a part in the motive for Denis's killing, maybe all the property in the shed should stay right there and the gendarmes should try to trace the owners. And how come the gendarmes hadn't uncovered the blackmail angle? What were they working on for a motive besides the fact that Annee and he didn't get along or that Denis and his son had had a falling-out?

As soon as I got a chance, I called the Toutes' house. I got lucky and Niki answered the phone. What I would have said if someone else had answered, I don't know. I hadn't prepared any lies. I would have had to wing it.

And then I worried about something else. If Jacques took the trouble to follow Niki, he also might have bugged the phone. But I got that thought too late, and I had to wing it anyway to keep Niki from giving away the fact that I was working for her.

Talk fast, I told myself. And I did. I started blabbering. "The baby is so cute. She's sleeping in an old basket. I don't know what to tell you to get for a christening gift. Maybe we should get together, and if we put our heads together, we could think of something."

I hoped Niki was too puzzled to say anything that I wouldn't want Jacques to hear. I didn't know how I was going to explain my strange behavior, either, unless I told her that her husband suspected she was running around.

"I am having trouble understanding," she said.

"Why don't you come to the inn sometime this evening? I'll be working at the bar. I'll buy you a drink."

She paused. I was sweating it out, hoping that she wouldn't mention anything that would get her, or me, in trouble. "I must drive Odette home tonight. I will come early."

"Great. See you later," I said, and hung up with relief.

My reflexes must be getting slow, I thought. Why hadn't I thought about a bugged phone before I called her? While I was going over this bugged material, I came up with an almost plausible way to alert Niki to the possibility that her phone was bugged. I'd just say I heard something funny on the line and wondered whether someone was trying to find out what Jacques was doing. After all, he was a bigwig with the Paris police, and they were always into secret operations.

The more I thought about it, the more sure I was that Jacques wouldn't let an opportunity like that pass. Especially since he thought his wife might have clobbered me.

If he had come to me with that story before Niki talked

to me, I probably wouldn't have gotten as far as I did with Niki.

My mind was so busy running over the Jacques-and-Niki problems that it took me some time to realize that the atmosphere in the bar had changed completely in the two weeks I was away. There was a bigger and younger crowd, a leather-and-earring group, and the remaining old souses sat together in a corner. The music was different, too—louder, younger, and some of it in English. Yves was often the center of attention, and he seemed to enjoy it. He even looked less tired when he was talking to the bar crowd.

Whenever Clarisse had to come to the bar for an order, many of the patrons spoke to her as if she were a buddy. And Yves treated her as if she were under his personal care. The connection between them was so obvious.

M. Saverne came out to the bar several times, probably to check out the crowd for any tendency to get rowdy, I thought. He greeted me warmly, in French. He was still keeping a lid on the fact that he spoke such good English. I wondered whether it had anything to do with his secret.

Odette also enjoyed the new crowd. I figured that she knew a lot of them because they were her brother's friends and acquaintances.

The dining room clientele hadn't changed much, but I could see that Annee or the Savernes had put some energy into giving the place a cleaner, neater look. Not that it hadn't been clean before, but it had had a cluttered appearance. I tried to remember what was different, and it took me all of about five minutes to realize that the window curtains had been removed and now the leaded-glass panes were visible, and clean. I was sure that that was not all that had changed, but I couldn't think what else was different. I would have to ask Annee.

Of course, Annee was different, too. She glowed. I noticed, too, that she had on a dress that must have been new. It showed part of her arms. And all I could think of was that the marks had healed and now she could uncover her arms. Her legs, too. They were encased in regular sheer stockings instead of the dark hose she had worn before.

During the course of the evening, I made a number of trips to the kitchen and the dining room. I was easier now with the routine and understood some of the basic words that I needed to know to be helpful. But most of the time I was among a clatter of voices with no meaning whatsoever for me.

On one of my returns to the bar, a new customer had shown up and was talking loudly. The younger people hung back and gave him room. I didn't understand what he was saying, but everybody was listening. He was gray-haired, bearded, and wore tinted glasses. He also wore a fedora that he didn't remove.

When Clarisse came into the bar on one of her many nonessential trips, I saw Yves give her a nod that sent her running to the kitchen. She was back in a few seconds with M. Saverne and Annee.

They were a great team. M. Saverne supplied the muscle and Annee supplied the diplomacy. The loudmouth was quiet and sitting at a table in no time. Annee offered him a drink, and M. Saverne offered him an unspoken threat.

Several minutes later, the three of them had come to some sort of meeting of the minds, which I assumed had occurred, because I saw them all smiling. M. Saverne got up and went back through the swinging door to the kitchen. Then the door swung out and Vincent, clad in an apron, came out smiling.

He double-kissed the stranger and sat down with him and Annee.

All this time I was helping Yves serve drinks to the young crowd, who now had another topic of conversation, and they were busily buzzing about the loud newcomer. When there was a lull in the drink orders, I asked Yves what had happened.

"He says he's Denis's brother, Paul, and he's outraged that his brother was murdered and that no one notified him, and he wants his share of his brother's property. He says he has a copy of a will that gives him half of everything that belonged to Denis."

"And Annee didn't know anything about this brother?"

"Well, she acted surprised when she first heard it," Yves said. "He could be an impostor, of course."

"I've heard of people who present themselves as long-lost relatives after the person who could identify them has died,'' I said.

Yves poured another carafe of wine while I took a closer look at the fellow sitting at the table with Annee and Vincent. I knew Denis only from pictures. But in the pictures Denis had no beard, so it was hard to see whether there was a resemblance. The new arrival's hair, although ample, was totally gray, but the hairline was the same as Denis's, and maybe the nose.

"He does look like Monsieur Rien," Yves said when he came back to the end of the bar where I was standing. "Except for the hair color. And he's a bit heavier. And the expression on his face is more pleasant."

Yves curled his lip when he made the comparison, and I was reminded of the night he had as much as told his father of his affection for Clarisse. I also remembered what M. Saverne had said about Denis giving Clarisse money. "Denis was not a pleasant person to work for?" I said.

"I did not work here very often while he was alive. I did not like him and only helped when Madame Rien asked me to come, usually on Mondays, when he wasn't here and the place was closed."

"Why didn't you like him?" I said.

"He was a pig," Yves said.

"A pig?"

Yves walked away and wiped up the bar and asked people if they needed anything. Some did, so he didn't come back to finish the conversation. Too bad; I was just warming up to it. I wanted to know what he knew or suspected about Denis and Clarisse. But I didn't get a chance to get back to the subject.

Annee got a call from Laurence that Fanny was awake and acting hungry.

"Fran," Annee said, "I must go home and feed Fanny. But you mustn't stay if you are tired."

"I'm not in the least tired," I said. It wasn't accurate, but I did have to wait to speak to Niki.

Vincent and Paul, Denis's alleged brother, went home with Annee. She was treating him like family, something I wouldn't have done on such short acquaintance. Perhaps she wanted Laurence to have a look at him.

As they were leaving, Odette came into the bar and did a double take when she saw Paul. Yves told me later that Odette thought she had seen a ghost.

Niki, as she had promised, arrived about a half hour before Odette was due to go home, causing some confusion for Odette, who hung up her apron and was ready to leave as soon as her mother came in. Niki explained to her, I think, that we were going to chat about a present for Fanny.

Yves thought it was amusing that his mother was going to have a drink with me. I got the idea that Niki was supposed to be at their disposal and not have a life of her own.

Once we got her kids straightened out and got rid of them so we could talk, I told Niki that I thought I had found the necklace.

She smiled happily and looked excited, but I couldn't very well show it to her because there was no privacy, even though we were in one of the corners of the room.

We finally worked out our version of the spilled-drink ploy with her purse hanging from a chair and me dropping the necklace into her purse while we bumped and stood up and started wiping up the wine.

She went to the bathroom shortly afterward and came back looking radiant. "Thank you, Fran," she said, and slipped something into my pocket so deftly, I wondered why we hadn't let her pick my pocket to get the necklace. "Where did you find it?" she said.

Her question sounded innocent enough, but I wasn't about to give away the secret of the shed. Who knew what else he had there? And I felt guilty about giving it to her. If she were accused of killing Denis, I would have tampered with evidence. I didn't know what the punishment for that was in France, but I figured it was something a little less harsh than the now-abandoned guillotine.

I moved the conversation to the subject of a tapped telephone, telling her that I had heard a peculiar sound on her line.

"I have heard a sound sometimes," she said.

"When did you first notice it?"

"Perhaps one month," she said.

"And you haven't told Jacques about it?"

"No. I will have to tell him."

"But then you will have to tell him that we were talking. Will he ask questions?"

She frowned. "What will I do?"

"If he hears the noise, he surely will suspect," I said. "He is a policeman."

That seemed to be all right with her, and I figured another crisis had been averted.

Eighteen

Later, back at Annee's, Marsha and I walked in on a strange scene. Annee was holding the baby, Vincent was scowling at his newfound uncle, Laurence was looking very uncomfortable, and Paul was sitting in the big armchair as if he owned the place. His elbows rested on the arms of the chair, his hands were folded over the bulge of his stomach, his legs were apart, and his feet were flat on the floor, not the position of someone who is at all uneasy.

Even Annee's composure and good temper seemed to be taxed. Laurence, as soon as we entered the living room, got up and steered us toward the kitchen, saying something about making coffee, a phrase that I had become familiar with while working at the inn.

"He expects to stay here," Laurence said as soon as we were out of earshot of the living room. "Annee doesn't know what to do."

"Is that why Vincent looks so angry?" Marsha said.

"He tried to tell Paul that he couldn't stay here," Laurence said, "and Paul told Vincent that he had no more rights to the house than Paul did."

"He needs to have a document and the document has to be authenticated," Marsha said. "He can't just come in here waving a paper and expect people to make him feel at home."

"He looks like he feels right at home," I said. But in the back of my mind, I was making a decision to call another man who pushed people around. Fight fire with fire, I thought.

I dug around in my things up in my room until I found Jacques's phone numbers. If he wasn't home, I'd track him down.

He answered the phone when I called the house. "Fran," he said, "I hear that you and Niki have been drinking together."

Hmm. He didn't know that Niki hadn't clobbered me. And I wasn't about to tell him right away. "There were some things I had to talk to her about," I said, at my enigmatic best.

"Yes?" he said. "What did you find out?"

"I can't talk about that right now. We have a problem here, or rather, Annee has a problem."

"Annee? What's the matter?" I knew I had said the magic word. I told him about Paul's arrival at the inn, some of which he had already heard from his children. Then I told him what had happened since Paul arrived at Annee's.

"I'll be right over," Jacques said. "He can't expect Annee to give him a place to stay. Has anyone seen this will he is talking about?"

"Not that I know of," I said.

When I went back to the living room, Laurence and Marsha were serving coffee, and Paul was saying something about having plans for the inn. Annee was practically squirming in her seat.

"Where has Paul been living all these years?" I asked Annee.

"In Marseilles," Annee said. Then she translated for Paul, who looked at me with a sneer.

"When did he hear about Denis?" I said. "And how did he hear?"

Annee turned to ask him the questions I had asked. He turned red and started shouting at me and stood up and came toward me. He definitely looked threatening.

Since I had had a husband who had played all those intimidating games, I was familiar with the stance. Familiar, but not comfortable. I knew that backing off would only make him worse.

So I stood up to face him and braced myself to fight him

with every bit of energy I had. I am sure that my fingers were set in a claw shape, and I gritted my teeth as if I were a wild dog.

He stopped in his tracks. Vincent had risen from his chair, too. But Paul was looking over my shoulder, and I never got to find out whether my display of grit would have worked.

"Allow me to introduce myself," Jacques said to Paul in a voice that was polite and almost mocking. Then he said the same thing in French, and followed that with an introduction of himself, complete with his police department titles, one of which was *commissaire* (superintendent). Their handshake after Paul had introduced himself was cold and stiff.

Jacques continued to say everything in two languages, English first—"What is your name?" "When did you arrive in Vaudoy?"—then French. It took me a few minutes to realize what he was doing. He was getting ready to arrest Paul and he wanted to have witnesses in both languages. I thought it was because he didn't have one of those papers that the gendarmes bring along when they are going to arrest someone. In French it's a *mandat*, what we call a warrant in English.

But I wasn't the only one who realized what was coming next. Paul was right on top of the situation, and since he was standing right near me, he grabbed me and held me in front of him like a shield. His beard bristled against my neck and he started shouting in my ear. I hadn't the least notion of what he was saying. He started to pull me backward, heading for the door.

Panic was rising in my gullet and my mind was starting to feel the way it had felt in the hospital. Even my tongue was starting to feel thick. I was wishing I were healthier, because I had better coping mechanisms for this type of situation when all my systems were working.

I came up with a plan anyway. It wouldn't work, I knew, if Paul was well coordinated and fast on his feet. I was hoping for clumsy and slow.

My heel went down hard on his foot. This obviously surprised the heck out of him, because he cried out, started muttering, and loosened his grip on my arms. I wheeled around and lifted my elbow at the same time and whacked him on the side of his head. It made a satisfying crack, and hurt me only a little bit.

He turned and ran right to the kitchen, like someone who knew where he was going, I thought. He was favoring one foot, but I was in no condition to pursue him, and apparently nobody else thought it was a good idea.

Jacques got on the phone, and Annee locked the doors.

As soon as there was a quiet moment, I asked Laurence if she knew Denis had a brother.

"I did not see the family for many years. There was a disagreement. They were living in the south and had a little auberge."

"Ah, so that's where he learned to cook," Marsha said.

"But you would have heard, wouldn't you, if there had been another child?" I said.

"Something so important," Marsha said, "they would have told you."

Laurence thought for a minute and then shook her head. "Since we did not speak, it is possible that they did not tell me about him. And Denis and I did not speak about the family."

"So we can't assume he's a phony," I said.

"But he looks so much like Denis," Annee said. "Are there any cousins?"

Laurence brightened. "But yes," she said. "A cousin. Marcel. He was looking like Denis very much."

"But why would he say he was a brother?" I said.

Annee's face was going through one transformation after another. We all watched her. "I'm trying to remember the night he supposedly died," she said.

"You think that Paul might be Denis?" I said. "He's that much like him?"

"I don't see how. Of course, he could have planned it all and then, when I went to call the ambulance . . ." She shook her head. "No, I don't think it's possible."

"Unless he had help," I said. "But why?"

"We have to find this man who calls himself Paul Rien," Jacques said.

If Denis's blackmailing had backfired on him, I thought,

he might have faked his death because he was afraid someone was going to kill him.

Then he could wait a couple of weeks and return as Denis's brother and start the blackmail all over again. If Arnaut and Foyer had helped Denis fake his death, they might have been in the way when Paul appeared. But who was the man in Denis's grave?

Or maybe Arnaut had double-crossed Denis by giving M. Saverne the key. And what about the attempt on Laurence's life? Was she going to be sacrificed, too? And would Annee have been on the list, too, as well as Vincent, and maybe Niki?

Of course, I told myself, this is all predicated on the theory that Paul is Denis. Suppose Paul is Paul, brother of Denis, who is just another opportunist.

Vincent hadn't said a word since the man who called himself Paul had left. "What did you think?" I said to him.

"I was getting the same feelings toward him that I had for my father. He made me resentful, angry, outraged. But the gray hair and beard was not like Papa. But he moved the same and his face had the same unevenness when he lifted one eyebrow."

"He smelled like Denis," Annee said. "When he bent over to look at Fanny, I could smell him." She looked distressed. "I don't know whether I am a widow or not."

"We can get an order to dig up the grave and see who's in it," Jacques said.

The evening was shaping up to be another night with the gendarmes. I was tired, but I knew I wouldn't be able to sleep anyway.

The blackmail was looming larger in my mind and I was getting edgy about keeping it secret. It was a secret worth killing for, and the more people who knew about it, the safer I'd feel.

Before the gendarmes get here, I told myself, I've got to get Jacques aside and tell him. The resolve was no sooner made than I was rescued from having to keep it by the appearance of M. Saverne at the door.

He was tired of keeping secrets, he told Jacques. Then he told everyone in the living room the same things he had told me about the night I got clobbered and the blackmail.

Unfortunately, he also told them that he had already told me the story. I got a few fisheye looks on that score.

But M. Saverne was the one who had the surprises that night, and his knowing English was only the first.

The secret that had cost him so much, that Denis had held over his head, was that he was a deserter from the Canadian Army in World War Two and that he had assumed the identity of a dead French soldier, Jean Saverne, who wore Jean Leclerc's dog tags to his grave. He was raised in Quebec, he said, and got into the army at sixteen by lying about his age. His parents were dead and he had been living with a drunken uncle who was glad to be rid of him.

The captain of his unit, he said, was a homosexual and used M. Saverne ''badly,'' M. Saverne said. He hung his head as he told his story and I could see drops falling to the floor.

''I don't know how Denis found out, but one day he called me by the name I was born with. I have been his slave ever since. More than once I wanted to kill him, but I didn't. And then, tonight, seeing that man at the inn who said he was Denis's brother, I knew it was time to tell.''

''Did he look like Denis to you?'' Annee said.

''Yes. He looked exactly the way he looked often when he had flour in his hair in the kitchen, when he would be making that thing he makes when he tosses the dough around.''

Annee smiled. ''He does pizza the way he saw it done in America years ago.'' She got a funny look on her face. ''Did you hear what I said? I used the present tense. As if Denis were still alive.''

Jacques didn't look too happy just then. And during M. Saverne's story, Jacques had looked at me with questions in his eyes more than once. I already knew one question: Why hadn't I told him that Niki didn't bang me over the head?

By the time the gendarmes arrived, Jacques had given M. Saverne a new lease on life. He explained some of the legal ramifications and told him that extenuating circumstances could erase the crime or make the penalty less severe.

"Will all the children and grandchildren have to change their name?" M. Saverne said.

"That's the easy part," Jacques said. "You go to court and legally change your name. The others were given that name on their birth certificates."

I kept mum about Niki's necklace and dreamed about it all night while the police hauled away the contents of the shed.

Jacques had put a guard on the house to keep Paul away should he get it in his mind to return. Sometime before we all went to bed, Jacques told Annee that he had put in a request to have Denis's grave opened. And sometime during the night, while I slept, safe, I thought, in my bedroom, with a guard outside the house and police packing up the shed, someone pushed an envelope under my door.

Nineteen

When the light seeped through the cracks in the shutters next morning, I thought it was earlier than it was. The sunshine was gone, replaced by a gray, cool drizzle. I had been in the habit of leaving the windows open inside the shutters, because the nights had been fairly warm. But this morning I closed up the windows and slid back under the blanket.

It was while I was lying there, luxuriating in the coziness of the bed, that I noticed the white rectangle under my door. Since the doors to the bedrooms were usually not locked, I thought it was a strange way for any of my housemates to communicate. I wasn't in any hurry to get up and see what it was. I was too chilly to succumb to a little thing like curiosity. But it kept catching my eye and I figured someone was playing a joke.

When I finally got out of bed, I picked up the envelope and took out the piece of paper inside. Even after I read it the first time, it didn't sink in. I was waiting for the punch line. But sink in it did, and I was colder than ever. Someone had written in capital letters: MADAME KIRK, GO AWAY WHILE YOU CAN. GO BEFORE YOU ARE BURIED IN FRANCE.

Threats always get to me. They don't roll off my back like so much water off a duck. They scare me and make me mad. This time it made me cry. I am not given to tears very often, but in the state I was in, I was vulnerable. While I was standing by the door gritting my teeth and wiping away tears with the sleeve of my nightgown, there was a noise in the hallway.

Yes, I screamed. And in seconds I was no longer alone. Marsha and Annee were there, clucking and caring. They looked at the paper that I waved at them through the blubbering. Annee immediately called the police, who had not stayed all night to sort out the shed, but had gone home to bed after cordoning off the backyard. They did leave a guard at the front and one at the back of the house, though. These two looked over the note, and I was starting to count the number of sets of fingerprints that would be on it.

I mentioned this to Annee, who translated for the guards, who immediately began handling it with a handkerchief.

"They just came on duty," Annee said. "They haven't seen anyone."

"How did anyone get in?" I said. "You locked the doors and the house was guarded all night."

"The guards might have been easy to get past," Annee said, "but I can't think how anyone got in."

By this time Laurence had come out of her room and joined us. Vincent must have still been sleeping, as was Fanny. "We'll check the whole house after breakfast," Laurence said.

Spoken like a true Frenchwoman, I thought. Food first.

But we were only half through breakfast when the investigators swooped down on us again. Annee got out more cups and bread and croissants and the officers sat down at the table and asked their questions while they buttered their croissants, sugared their coffee, and knocked crumbs off their ties.

Vincent toddled in with his hair sticking out at odd angles and his eyes half open, or half closed, depending on whether you're an optimist or a pessimist. His shirt, which I remembered from the night before, was buttoned wrong and one tail was higher than the other in the front. I thought he looked kind of cute.

He dutifully stayed awake long enough to answer the officers' questions and scarf down some pastry and coffee. Then he went back to his room. Young folk can really log in the zees when they put their minds to it.

After breakfast was over, Annee and I went with a couple of the investigators to check the windows and doors for any sign of a break-in. We didn't find anything, and I have to say I would have felt less nervous if we had. As it was, we had no idea how anyone who would want to threaten me could have gotten in.

After the police left, Annee and I put our heads together and went over everything we knew, or everything we were willing to tell about what we knew, and I got a glimpse into the way her mind worked. I bet she made a great detective. She might have been gullible, as M. Saverne thought, but she didn't miss much.

She said she always knew there was something in the shed that would have to be reckoned with, but she never had time or the opportunity to get a look at it.

When I told her that I thought there were things there belonging to many people, she shook her head. "No, I don't think there were a lot of people he was blackmailing. Otherwise he wouldn't have needed to hide the money he got from Laurence. The things in the shed are probably things he found." She paused before she said, "Or stole."

I was feeling so disloyal because I had held back the story about Niki, but I couldn't think of a way to bring it up so that I wouldn't seem to be such a rat. "Stole?" I said. "Seems he had a long list of faults."

Annee frowned, probably at my bluntness. "I was a fool," she said. "If this man Paul turns out to be Denis, I will divorce him. I didn't know or couldn't let myself know before."

"Suppose it is Denis," I said. "What was his intention when he faked his death? Did he plan to show up again as his own brother? And did he expect to kill off everyone who knew him so that he wouldn't be discovered? And did something go wrong with his plan?"

"I've been trying to come up with a scheme that would fit the situation as I can imagine it," Annee said. "But every time I think I've got it, something else crops up that doesn't follow."

"Did Denis know Arnaut and Foyer well? Could they have helped him put someone besides himself into the grave?"

"I still don't see how it could be anyone else. His body was at the police lab for days, I saw him fall down when he was stricken."

"When he was stricken," I said. "Did he just fall over dead?"

"No, no. He writhed in pain and screamed and kicked."

"Did he throw up? Was he gasping for breath?" I said.

"The gendarmes asked me those questions after the poison was identified. I told them what I just told you."

"So perhaps Denis wasn't poisoned," I said. "Did you leave the kitchen?"

"I went to the phone and called the gendarmes and told them I needed an ambulance." I waited for her to go through the story. "When I finished the phone call, I heard no more thrashing. Before I could get to the kitchen, though, I heard someone tell me to stay in the living room. I assumed it was the police."

"But wasn't it too fast for them to have gotten there?" I said.

"Yes, but I didn't question it then."

"And did you ever see Denis again?"

"No."

"Why was the coffin closed?" I said.

"That was always his wish. He used to say that he didn't want Arnaut or Bouton to look at his corpse and gloat. I told them to close the coffin."

"And who told you he was dead?"

"The voice from the kitchen. The one who told me to stay in the living room."

"You didn't recognize the voice?"

"I remember thinking it was a policeman."

"So maybe he had help in pulling off this ruse. We can ask the police who was here when they arrived."

"It will be difficult to question the police about what they did," Annee said.

"Maybe Denis and his cohorts counted on that," I said. But I still was shaky on why he would want to fake his death. And I couldn't figure out who had shoved the note under my door, either.

"Have you discovered anything unusual in his records?" I said.

"Laurence and I went over the books as well as we could, but there must have been things that he didn't write down. For one thing, I don't think he reported all the income he made from the inn. Since he died, the income has been much higher. And it isn't that there are many more people or that we are charging more.''

''Where did the money go?''

''I don't know,'' she said.

''Maybe he had a Swiss bank account and was planning his getaway for a while. Maybe that's what he did with the money from Laurence and with the blackmail money, too.''

Annee thought about that for a few seconds. ''That fits with our theory,'' she said. ''But I don't think it fits Denis. I don't think he would want to go away from his town.''

I wasn't at all sure that Annee was reliable when it came to what Denis might do, but I went along with it. ''Then if all our suppositions are on track and he didn't want to leave town, he must have been planning on coming back as Paul, with gray hair.''

''And maybe he planned to bully me into letting him take over.''

Just like he'd been bullying you for years, I didn't say. ''But it won't work now,'' I said. ''Laurence and you and Vincent and M. Saverne all suspect that he might be Denis. And when they open the grave, the ruse will be uncovered.''

''Assuming we are right,'' Annee said.

''But what about the note under my door? Could he have gotten in the house?''

''I have lived here for more than twenty years,'' she said. ''I have cleaned every spot in the house. There is no way he could have gotten in except by the doors. The shutters were all closed last night.''

''He would have had to get past the guards going in and coming out.'' Then a chill took hold of me. ''Unless he's still in the house,'' I said.

''But we looked everywhere,'' she said. Then she got a look on her face that told me she felt the same chill. She was thinking something else. ''No one followed him out of the living room last night. He might not have left. He might have gone to the cellar.''

''How many ways are there to get to the cellar?'' I said.

''Two. One outside and one inside. But the outside door is usually locked.''

"But Denis would have a key."

"Yes." She got up and started toward the kitchen, with me behind her. I recalled the door in the kitchen that I had never seen opened, and knew that was the other entrance to the cellar.

She opened it and in the dark on the other side I could make out a banister and a stair pad on the top step. I heard a click, and Annee said, "*Merde* [Shit], the bulb has blown out."

"Wait," I said. "Get something. A rolling pin."

Annee grabbed a heavy iron frying pan off a hook over the stove and a flashlight from one of the drawers. I grabbed a knife and lit a candle. I really didn't think we were equipped to handle a trapped felon, but we started down the steps.

We had gone only a few steps into the darkness, carrying our halo of light, when Annee stopped. "Someone's down there," she breathed.

"Maybe we should send Vincent to guard the outside door," I whispered.

Before she had a chance to answer, we heard a crash and a thump. I felt that if I didn't swallow hard, one or more of my organs would jump into my throat. Annee gasped. We were reluctant to go any farther.

I was thinking that we should get back upstairs and bar the door and then barricade the outside door to trap whoever it was. But I knew it was too late when I saw the swath of light on the basement floor.

"He's escaped," Annee said.

At that point we started to scream in two-part harmony. Everyone came running, but not one of us got to see who the intruder was or which direction he had taken.

Annee said she knew the police couldn't do anything about it, but she called them anyway.

Whoever it was might have been in the house all night, wandering around. He could have killed any one of us or all of us, I thought. But the only thing that had happened was that a note had been slipped under my door.

While we waited for the gendarmes to arrive for another go-round, I tried to sort out what had happened. Usually when I felt stuck, I would go back to the beginning, but this time the beginning was all turned around. What we thought had happened might not have happened.

I tried another approach. What did we know that was certain? Whoever was killed, Denis or someone else, had died from eating poisonous mushrooms in a pâté. Was there something I could find out about the mushroom that would point the way to the killer? Annee would have to help me on this, because I didn't know enough French to ask the questions I had.

Before we were invaded by enthusiastic policemen, I managed to tell Annee what I wanted to know. She said she would ask Jacques to get the information from the lab about the type of mushroom that had killed the three men, and she told me that Laurence could tell me a lot about mushrooms.

I decided to go ahead and ask Laurence about the kinds of mushrooms that grew in the area and which ones were poisonous, even though I got an uneasy feeling when I thought about Laurence eating a pâté poisoned with mushrooms when she was supposed to know so much about them.

She had a new bit of information for me when I asked her, which I had a chance to do because the gendarmes were slow to arrive.

"There is one mushroom"—actually, she called it *champignon*, which is the French word for "mushroom"—"that can poison the whole sack."

"Oh," I said. "Is that what you think happened to you? You ate one that had been in the sack with a poisonous type?"

"*Exactement*," she said. "That is what I think."

She spelled out the name of the mushroom that she thought was the culprit: Amanita phalloides. "Many deaths are from this mushroom," she said.

By then Marsha was listening, and she had more information. "But, Laurence, I read about that mushroom. It doesn't kill people right away. They don't even get symptoms right away."

Laurence hit herself on the forehead. "*Mais oui*," she said, then spoke in French, first to herself and then to Marsha.

"Inocybe de Patouillard," Laurence said several times

before I realized that she had come up with another mush-room name.

She and Marsha babbled some more and then Marsha said, "That one can kill right away, but you have to eat a lot of it, Laurence says. Maybe that's why she didn't die."

"Do these mushrooms grow around here?" I said.

"*Oui, oui,*" Laurence said.

"Could you show them to me?"

"*Mais oui,*" she said. "The Inocybes are growing under linden trees and by the woods."

Marsha suggested that I come with them when they took their walk. "We'll walk in the woods today. Now that the rain has stopped, it's hot again. It will be nice to walk under the trees."

Jacques arrived with the police when they finally came. They looked around the house for footprints, but they told Annee there were too many to tell which ones were the intruder's. Most of them were from the gendarmes, I thought.

When they finished their discussion of the footprints, An-nee asked Jacques about the mushroom that the lab had found.

"I will call the lab. I don't remember the name, but I know it wasn't the one that we get so many calls about every year. The one that causes so many accidental deaths."

I mentioned the name Laurence had given me. "Inocybe de Patouillard?"

"Yes," he said. "I think that's it. How did you know?"

"Laurence suspected that was the one," I said. "She's going to show me one this afternoon."

"Many people know mushrooms," he said. "Niki and her parents have picked them in the woods for many years."

Niki again, I thought. Maybe I shouldn't have taken her off my list of suspects. Maybe I shouldn't have given her back her necklace.

Jacques called the lab and told us that the poison was muscarine and that the mushroom Laurence had mentioned was one of many that contained the poison. I didn't know what good it would do me to actually look at the deadly mushroom, but I was curious to see the instrument that the killer had used.

There was more news from Jacques, too. "We've got permission to open Denis's grave," he told Annee. "Because Paul acted so suspiciously and you suspected that he was Denis, we had no trouble getting the order. You know, Odette was afraid that she had seen a ghost."

When Jacques left, Marsha and Laurence hurried me to go for the walk.

"We have to get back to watch Fanny," Marsha said, "so Annee can go to the inn."

I quickly got my running shoes on, hoping that I'd get a chance to jog a half mile or so. If I could run, I knew I would feel healthier, more like myself.

We got to see more than mushrooms on our walk.

Twenty

The day had taken on an entirely different character. The July sun had burned off the dampness and a dry wind drove small puffy clouds across the sky from the west. Marsha was right about walking under the trees. As soon as we got into the woods, we were enveloped by the coolness of the greenery.

One thing I had noticed since I'd arrived in Vaudoy was how many doves one could hear around the town. They were always making their coo, coo, coo sound. They were in the woods, too, but other birds joined the chorus there, making their coo, coo, coo less noticeable.

Laurence was walking so much better I was again tempted to tell her so, but again I didn't for fear of insulting her by indicating how badly she had walked before. At one point, walking behind her, I realized that her backside, which formerly was of a size that my mother used to call a "bushel boomy," had been whittled down to a half bushel. The walks hadn't been bad for Marsha, either. Although the difference in her silhouette was not nearly so marked, there had definitely been an improvement.

I didn't want to think about what I looked like to someone approaching from the stern. I imagined cellulite, soft lumps that shook with each step, thickening in the outer thigh and rubbing together on the inner. Unconsciously, my hand ran over my backside and legs. When I realized what I'd done, I put my hands in my pockets.

We were nearing the area where I had seen Arnaut pacing the day before, at the edge of the little hollow where

Odette and Bernadette made their magic. There was no one around now. The girls would practice later in the day, I assumed, and then people from the village would gather to watch. I wondered whether they practiced in the winter, and asked Laurence about it.

"No, they have not done this in the winter," she said.

"They just started this spring," Marsha said. "At first, people whispered about it, and then some started to sneak into the woods to watch them. But now it is an event. People are coming from other villages."

"It won't be long before the television cameras arrive," I said.

"Television, *ooh là là*," Laurence said. "Here in Vaudoy? Maybe the town would become rich and could repair the church."

I had noticed the holes where the old stones had fallen out of the church walls and birds had taken advantage of the shelter that the holes afforded. Laurence had told us that the oldest parts of the church had been built in the twelfth and thirteenth centuries. It had been restored, she said, in the sixteenth century and repaired in the 1700s and again in the 1800s, but the twentieth century had not been kind to the old edifice, and the few places where modern improvements had been affixed to the old stones looked tacky and impermanent, not to mention ugly.

We spent some time imagining what the glare of publicity would do to the sleepy town of Vaudoy, and then Laurence suddenly stopped.

"Here is where I have seen the most deadly of the mushrooms," she said. She pointed to a mossy area near an outcropping of rocks. "Not today. Not enough rain, perhaps."

I was wondering when she had seen the mushrooms. Certainly, when I arrived in France, she was in no condition to walk this far. So I asked her.

"Spring," she said. "Before I was feeling bad."

Oh, I thought her condition had been a permanent thing before we arrived. But she'd been able to walk in the spring. I wondered whether that was important in the scheme of things.

I went to the spot where Laurence said she'd seen the

mushrooms growing and bent over to look at the ground. I didn't expect to find anything, but detectives are always looking at the ground for something.

In between a couple of rocks, however, I did see mushrooms growing. "Laurence, can you look at these?" I said.

She half busheled over to the spot and bent over. Then, without taking her eyes off the spot, she grabbed my arm and lowered one knee to the ground.

"Yes, yes," she said. "These are Amanita phalloides."

"But this isn't the type that the lab says killed Denis and the others, is it?"

"But no."

"Have you seen the other kind?"

"This year, no."

"But they do grow around here?"

"*Oui*, by the linden tree," she said slowly.

Apparently more people are familiar with mushroom lore in France than in the States, where only a few people delve into it.

"Can you show me?"

"Let us see."

She walked into the woods, looking up, not down, trying to locate a linden tree, I guessed. Not far into the woods, she pointed to the base of a tree. "There. Inocybe de patouillard."

"So the murderer wouldn't have had any trouble getting his hands on the poison," I said.

"No, not at all," Laurence said. She jumped from French to English, sometimes saying "*non*," and sometimes "no."

"Wait a minute," I said.

Marsha and Laurence looked at me.

"We're not going anyplace," Marsha said. "What's the matter?"

"If Paul is Denis, and someone else is in Denis's grave, then Denis could have made the deadly pâté. And he could have put the pâté on the kitchen table the night Laurence got sick."

Their heads rocked, together, like a couple of plastic creatures on the back shelf of a car.

"Yes," Marsha said. "That could explain part of it."

"Yeah," I said, "he could have. If he wasn't dead and was hiding."

I was feeling strangely agitated. That scared feeling, no, make it that panicky feeling, was making me tingle all over, making me want to run or cry or scream. It was all I could do to make myself stand still and act somewhat normal. Marsha and Laurence kept going over the events, bringing up possibilities, but I was tuned out, lost in my own little battle to control myself. I would have something else to tell Dr. Berenger about when I saw her.

When Marsha and Laurence decided to continue the walk, I followed along dumbly, not thinking of anything, but worrying over my state of mind.

We'd gone only a short distance when we heard the unmistakable sound of Bernadette playing the flute. We, all three, stopped, and then, as if we had agreed upon it, stealthily proceeded toward the sound.

I guess I expected that when we got close, we'd see Odette dancing, but Bernadette was alone. We got to the edge of a small clearing, not big enough to part the branches and let the sun in, and stood there listening and watching Bernadette, lost in the music. Her eyes were closed and she neither heard nor saw us.

The music was melancholy and its rhythm was uneven. When I looked closer at her face, I could see why the rhythm was off. She was crying, her sobs breaking up her breathing.

I motioned to the others to back off. I suddenly didn't want this girl to know we had seen her. But one of us must have stepped on a twig or something, because her eyes snapped open, her mouth did likewise, and she got up and ran away. From out of nowhere, Odette appeared and ran after her, calling, "Baba, *attends* [wait]."

"Where was Odette?" I said.

"I didn't see her until she ran," Marsha said.

"She must have been watching us watching Bernadette," I said. "It makes me feel creepy." But that was nothing new. Everything was making me feel creepy.

"I like to see them happy," Laurence said. "They are angels."

I wasn't sure my notion of the Toute girls included halos,

but they did do something magical when they played and danced.

"I wonder what's the matter," Marsha said. "Bernadette looked so unhappy."

"They are young, artistic," Laurence said. "Many things make them unhappy."

Laurence sounded like a romantic.

We trudged on a little farther, heading for the path that Odette and Bernadette had taken the day before. The woods seemed a little less daunting now that I'd been on the path through them twice.

We were making no effort now to be silent, so when I first heard the sound behind us, I wasn't sure it wasn't one of us. But the second time I heard it, I stopped and hushed the others.

There was one more sound of something crashing through the brush after we stopped. Then another sound sent us running as fast as we could go, which meant that I led the pack. The sound was definitely a shot and it had hit the tree near where I had been standing. I broke into the open field screaming, and frightened an old man walking his dog—the man hustled away, carrying the trembling dog.

"Gendarmes, gendarmes," I hollered after him. I looked back and Marsha, followed by Laurence, was just coming out of the trees. Laurence saw the man and apparently knew him, because she started speaking to him in an animated way and he was answering her. Then he hustled off in the direction that he'd been going before.

"He will call the gendarmes. He lives just there." She pointed to a small stone house whose shutters were all closed.

"Let's get away from here," Marsha said. "Whoever is shooting can still take aim at us, and maybe stand a better chance of hitting us in the open."

We walked away quickly, and since we were closer to the inn than to the house, went there. I was thinking that whoever was in the woods didn't want to hurt us, but did want us to go away.

We called Annee to tell her what had happened and that we were at the inn and would wait for the gendarmes.

"I must go this afternoon and see whoever it is in Denis's coffin," she said, her voice tight and squeaky. "I was going to have Bernadette walk Fanny in the pram. Do you think the girl is all right?"

"If she's like most teenagers, she'll be in an entirely different frame of mind by this afternoon," I said.

"I'll call the house to make sure," Annee said.

A few minutes later, we saw the police van going by and we went out to flag it down. I let Marsha and Laurence do most of the talking, and it wasn't long before a second carload of gendarmes arrived and all of them were combing the woods.

Just about the time we were going to go back to the house, Odette arrived at the inn, not to work, because she usually worked the supper shift, but to apologize to us for being rude. Laurence's pants were charmed off (what a stupid expression that is) and Marsha, too, was impressed with the girl's sensitivity. Odette, I felt, had layers of complexities that she kept hidden from most people. Especially her parents. Maybe that was what made her dance like some possessed sprite.

Before we left the inn, the inevitable happened: A TV reporter, who had heard that the girls danced every afternoon, stopped in front of the inn with his crew. Marsha, Laurence, and I were standing near Odette when the reporter came in and told Odette that he wanted to shoot the rehearsal. He mentioned money, too, a lot of it. Marsha and Laurence translated for me.

Odette, to her credit, remained calm and didn't jump when he mentioned money. She said something about Papa and ran a string of titles past the reporter, and I was guessing that the TV man would have to speak to Jacques before there would be any shooting.

Of course, the shooting that the rest of the police were concerned with just then was the shots that had been fired in the woods.

Odette left with the TV crew following her and filming her. Even her walk was good footage. If the TV crew was going to film the girls, I wondered whether Bernadette would be done in time to baby-sit when Annee went to identify the person in the coffin.

We got our answer when we got home. Bernadette was there. She also apologized for being rude, and then she told us that she and Odette were not going to practice today because the TV crew was in town and her father didn't want the girls to be exploited.

I didn't think that would keep the TV crews away. It would be only a matter of time. Maybe Jacques knew that and was holding out for the best price.

Annee dressed the baby and put her in the carriage. Bernadette was to walk her around the yard while Annee was away. Annee called me into the next room while Marsha and Laurence cooed at Fanny.

"Would you mind very much coming with me?" Annee said.

Actually, the prospect of looking at a corpse that had already started to rot was not high on the list of things I didn't want to miss in my life. But it didn't give me that dreadful feeling that I'd had so many times lately.

"Give me a few minutes to change into something presentable, and I'll be right with you," I said.

"You won't have to look," she said. "I just want someone to go along."

"I thought Jacques would be there," I said, and saw the look on her face that told me that was why she wanted me there. "Oh," I said.

She smiled a tight little smile.

When we got to the morgue, Jacques had another surprise.

Twenty-one

The gray cement building that housed the morgue was in Melun, the principal city of France's seventy-seventh department, which is called Seine-et-Marne. The casket had been dug up out of the little cemetery in Vaudoy and then taken by the Pompes Funèbres Générales (the company licensed in France to deal with dead bodies) the twenty-five miles to Melun.

I was glad I had come with Annee, because there was a little more hustle in the city than in the sleepy town of Vaudoy. One section of the city was closed to auto traffic and I could see as we passed that restaurants had moved their chairs out into the square and merchants were displaying their wares outdoors as well.

The French drivers were mostly rude, I thought, passing Annee and cutting her off, even though she was traveling at the speed limit. Most of the cars were small and buzzed around like so many angry bees.

The Seine splits around an island in the middle of Melun, creating several pretty vistas and, with the city's profusion of one-way streets, many problems finding one's way around the town. We finally found the building we were looking for, after having gone over one fork of the river and then the other and back a couple of times.

A uniformed guard at the gate told us where to park and which door to enter after Annee told him what we were there for. Jacques was waiting just inside the door.

I sat down in the hallway, where a line of chairs ran along one side. Jacques took Annee by the elbow and guided her through a wide door at the end of the corridor. Annee did not look steady on her feet. While I sat there with nothing to do, my body started complaining about its neglect. My mouth was dry because I hadn't had nearly enough to drink that day, my stomach was growling because lunch had somehow been skipped, and my bladder was annoyingly full. The last item I thought would be an easy one to remedy.

I got up and walked along the corridor, looking for the international symbol for the ladies' room, and found nothing. Then I looked for the international symbol for the men's room, and still there was nothing. I went up a flight of stairs to another corridor and still found nothing. So I went back down and sat, uncomfortable and impatient for Annee's return. As I sat there, my eyes fell upon the door opposite where I sat. On the door were two small letters about eye height: WC. I hadn't noticed them before. I still wasn't used to calling a bathroom a water closet. And even though the expression wasn't French, some of the toilets were so marked.

Well, one of my body's complaints was taken care of. And Annee showed up a short time later, looking slightly green. Jacques's coloring wasn't exactly rosy, either.

I stood up, thinking that we would be on our way. But when Annee got to where I was standing, she sat. So did Jacques.

"It looks like Denis," she said, "but it is so distorted I can't be sure."

"What did you think?" I asked Jacques.

He looked tired and edgy. "Yes. It looks like Denis. I don't know. We will wait."

"Wait for what?" I said.

Annee put her face in her hands and began sobbing.

"They are going to open his mouth," Jacques said. "Annee will look at his teeth."

I looked at Jacques to see what he knew about Denis's teeth, or what he knew about what Denis had done with those crooked teeth, those teeth that had left so many marks on Annee, on Niki—and on how many other women?

"That's the only way I can be sure," Annee said, sniffling.

And I imagined the morgue attendants taking the stitches out of the mouth of the corpse so that Annee could look. No wonder she was greenish.

While we sat there silently with our separate images of the ghoulish procedure taking place behind the big door, Jacques was called to the telephone. He wasn't back yet when the big door opened and Annee was called to come in.

She grabbed my hand and I stood up and walked with her. I didn't want to go, but I couldn't let her go alone. My legs were not doing a first-rate job of transporting me.

When we entered the room, there was a big white drape covering something on a table. It looked too big for a corpse.

It was the whole coffin. I stood next to Annee, averting my eyes. Her hand was clutching mine so hard I thought my fingers would go numb. The attendant, or whatever he was, said something to Annee that I interpreted as ''Are you ready?''

She said, ''*Oui*.''

She let go of my hand and let out a screech. I turned my head and saw the teeth gaping from the shadows of the coffin.

I gasped and headed for the door. Before I got there, another attendant materialized, holding a bucket in front of me. I guess they were used to reactions like mine. It was just what I needed. What little food I'd had that day, I left behind.

When Annee and I were in condition to converse once again, she said, ''It's not Denis.'' She shook her head. ''I don't know what all this will mean. If he is alive, I will never live with him again. That man last night, that man who called himself Paul, now I'm sure that was Denis. I will get a lawyer and keep him away from me.''

She looked so determined, so angry. But I couldn't blame her. He was no bargain to begin with, and she had found out so many rotten things about him since he supposedly died—and now he was back.

Jacques came back with more news. The man called Paul had been found in the woods after Marsha and Laurence and I had been shot at.

Annee told Jacques that the teeth she saw weren't Denis's, and I almost started retching again.

"Can you drive home?" Jacques said. "Or shall I have someone drive you?"

"I'll stop at a café before I try to drive all the way home," Annee said. "Then I should be better."

"I will call the officers in Vaudoy and tell them that you failed to identify the corpse. That may help us question the man we arrested. I will call you later."

"Thank you," she said. "I wonder if he is the cousin. He looks so much like Denis." She gestured toward the doors at the end of the hall.

Annee and I got in the car and drove around on the one-way streets, looking for a place to park and a café. We found a little plaza where cars were parked around a fountain and where the café's tables were practically in the road. At first glance we saw no parking places left, but luck was with us and a car pulled out of a spot just as we approached it.

"You look a little green still," I said.

Annee laughed. "I look green? What color do you suppose your face is?"

"How many guesses do I get?" I said.

A waiter appeared next to the table, carrying a tray with little slips of paper and dirty glasses on it. Annee ordered port wine and I ordered Martini *blanc*, which is a semisweet vermouth.

Sitting there under the umbrella in that sunny plaza, watching the French do what they do so well—sit in cafes and nurse their drinks—I almost forgot the grim events of the past few weeks. Almost.

We were halfway through with our drinks before Annee got back to the subject of Denis. "I knew as soon as I saw the teeth from the front that it wasn't Denis," she said. "That's when I screamed. But when you ran, I made them open the mouth wider to see all the teeth. I didn't want to make a mistake. There is no chance at all that the man in the coffin is Denis."

"But you said he looked like Denis."

"He did. I thought he did. As Denis might look after he had been dead for three weeks. I didn't see him after he

started rolling around on the floor that Monday. I didn't see
him in his coffin. It was sealed, you remember."

"And you are sure it was Denis who was having supper
with you that night?"

"I've thought about that. I've wondered when the switch
was made. There surely was a switch. I can't believe that
the man in the coffin was so like Denis in life that I
wouldn't have noticed the difference."

"And last night, the man called Paul?" I said.

"I thought he was like Denis, but I couldn't see his teeth.
There was something different about the mouth. Perhaps it
was just that he was heavier than Denis was the last time
I saw him. But the smell of him, I mentioned last night,
was like Denis, and he moved the way Denis moved."
Annee sat there at the table in the middle of the square, but
she was somewhere else. Her left hand was balled into a
fist pressed against her mouth, eyes staring into a dimension
where no one else could see, shoulders rounded.

The northbound main road ran through the city on the
side of the plaza where we had parked. On the other side,
the street was closed to automobile traffic, and pedestrians
and shopkeepers alike availed themselves of the narrow
cobblestone road. I couldn't believe all the T-shirts with
American messages on them: the names of Western states,
the names of American football teams, messages in English
urging the saving of the planet.

The women dressed in very alluring clothes, I thought,
and many of the women were narrow-shouldered, narrow-
hipped, small people. They made me feel quite bulky, even
though, at five foot seven, I am not overweight. There were
loads of shoe stores and women's clothing shops, and all
of them had sales racks and tables on the street in front.

Annee and I wandered through the pedestrian mall for
twenty minutes after we had finished our drinks. It took me
a few minutes to realize that the number one hundred didn't
mean dollars and that some of the things on display were
pretty inexpensive, even though, as Marsha told me daily,
the dollar was weak.

Annee was pensive, but she answered my questions with
good humor. However, twenty minutes of browsing was all

she could take in her present state, so we returned to the car for our trip back to Vaudoy.

Her mood didn't lighten except when she spoke about Fanny, who was gaining weight faster than the doctors had expected her to.

"That's because I am gaining weight, too," Annee said. "I am eating much more cream and meat than I usually do. Milk, too. But I will cut back when she is a little bigger."

Then she sank back into her thoughts. That was how the trip went, all the way home. I'd bring up a subject, she'd say something about it, I'd add something else, and then the conversation would die. Finally I got sick of trying to pick the topic of the minute and I shut up.

My neglected stomach broke the silence. "I should have had something to eat," I said.

Annee said, "Oh, dear. I haven't eaten in hours, either. I'll have to give Fanny a bottle. I'll have nothing to feed her."

It seemed that she picked up speed at that, and suddenly all the macho males were no longer passing her, but were throwing her the finger, which seemed to be a universal signal, as she zipped past them. Frenchmen didn't like women passing them, and a couple sped up and rode right behind her, trying to pass, but she would have none of that. She was in the mother-tiger mode and her baby would be hungry.

I tried not to giggle. Annee definitely had different sides to her personality. If I had doubted her before when she vowed to keep Denis away from her, I doubted no longer. The wimp is dead, long live the tiger.

Another thing Annee was good at was getting a meal together, fast, which she did without making a fuss or a mess as soon as we walked in the door. Nor did she stop her preparations when Marsha told her that Jacques had called and wanted her to call back as soon as she got home.

"Later," she said. "I have to eat. And Fran is hungry, too. It's three already."

I was thinking that I probably couldn't have eaten earlier, but now I was ready to tear into a bare baguette (very French). Annee didn't ask for help, and I couldn't figure out what to do to pitch in, so I set the kitchen table and filled up the water pitcher.

Marsha and Vincent had just finished their lunch shift at the inn, and they reported that the inn hadn't been very busy.

"It wasn't worth opening for lunch," Vincent said.

Annee smiled. "I've been telling your father that for years. The town is too small to have a restaurant that opens for lunch."

"Why don't you do take-out food for lunch?" I said. "Like soup and sandwiches."

"Good idea," Vincent said. "We could price it low enough to make a go of it, I'll bet." Vincent was sounding definitely entrepreneurial.

I could see that Annee was getting a kick out of him. "Why don't you price it out for me? Consult the Savernes, though, because it will change their lives."

"What about Clarisse? We might not need her for lunch."

Annee didn't say anything right away, but the look that crossed her face told me that she had some not-too-pleasant thoughts about Clarisse.

"Don't say anything to her yet," Annee said.

"The way news travels around this village, I wouldn't be surprised if half of it knows about this conversation already." Vincent laughed, a deep baritone that I hadn't heard before. Maybe it was because he hadn't been laughing.

I noticed that Annee hadn't said anything to him about what she had seen at the morgue, and he hadn't asked. If I were back in the States and in Delia's company and tried to make something out of the fact that mother and son hadn't communicated about something so vital to their lives, Delia would have said, "Stop being a shithouse analyst." But I wasn't back in the States, and Delia wasn't anywhere around, and I let myself dwell on the psychological meanings of the moment.

Deep denial? That's an explanation that's very fashionable.

Enjoying the moment and to hell with tomorrow? Very retro.

Waiting until after the meal to talk about something unpleasant? Very French.

Marsha and Laurence and Vincent joined us at the table, even though they had already eaten. Most of the conversation was about Fanny. She had overnight acquired a little mole on her right cheek.

"It will be *très chic*," Laurence said.

"Her grandfather Kirk had a lot of moles," Marsha said. "Do you remember, Annee? I remember the first one I discovered on Richard."

Richard was my not-so-dear departed ex-husband, whom Marsha kept referring to as an eternal baby. Of course, he had never got as far as thirty, so maybe that was valid. I tried to remember whether he had any moles, but my mind wouldn't open the file on "Moles, Dick Kirk."

"Maybe it will go away," Vincent said, which, it occurred to me, was his take on difficulties in life. Maybe he had watched his mother's passivity too long. Maybe her new strength would inspire him. Maybe it would all go away.

By four-thirty, the meal—tomatoes and lettuce from the garden with a vinaigrette, fresh bread, *saucisson sec* (sort of a salami, but better), a couple of cheeses including a delicious Roquefort, coffee, and *tarte citron* (lemon tart)—had been eaten, the dishes had been washed, and Fanny had been fed and changed.

Then Annee told Marsha, Laurence, and Vincent about our trip to the morgue. I don't know how they waited that long, but Annee had fended off all their questions, I didn't feel it was my place to tell them, and they finally stopped asking. When she had finished telling them all the grisly details, Vincent said, "I'm glad I did not come."

Laurence said, "He was like Denis? The dead man?"

Annee nodded.

"The cousin," Laurence said. "It must be the cousin. They were very alike."

"But I never heard of him," Annee protested.

"I haven't thought of him in years," Laurence said.

When Annee called Jacques, the conversation was short and Annee didn't say much on her end. We were all sitting in the living room, sort of eavesdropping, but we didn't learn anything until she had hung up.

The tension in the room was horrid. If I had listened, I probably could have heard the sweat oozing from the pores.

Annee's face was colorless, drawn, dried-out-looking, as she stood facing us.

When she told us, we all shouted our demands to know.

"The man who called himself Paul has admitted he is Denis."

When we had finished our protests, Annee said, "Jacques wants me to come to the gendarmerie. Denis has explained why he let the farce go on."

"What possible reason could he have?" Marsha said, expressing the outrage that we all felt.

"I will find out when I get there," Annee said. "But I am not going without a lawyer."

"Good for you," I said. I didn't care what anyone else's opinion was on that.

Laurence spoke then, as if in a different key. Marsha noticed it, too. "I understand," she said. "But, of course, he is my nephew."

"You will have to make your own decisions about Denis, madame," Annee said, returning the formality that Laurence had projected. "I buried my marriage more than two weeks ago."

"But what if he has a good explanation?" Marsha said.

"It doesn't matter," Annee said. "There are many reasons."

"I'm on your side, Mom," Vincent said.

Laurence said nothing, but her eyes grew watery and she clenched her lips hard.

"I'm sorry, Laurence," Annee said. "But Denis wasn't a good person before this happened. If you feel loyalty toward him, I won't condemn you for it. He'll need a lawyer now, because he will be prosecuted for perpetrating a fraud. But I will not have him in this house, and if I can get the law on my side, I'll keep him out of the inn."

"But where will he go?" Laurence said.

"Why don't you ask him where he's been?" Annee's determination had turned into something that looked very much like rage.

Annee went back to the phone, and from what I picked up, she was speaking to a lawyer. Then she called Jacques and I heard her tell him that she would be there at six o'clock with her attorney, M. Simon Quiniou. There was more conversation after that, which seemed to indicate that Jacques was giving her an argument. Just before she hung up, she said, ''My mind is made up. I will not enter a room where Denis is unless my lawyer is with me.''

I didn't know what Jacques had been trying to persuade her to do, but I figured it had something to do with her helping the cops get more information out of Denis.

Marsha and Laurence, who had been getting along so well, now had their loyalties standing in the way of their friendship. I heard Marsha trying to smooth things out, but Laurence hadn't thawed.

Laurence, I thought, was having a tough time trying to figure out where her own loyalties lay. She had already been sending money to Vincent after he'd had a split with Denis. And now there was Fanny as well as Vincent on whom she could lavish her great-aunthood. But maybe she didn't want to abandon Denis altogether, now that Annee was set on kicking him out.

Annee again asked me to accompany her. ''I know that you will notice things that I miss,'' she said, flattering me with her confidence.

''I'll try to catch what's going on,'' I said. ''But I still don't understand much of the French.''

''I'll listen,'' she said. ''You watch.'' Then she smiled as if she were her old self and not the war-horse that had called a lawyer and spoken up to Jacques and Laurence for the first time in her life. ''Besides, I like having you with me. You give me confidence.''

I thought about how hard it had been for me to assert myself after I had spent ten years with Dick Kirk sitting on me, and it was true, I had come a long way. And maybe I could help Annee on that road. I'd had a lot of help from the battered women's group and Polly, the leader, who made us take a look at ourselves and find those things that kept putting us in harm's way.

When Annee asked Vincent if he wanted to go with us, he shuddered. ''I don't want to go near that place,'' he said.

Annee looked sympathetically at her older child. "Poor fellow," she said. "What a thing for you to have to go through. For us all. And he was alive all the time."

"How could he possibly explain it?" Vincent said, and he looked more like a boy than a man at that instant.

When the lawyer arrived, there was some hemming and hawing about how we were going to ride to the gendarmerie. Annee wanted to talk to the lawyer before they got there, and the lawyer wanted to stay on to talk to the police after Annee was done.

"Anything he will be charged with, anything he has admitted, will be helpful in your suit to keep him away from you," M. Quiniou said in perfect Oxford English. "You do intend to file for divorce, don't you? It will make keeping him away easier."

"I have ample grounds," she said.

It was decided that Annee would ride with M. Quiniou and I would follow in Annee's car. I imagined all the way how the conversation would go, and I wondered how sympathetic he would be. In the States, there are legions of women lawyers who do this kind of work, I thought, because women have had so much trouble getting men to understand. And then I wondered how much she'd tell him.

Twenty-two

The room to which Jacques escorted M. Quiniou, Annee, and me when we arrived at the gendarmerie was the same one to which the officers had taken Marsha and me the night Laurence was poisoned. This time, though, we weren't being grilled, we were being informed.

Denis had told the cops a long story that seemed to make him an innocent party. That was the story Jacques told Annee while M. Quiniou and I listened.

Annee's face betrayed almost nothing of what she felt during the recitation. I don't know how she did it. I'm sure she must have been feeling some of what I was feeling and much more so. I don't know what my face looked like, but the inside of me was churning, and my face is not exactly designed for poker playing. It took all the control I could muster to keep from shouting questions and calling the story a pack of lies.

The first part of the story rang true, partly because it explained the presence of someone else in the coffin.

"Denis told us," Jacques said, speaking in English because Annee had told him that she wanted me to hear, "that the man in the coffin is Marcel Gris, a cousin who has often put in appearances for him. M. Gris and Denis started doubling for one another years ago."

Annee's hands were folded in her lap. She didn't ask when Marcel Gris had stood in for Denis or how often. M. Quiniou took notes.

"On the Monday that Denis supposedly died of poison, Monsieur Gris and Denis were to meet in the shed behind the house, apparently to arrange for the next time he would be Denis. But when Denis arrived at the shed, Marcel Gris was dead.'' Jacques stopped for a minute and waited, but Annee said nothing.

''Denis was alarmed, and was convinced that whatever had killed his cousin was meant for him. Denis recruited M. Foyer to help him make the switch that night at supper.

''The subsequent poisonings of Madame Morvel and Messieurs Foyer and Arnaut only made Denis more convinced that he should stay in hiding. But he missed his family, he said, and then decided to assume the identity of his brother, Paul, who actually died in infancy, but whose death took place far from where he was born, so Denis thought he could get away with producing the birth record and be fairly safe that the death certificate would not show up.'' Jacques sat back. ''Of course, the story is longer than that, but basically, that's it.''

Annee looked at M. Quiniou, which I guessed was the signal for him to take over.

''Madame Rien's position on this is that she wants nothing to do with Monsieur Rien. Since his supposed death, she has discovered a number of his misdeeds, and she no longer wishes to be married to him. And, of course, the fact that he would pretend he was dead and not tell her indicates the utmost in distrust.''

Jacques looked at Annee. ''He expects you to get him a lawyer and to put up whatever money will be needed for a bond.''

Annee again said nothing, but looked at M. Quiniou, who said, ''Monsieur Rien, if that is indeed who he is, will have to get his own lawyer. If it is ascertained that he is who he claims to be, his lawyer will have to contact me regarding financial matters. Again I must stress, my client wants no contact with the man who now calls himself her husband.''

''So you won't see him?'' Jacques said. ''He has been asking for you.''

Annee shifted in her chair, her composure almost intact. ''Monsieur Quiniou and I have conferred. He has told you my wishes.''

''We will have no choice, then, but to keep him in jail until his lawyer can verify his identity. But you already said

that the man in the coffin was not Denis.'' Jacques was in
the peculiar position of pleading for Denis. Perhaps he
didn't like Annee as well when she displayed a little starch.

"That is police business," M. Quiniou said.

After all that was made clear, M. Quiniou told Jacques
that he would like to discuss the matter further with him.
He also said that he would meet with the man who was
calling himself Denis Rien and inform him of Madame
Rien's decision. Jacques got a crease between his brows
and then nodded.

Annee and I went home to await M. Quiniou's return.
From what I'd heard of Denis, the police would have to
hold him back from tearing into M. Quiniou when the lawyer told him what Annee was going to do.

When I asked Annee about it, she said, "Monsieur Quiniou won't have to take my word for Denis's disposition if
Denis shows his temper.''

"What are you going to do if Denis gets out of jail?"

"I hope the courts will keep him away from me."

"And if they don't?"

"I don't know." What recourse would she have? It was
the same everywhere. If the courts and the police couldn't
keep him away, she could flee or fight. Neither alternative
was satisfactory.

"Do you believe his story? Do you think someone was
trying to kill him?"

"If his story is true, you'd think he would want to stay
in jail until the murderer is caught," Annee said.

When we arrived at the house, only Laurence was there,
sitting in the living room, holding Fanny, who was making
hungry-baby noises. Marsha and Vincent had gone to the
inn.

Annee fed the baby and then took her upstairs to change
her and put her back to bed. When she came down, she
was smiling. "She eats so much, I can almost see her growing.'' Annee was doing it again: pushing away the unpleasant things and focusing on Fanny and what fun she was to
have around.

I went along with the mood and talked about Fanny. So
did Laurence, who, I imagined, really wanted to ask about
Denis.

I had some questions, too. One of them was why M. Foyer had consented to help Denis substitute the body of Marcel Gris for that of Denis. Of course, we had only Denis's word that M. Foyer had done that. And what if Denis himself was responsible for all the poisonings? M. Foyer might have found out about the switch and then Denis killed him, too. If Arnaut had a key to the shed, he might have found out something he shouldn't have and become another candidate for murder.

My questions weren't going to get answers this night, but when M. Quiniou arrived, Laurence was able to ask some of hers. Maybe that was what Annee had planned. Maybe it was better to have some of the unpleasantness come from a stranger.

In any case, after M. Quiniou walked into the living room, the atmosphere got thick with tension, and it didn't get any friendlier as the moments wore on.

When I offered to get some tea or coffee, Annee quickly took me up on the offer and then followed me into the kitchen.

"You're not obliged to stay," she said.

"Good," I said. "Why don't I go to the inn and see if I can be helpful there?"

"I wish I could go, too," she said, a wry smile replacing the worried look she had been wearing. "You go on. I'll get the coffee." And I was out of there.

It was almost dark and the streets were deserted. The dogs barked as I passed the fenced-in yards. It was a fairly warm evening and some doors were still open to let in whatever breeze might stir the air. Television sets were on; I could see the colors flashing inside the darkened rooms.

I passed a man walking two dogs, one a small black poodle and the other a black Labrador who was not on a leash, but hadn't the slightest interest in me. He didn't even bother to sniff me.

I had already decided to stop in the kitchen and have a word or two with M. Saverne about the latest developments. It had occurred to me that if Denis had used his doppelgänger at the inn, M. Saverne might have noticed some oddities that he had attributed to Denis's idiosyncrasies when Marcel Gris had taken Denis's place.

There were three doors to the inn, one to the restaurant, one to the bar, and one at the back that entered the kitchen. I turned into the alley at the side of the building. The garbage cans were kept in back, too, and late at night, a number of creatures had been known to visit the *poubelles* (garbage cans).

As I made my way up the alley, I didn't try to be quiet, because I wanted to frighten away any rodent types that might be getting an early start on their dinner. I guess I wasn't noisy enough, though, because when I turned the corner at the back of the building, the corner where the kitchen door was usually standing open and where there was usually a light, a couple were leaning against the building just beyond the doorway, too involved in their activity to notice anyone else, human or rodent.

I caught a glimpse of most of her leg and noticed that his trousers weren't belted at the waist but hung rather farther down on his leg. As I backed off down the alley, I could hear their moans.

Once inside the bar, it didn't take me long to realize who was missing. Yves and Clarisse were nowhere in the restaurant or the bar. Since it wasn't busy, most of the diners were on their coffee, cheese course, or dessert. Odette was taking care of the dining room and Vincent was holding forth in the bar, while Marsha seemed to be shuttling back and forth from dining room to bar.

When I went into the kitchen to see whether the Savernes were busy and to hint to them that some of the help weren't at their stations, I found only M. Saverne, who seemed to be doing three things at once. He was putting the finishing touches on a dessert, stacking dishes that came in from the dining room, and hanging up pots and pans that had been cleaned up.

I could see right away where I would be most useful, so I started work on the dirty dishes. There was an ancient dishwasher that had to be loaded just so in order to get the dishes clean, but Annee liked it to be used because the dishes got sterilized.

"Where is Madame Saverne?" I said, when I had gotten the first load of dishes into the machine.

"She is not well," he said.

My face must have expressed something like alarm, because I was thinking that a poisonous mushroom might have gotten into Mme. Saverne's food.

"She hasn't gotten into any poisoned pâté," he said, smiling. "She gets aches and pains when it rains."

"I don't want to interfere with young love," I said. I wasn't going to say that Yves and Clarisse were going at it on the other side of the kitchen wall; I was just going to mention that they were missing from their posts. Before I could finish what I had started to say, M. Saverne marched to the back door, flipped the switch, which I assumed turned on the outside light, and banged on the door once before he opened it.

When he opened the door, he said something to them in French. It was brief and it mentioned Madame Rien.

The two rumpled lovers came in, tucking in and smoothing out and trying to look like they weren't doing what they were doing. I blushed for them.

After Clarisse went into the dining room and Yves to the bar, M. Saverne told me that it wasn't the first time he had noticed them missing and they had been warned enough. This time he was going to recommend that Annee fire them.

"The girl is stealing, besides," he said.

Another couple of groups came in for dinner and M. Saverne and I were very busy in the kitchen, so it was an hour or more before I got around to telling him about Denis being alive and having had a double.

M. Saverne was at first shocked and then pensive. "I thought that man Paul was too much like Denis," he said. "Did he think he would get away with it?"

I asked M. Saverne whether he thought Denis's double had ever put in time at the inn.

He was dolloping cream onto a charlotte and stopped in mid-dollop. "That would explain it," he said.

He finished dolloping and put the dessert where it could be picked up by Odette or Clarisse. "The strange Tuesdays," he said. "Madame Rien did not come here on Tuesdays."

I thought for a minute about the significance of that and wondered whether on Tuesdays she was nursing the bites on her arms and legs after the festivities of Monday, Denis's day off.

M. Saverne was saying, "And on Tuesdays, Denis wouldn't let me in that section of the kitchen." M. Saverne pointed to the other side of the kitchen, where the big range was. "He would be busy cooking his specialty, he said."

"Did anything else happen on Tuesdays?" I said.

"Sometimes Clarisse was not here on Tuesdays, but I was not suspicious of that. Not then."

But surely now, I thought, you can figure out where Denis might have been some of the time. "How long has Yves been going out with Clarisse?"

"I don't know. It seems the interest was there a long time ago, but since Yves has been working here, they can't leave one another alone. I have seen them in the middle of the night."

"So have I," I said, and told him about seeing them walking near Annee's house. But I realized that he had just told me something about himself. He was a man who didn't sleep at night sometimes. I wondered whether he wandered around the town every night. He had been in Annee's yard and clobbered me in the wee hours.

I heard a rustling sound and turned toward the door. M. Saverne also looked in that direction. Odette had just moved from behind the door and was standing there with her eyes wide open. I was sure she had been listening. For how long, I didn't know.

When we turned to her, she said, "Clarisse?"

Why was she surprised? Wasn't she pretending to ride with Yves to school and getting a ride with someone else so that Yves could be with Clarisse? Hadn't Clement told me that? "You didn't know?" I said.

"I thought he, no, not Clarisse." Odette's confusion gave way to anger, which she manifested only with a sternness about her face and a tensing of her shoulders. Maybe she shared her father's opinion of Clarisse. Obviously Yves hadn't confided in her, but had enlisted her help with his assignations.

I had other questions about Odette. Why had she been listening to M. Saverne and me? What was it that she wanted to know about? She might have gone on listening,

I thought, if we hadn't gotten on the subject of her brother and startled her into making the noise that gave away her presence.

"How long have you been standing there?" I said. No sense letting her believe she had gotten away with her eavesdropping. She hadn't come through the kitchen door; she had to have come around the building to get there.

"I have only just arrived. You were talking about Yves. I listened. I'm sorry. I went out from the front door to breathe the air. Then I came in the back to get a dessert for a patron. It is very warm in the dining room."

Smooth liar, I thought. Maybe that's the way kids get when they have a father as strict as Jacques.

"There is no order waiting," M. Saverne said. His face was stony, and he apparently had decided to let people know that he spoke English.

She took out her order pad. "But yes, a chocolate mousse," she said. Then she held out the pad for him to see.

He looked at the pad and went to the refrigerator and pulled out the bowl of mousse. "With or without cream?" he said.

She consulted her pad. "Without," she said. Her face had reddened slightly, but she was keeping the lid on.

When she left the kitchen, M. Saverne stood in the doorway to the dining room and watched her. I watched over his big shoulder.

Odette put the chocolate mousse down on the sideboard and walked out the front door, passing Clarisse on the way and saying something that turned Clarisse's face magenta.

Why would Odette eavesdrop on a conversation between me and M. Saverne? And why did she seem so angry that Yves was seeing Clarisse? Was it only because he lied to her? Shouldn't she have been able to see the connection between Yves and Clarisse, with all the trips to the bar that Clarisse made? Odette was right in the dining room with Clarisse every night. Shouldn't she have noticed?

It seemed to me that ever since the day that Arnaut had followed the girls in the woods, Odette and Bernadette had seemed more emotional. Had the experience been so frightening for them? If it had, why did they continue to go to the woods?

As these thoughts tumbled through my mind, I started moving toward the door.

"I'm going after her," I told M. Saverne. "I'll be back, though, to help you."

But I wasn't going to be any more help to him that night.

Twenty-three

When Odette looked back and saw me come out of the inn, she started running. I ran after her. I was a fast runner, but I wasn't gaining on her. I wasn't losing ground, either. She had the advantage, though, of being younger and in better shape.

She hadn't spent a couple of weeks padding around a hospital with her brain fried. It still galled me, though. Running is one thing I do well, and I don't like it when I can't outrun somebody.

She seemed to be heading toward her house. Good, I thought, then I won't have too much farther to run. But just as she reached the house, she looked back and saw me as I passed under one of the few streetlights. Maybe she thought she had outrun me.

She didn't stop at her place; she kept running, and I knew she was headed for the woods and that I'd never find her there, in the dark, in a place she had known since she was an infant.

I stopped when I got to the Toute house, though. I was panting and miffed. There were too many secrets, too many odd happenings, too many ways to hide things because nobody talked about the secrets. Conversations stopped at these walls. It was time to do something about them. Knock them down.

I don't know where my nerve came from, but suddenly, crazily, it was there. And so were Jacques and Niki, both of whom had secrets I was privy to.

The smiles that greeted me faded when I started going through my list.

"Why didn't you tell your husband that Denis raped you?

"Why were you following your wife? Why were you bugging the phone? How come you're making eyes at Annee all the time?"

I gave them both barrels.

They denied everything at first. Then they started shouting at each other. I could hear noises outside the door to the living room. More eavesdroppers in the Toute clan.

When I was done, Niki's affair with Denis, as reluctant as she had been, was out in the open. Jacques's long-simmering pursuit of Annee and his following Niki the night I was hit, and the goings-on between Yves and Clarisse, also were on the table.

Niki cried. Jacques turned red.

I was glad to have it off my chest. Even though it might have broken up the family. Even though I had my own culpability in the necklace affair to answer for. I didn't care.

I didn't think much of that family anyway, and I was really steamed. I felt I had been cornered. That was it, cornered. And I acted like a rat in a corner, striking out at what was keeping me there.

"I got whacked and the two of you were there," I said, "for your own reasons. But neither of you was any help to me." I continued to rage at the Toutes.

"I'll give you back your money," I said to Niki, "but you'll have to turn over the necklace to the cops."

Then I turned to Jacques. "And you'd better tell your colleagues that you were there in the yard or nearby, too.

"And while we're on the subject of sneaking around," I said, and then I told them why I happened to be at their house with a string of grievances. I told them about Odette listening in on the conversation in the kitchen at the inn.

"And speaking of the inn, I have to get back and help. Not only does your son take time off from work to play with Clarisse, but your daughter eavesdrops and then walks out."

At that I turned and left the house and started back to the inn. I was halfway there when I heard footsteps behind me and turned. Clement, in a rage, ran at me and caught my shoulder with the fist he had aimed at my face.

My adrenaline had not subsided after my harangue at the Toutes. I started flailing against this boy, who had probably been eavesdropping, as had his sister before him. Clement's rage was a match for my own. He pummeled me. He pushed me down. I grabbed his foot as he aimed a kick at me. I pulled him down to the ground and sank my teeth into his leg.

He howled and scrambled away from me, getting to his feet in the process. I wasted no time in standing up to face him again.

We were back at close range, pummeling, but with little room to swing. I was so close I could smell the boy of him.

But I was tired and he was full of energy. Losing ground, I did what I could do to disable him, and aimed my knee at his groin.

As he writhed on the ground, I stumbled to the inn and fell in the door to the dining room before I blacked out.

I wasn't out long, and I came to with smelling salts under my nose. Very unpleasant, much more so than the name "smelling salts" seems to indicate.

Clarisse and M. Saverne took me to the kitchen and looked over my cuts and bruises as I gave them an abbreviated version of what had happened. Clarisse, luckily, didn't know what I had done to mess up her life—she had been doing a bang-up job of messing it up herself—and couldn't understand what I was saying anyway, so she treated me carefully.

I was feeling rocky, and getting the feeling that I ought to go back to the hospital, when Clement came into the kitchen. I screamed, because I had no strength left, and blacked out again.

I woke up in the hospital, and Annee was there.

"I had a busy night," I said.

"I heard," she said.

That was all. I fell into a deep sleep, more than likely drug-induced.

The next day, Dr. Berenger walked into my room. "I see you're on time for the appointment," she said.

I had forgotten the appointment, had almost forgotten the

things that I wanted to tell her. But I hadn't forgotten my rage of the night before.

And when I started to talk to Dr. Berenger and the fears and anger came pouring out, I began to understand what had happened to me, how deeply I had been affected by the attack, by the loss of my memory.

And Clement's attack, by no means as deadly, had brought it all back, had even straightened out the lines of thought that had curled around and confused me.

And at the end of one of those lines, there was something else, something that I hadn't let myself remember about the night I was attacked. It was the face of my attacker.

And it wasn't M. Saverne's.

Twenty-four

I guess my mind had turned off, because the face that I remembered quite clearly now was that of Denis Rien, the man I'd seen in the pictures in Annee's house, the man who was supposed to be dead.

"Perhaps," Dr. Berenger said, "because you know now that he isn't dead, your mind permitted that door to open."

But solving one problem only created others. M. Saverne had confessed to hitting me. That meant he had lied and also that he knew Denis was alive when everyone else thought he was dead. But hadn't M. Saverne told us his story, the reason that Denis had blackmailed him? What further hold did Denis have over him?

And then there were the Toutes. Did they, too, know that Denis was alive?

Dr. Berenger told me that my rage against all these people with secrets was compounded by more than my injury. "You haven't been able to speak to people or tell them what you have been thinking because you don't speak the language. And so, few people understand you when you speak English," she said. "This would make you feel isolated. Secrets would only make this feeling worse. You can't tell what you know even to the people with whom you can communicate."

Our talk went on for a couple of hours, and I did feel better when she left. But I didn't have enough information to straighten out the confusion created by the events.

The first thing that had happened, we all thought, was that Denis was killed when he ate a pâté that contained a poisonous mushroom. The pâté was purchased at the Bouchegrandes' *épicerie*, where Niki worked.

Now we found that it wasn't Denis who was killed, but that Marcel Gris was already dead by the time Denis's suppertime rolled around.

Denis had reason to believe that the mushroom was meant for him and faked his own death by substituting Marcel Gris for himself sometime between the time Denis was rolling around on the floor and the time the gendarmes arrived.

Where was Gris killed? Did someone carry him to the shed? Where had he been that day? Did Denis have a suspicion about who was making the poison pâté? But Denis might be lying. And whom besides M. Saverne and Niki was Denis blackmailing?

Then I remembered that Annee had been concerned about money missing from the inn and had sent Marsha there to keep her ears open. It didn't take a genius to figure that the money was going to Denis with M. Saverne's connivance.

And then he blamed Clarisse. Poor Clarisse had enough trouble without being called a thief, too.

My mind seemed to be working better, but not well enough to come up with answers. And I was starting to feel guilty about telling the Toutes the secrets they had kept from each other.

I brushed that one away as soon as it started to buzz around me. I wasn't the one with the secrets, but they had told me their secrets so they could use me for their own purposes. Niki wanted her necklace and Jacques wanted to spy on his wife, probably so he could get a divorce and then pursue Annee. Secrets. How did I know how many secrets they had from each other?

The necklace! I had been digging around in the shed looking for the necklace, and Denis, the one who had nearly killed me, was alive. He could have come back and finished me. No wonder I was so mad at Niki.

I had asked Dr. Berenger to call the police and get an English-speaking gendarme to come to the hospital and take my statement about what I remembered about the night I was attacked.

Jacques had wanted to talk to me right after the attack. I remembered that he scared me then. I'll bet that wasn't an official visit.

This time I'd go the official route. No more waiting around to ask someone if this or that was all right. I wasn't going to ask Annee or anyone else what I should do about what I remembered.

A thirtyish fellow in a suit showed up at the doorway to my room early in the afternoon. He was blond and looked more German than French. The suit fit him as if it were tailored, but I decided that no tailor had sewn it, because the fabric wasn't good enough for a made-to-order garment. He was one of those people who look good in clothes right off the rack.

He was thin, broad-shouldered, narrow in the hips, long-necked. He was long-legged, too, but not very tall, maybe five foot nine.

"Miss Kirk," he said, and he sounded like an American.

"Yes," I said, "I'm Frances Tremaine Kirk, and you are?"

He flashed a nice, even smile. "Detective Jefferson Pierce Starke," he said. "Call me J. P."

"With pleasure," I said. "Did anyone tell you why I wanted to see you?"

"I spoke to Dr. Berenger right after her session with you this morning," he said. "She said you remembered who hit you and it probably was the man we have in custody who is calling himself Denis Rien."

He didn't waste any time getting to the point. I went through the whole story, sparing no one, not even myself. I told him what had happened that night and what I'd found out since. It was cleansing to blat it all out.

And when I was finished, I got some answers from J. P. Maybe it was because I was so forthright with him, or maybe J. P. was just an open kind of guy, but I never expected to get that much from a gendarme. When I asked where Marcel Gris was killed, he told me what Denis had told the police.

"Denis was supposed to meet Marcel to change clothes. Apparently they did that often, just to make sure that no one suspected the switch. Another ruse they used was to slop something quite noticeable on a shirt and then switch clothes when they switched identities.

"When Denis arrived for the meeting on the fatal day, it was almost suppertime and Marcel was dead. He had done Denis's errands that day while Denis was off doing what he usually did. The food, Denis told us, looked like it had been picked up in the usual place."

"The usual place would be the Bouchegrandes' store," I said.

"Yes," he said.

"Who helped him carry Marcel to the house? He did have help, didn't he? He had to have someone there to tell Annee to stay out. You know what she said about the evening, don't you?"

"Of course. I've read all the statements. But we can't verify the statement of so-called Denis Rien because the men who he said helped him are both dead."

"Foyer and Arnaut," I said.

"Precisely," he said.

"And they helped him because he was blackmailing them?"

"The man who calls himself Denis did not exactly make that clear to us. Not yet," J. P. said, and he sounded then more like the gendarmes I had encountered thus far.

"And what about Monsieur Saverne? When did he find out that Denis's death was faked?"

"We have only this Denis Rien's story that it was faked. And we have not examined Saverne yet about the fakery, of course, since you have only told me now that you remembered who hit you," he said. Then, with a rather stern face, he added, "And you hadn't told us everything."

"Well, I have now. You know everything I know." I shrugged and took a deep breath. "For a while it seemed that I had to hold back some facts. For one thing, I was intimidated by Jacques Toutes."

"That happens with him. He is very imposing. But he has some things to answer for now. There will be a departmental meeting on this, I'm sure. But maybe he will not actually be prosecuted."

"More secrets, then?" I said.

"Let's just say there will be some adjustments." J. P.

was grinning as if he were enjoying the notion that Jacques would be subject to some adjustments.

J. P. was looking cute to me. Of course, he probably looked cute to most women. But he was in my room, smiling at me, and he spoke English like an American, and I could tell him the whole story and get some feedback as well. J. P. Starke. It had a nice ring to it.

But I snapped myself out of it and ran through the chronology again, the deaths, the baby, my getting hit. Then I wondered about all the stories I'd heard about Denis. Could one man be so wicked?

My thoughts were interrupted by J. P. "The TV people are still trying to get some shots of the Toute girls practicing. They've interviewed people in the village who have seen them. It's becoming a big story. And along with it are all the stories of the murders, which just happened to have occurred in the same village where these angels live who dance and play."

"So there's pressure," I said, "to solve the crimes because the publicity for Bernadette and Odette drew attention to the town?"

"That's it," J. P. said. "And now we have a guy who's supposed to be dead coming around and telling us that he had a cousin who was his double. It makes great TV. Now they're digging up photos of Denis Rien and Marcel Gris and running them side by side. You can't tell them apart."

"What have you heard about Denis Rien?" I said.

J. P. scratched his soft blond hair. "What haven't I heard?" he said.

"So tell me. Maybe I know some things that you'll want to add to your dossier on him."

"What's your connection to his wife?"

"My late ex-husband was her nephew. I'd never met her until I got here."

"You'd never met her, but you came to visit her?" He was sounding like a policeman.

"My former mother-in-law talked me into making this trip with her. Of course, I'd heard about Annee, knew she lived in France." I didn't know whether to say anything to him about Annee asking me to keep my eyes open or hiring me as a detective. My life as a detective was not an aspect of my story that I had emphasized when I told him about getting the necklace for Niki.

"Don't you think Madame Rien is a little thick?" he said. That got my attention. "If you'll excuse the expression. She had to be dead between the ears not to know what Denis Rien had been up to."

My face probably registered disapproval of his blunt appraisal of Annee.

"Maybe she didn't want to believe it." He waffled. "She wouldn't be the first woman to wear blinders."

"What was he doing besides the stuff I told you about?" I said.

"He was making his mark," J. P. said, smirking.

"You mean teeth marks?"

"So you've heard about his perversion?" he said.

"I saw the evidence all over Annee's arms and legs when she was in the hospital."

J. P. stopped smirking. "His wife, too, eh?"

"Maybe she got the worst of it," I said. "What else do you know about Denis?"

"We've been keeping a dossier on him for a long time. Rapes, attempted rapes, various complaints about assaults from women who wouldn't give their names, from husbands who suspected, from boyfriends and women friends of the women who were assaulted. Come to the gendarmerie," he said. "I'll show you some of the files."

Strange, I thought, this cop is being very open. Is he dopey or is he up to something? "Is it legal? Your showing me files, I mean."

"He's dead, remember? You may be sure he's Denis. I may even be sure he's Denis. But until he proves otherwise, he's dead."

"But he's confessed that he faked his death. Won't that make a difference?"

"It'll take a while to undo," he said. "This is France, the home of red tape." He sounded bitter. At some point I would have to ask him about red tape. I was sure that he had a grievance.

"So what would I see in the dossier?"

"In the part that I can show you are the complaints with

no names, what he was accused of, even some photographs.''

''Photos of what?''

''His marks.''

''You're talking about his teeth marks? You have pictures of the marks? Someone let you take pictures?''

''That time we thought we had him. The woman was
quite irate. But she didn't live in France, and she suddenly
dropped from sight. No one seems to know where she
went.''

''Do you think something happened to her?''

''Yes. Something like a couple of hundred thousand
francs.''

''Paid off? How did you find out?''

''We kept an eye on his bank accounts.''

Bank accounts, plural, I thought. How could Annee trace
money if she didn't even know how many accounts there
were? My respect for the French police was growing. They
had done a lot of homework on Denis. But he had kept
eluding them one way or another. ''This dossier on Denis,''
I said. ''Do many people know about it?''

J. P.'s mouth curled up at one corner. ''Every gendarme
in the Seventy-seventh knows, and probably their friends
at the cafés.''

''And you never arrested Denis?''

''Twice. But we got the wrong fellow once.''

''The double, Marcel?''

''We didn't know about him. But probably. And we
didn't know which was which. We think now that he made
sure that Marcel Gris was arrested just to confuse us.'' His
mouth was turning up at one corner again. ''It worked.''

''The list of people who would want to kill him could
be pretty long,'' I said.

''As long and twisted as the Seine,'' he said.

No wonder he thought Annee had her head in the sand.
In her defense, though, she did know about Niki. Now,
thanks to my big mouth, everybody would know about
Niki.

Then I remembered the notebook. ''Oh, and there's
something else.''

''Something else you haven't told me?''

"No, no," I said, and then told him about the notebook, which was in a pocket of the clothes I had on when I came to the hospital. "Could you step outside for a minute? I want to look for it."

The pause was significant. At first, it told me he didn't know whether he could trust me. When he finally realized that I wanted to maintain some modesty while walking across the room in the hospital gown, he made his exit.

The pockets of my clothes were all empty. But just as I was about to call the nurse and start screaming, I looked down at the floor of the little locker and saw a pile of small items, including underwear and shoes. The notebook was at the bottom of the pile.

J. P. took one flip through the pages and almost leaped for joy. "I think this will help us to prosecute Denis Rien. It is a diary of sorts and there are references to sums of money," he said, smiling.

I had been talking to J. P. for more than an hour when a nurse came in with flowers and a couple of packages. "For you," she said, in a way that told me that she had practiced those two words and wouldn't know how to say much else in English.

"*Merci*," I said.

Then she spoke to J. P. in French and he stood up. "They want me to step out so they can examine you," he said. "I'll come back tomorrow. Is that all right?"

Is that all right? In other words, he wanted to come back for an unofficial visit. I flashed my best smile, hoping that my teeth or gums hadn't been blackened in the latest fray or that a hunk of unidentifiable foodstuff was not lodged between two of my front teeth. "Of course," I said.

After J. P. left, a doctor came in and looked me over, with an especially hard look at my eyes. Probably because of the head injury I'd had before. Having him look so closely at my eyes made my eyes cross and I began to have difficulty focusing. I felt like telling him to back off. How could my eyes work right if he was sticking his face so close to mine?

The doctor used sign language to tell me to open my mouth and to turn my head first this way and then that way and to follow his finger with my eyes. He was there for about five or ten minutes and then left without saying anything to me or to the nurse who accompanied him.

He had no sooner left than J. P. returned, looking harried. He went right to the recently delivered packages and examined them one by one. He had gloves on, I noticed. "Do you mind if I take these?" he said, putting the packages carefully into plastic sacks that he had pulled from his pocket.

"What's going on?" I said. "Were you expecting these packages? Is that why you had gloves and plastic bags with you?" My fantasy had gone down the tubes by now. He didn't have to answer me. I knew why he had come rushing back. It was a jolt, though, because it hadn't occurred to me that someone would send me a lethal package. But it had occurred to the police.

"There may be no reason at all to examine these," he said, "but to be on the safe side, I want to have them looked at. I can return them to you in an hour or two." He grinned then, turning up the corners of both sides of his mouth. "Besides," he said, "I don't want you to be dead when I come and visit you tomorrow."

Fantasy again beginning to blossom. "What do you know that I don't?" I said. "Why the precautions?"

"You have made some enemies. And I don't know how dangerous they are."

"The Toutes? Jacques and Niki?" They had reason to hate me. Maybe Yves, too. But Clement was the one who had attacked me. And Odette was the one who had eavesdropped on the conversation about Yves and Clarisse.

"Them, yes," he said, as if they were only two of the legions of malefactors out there plotting my demise. "Please eat nothing but the food prepared by the hospital. I'll have this"—he lifted the bags—"sent back to you later, providing all is well."

"Thanks," I said, and watched him go. Why did I come to France? What have I gotten out of it besides a cracked head and a few educated taste buds?

I had a deep longing for Cheektowaga and a beef on weck sandwich, which around Buffalo is thinly sliced roast beef piled high on a roll that is coated with salt and called a kimmelwick bun. I like mine with horseradish, a staple on the table, along with salt and pepper and mustard, of any restaurant that serves beef on weck. Don't ask me why they spell "weck" with an *e*.

My mind started running on food from home, where foie gras was as unreal as chocolate-covered ants. Chicken wings from Frank and Theresa's Anchor Bar—the original Buffalo chicken wings, now famous all over—where they are served with celery sticks and blue cheese dressing and you can get the wings as hot as you like them. And even though I had had some terrific sausage in France, at that moment in the hospital, I would have given a month's pay for a good kielbasa.

My Polish mother used to make a dinner, the thought of which can still warm me on a cold night, of kielbasa, stuffed cabbage, and boiled potatoes. She'd drink a beer with hers and sometimes give me a sip. It seemed perfect to me, like wine and cheese for the French.

And then I was snapped back to where I was, in the hospital in Coulommiers, with the cops watching out for perilous packages. And the only person who knew everything that I knew was a nice-looking cop who had told me more than any of the other cops had.

I still hadn't squared things with Annee, didn't know if that was possible. I felt guilty about giving away her secrets, but, like J. P., I suspected that she was hiding from the facts or just plain hiding facts.

She had been in the house when Denis put on his death show. She would have been at the inn sometimes when Marcel Gris was there. She worked closely with M. Saverne, who had at some point discovered Denis's switch.

And she had asked Marsha to bring me to France to do some detective work. Instead of picking up clues, I was picking up scars.

And right on cue, Annee walked in, her second visit of the day.

"Thanks for coming again."

She didn't smile. Was she mad because I had done my stool-pigeon routine about the Toutes? Could she have found out about my conversation with J. P. so soon?

"I have something to tell you," she said. "I just found out about it myself."

Her face was so grave, so pale, I wondered if someone else had died.

"Denis has escaped," she said.

"How could he?"

"Someone hit the guard over the head. The guard was found in Denis's cell wearing Denis's clothes."

"Where do you think he'll go?" I said.

"I don't know. I don't know where he's been since he pretended to die."

"I have to tell you something, Annee," I said, and then watched her closely as I gave her the entire picture: everything that I'd told J. P. I saved until last what I remembered about who had hit me.

Her face hardly moved at all. She nodded a few times and her eyes grew a bit wider, but she said nothing. When I was done, she took a breath and said, "But if Denis hit you, why did Monsieur Saverne confess to it?"

"Is that all?" I said.

"All what?"

"Is that all you want to say to me?"

"No, but I don't know where to start. There's so much that's been left unsaid for so long."

"Are you angry that I told the cops everything?" There, I said it. That was what I wanted to know.

Twenty-five

"No, I'm not angry," Annee said. "I don't think I am angry. It's something else for me to think about."

"Annee," I said. Loud. "I told the cops something you've been hiding for years. How do you feel about that?"

Annee looked as if she wanted to duck. Her hands came partway up in front of her. Fending off. I recognized the gesture. I had perfected it over the years with Dick.

"I'm not going to hit you, for God's sake." I was getting angrier. I wanted her to talk. To get to the bottom of that pit she had been living in.

Then I felt contrite for hollering. Hadn't it taken me months to dig into the mess that was my life with Dick Kirk? Besides, contrition comes fast when you like a person and she's crying.

"I should have been more honest with you right from the start," she said. "But it would have meant showing the scars. I would have felt even worse. I was ashamed. I *am* ashamed. Yes. That's what I feel. Shame."

"Well, stop it," I said. "You didn't make those marks, he did. And now he's loose again. I've got to talk to Monsieur Saverne and find out what he knows about Denis and where he was hiding. See what you can do about getting me out of here."

"But are you well enough?"

"I feel fine," I lied. I was almost fine. But I was definitely itching to move. Something was bothering me and I had the feeling that it was urgent. I had no idea what it was, but I knew I couldn't do anything about it in the hospital.

Annee went to notify the floor nurse that I wanted to leave. She and a couple of others came to the room and protested, but the doctor apparently had not left any orders that would prevent them from dismissing me, and he had already ordered the medicines that I was to get on my release. The French doctors seemed to order a lot of medications, with lists of instructions to go with them, including side effects.

"Is Monsieur Saverne at the inn today?" I said, while I brushed at my clothes, which were dirty from rolling around on the ground with Clement.

"Yes. He and Vincent are working. They're planning the new lunch arrangement."

She went on about the plans for the inn while I tried to wipe the worst spots out of my clothes.

Just as we were getting ready to leave with the armload of medicines, J. P. returned.

"Fran, I heard you were leaving," he said. Who had told him? Did he have a snitch in the hospital? He looked at Annee. "Did Madame Rien tell you about her husband's escape?"

"She told me he had escaped. Was there something else?" I said.

"The guard may never regain consciousness," he said. "We may never know how Denis escaped." He was studying the medicine packages, actually two plastic sacks with lists pasted on the outsides.

Annee's free hand was in front of her mouth. The other one held one of the medicine sacks.

"Do they have any idea who helped him escape?" I said. I was wondering whether M. Saverne had a hand in it.

"No," J. P. said. "There was no record of any visitors." He turned to Annee. "Did your husband have friends in the gendarmes?"

"His only friend who worked for the police was Commissaire Toute."

"Ah, yes, of course," he said. The look on his face was peculiar. Bored? Snotty? Aloof? "Were they good friends?"

Then Annee surprised me. "You know by now that the Toutes were not real friends of Denis or me." Her face had reddened and her eyes had steely glints. "If you're asking whether Jacques would help Denis escape, the answer is I don't know what he is capable of."

"Nor do I," J. P. said. Then, to me: "By the way, one of those packages for you had in it a delicious pâté from Clement Toute. Here's the note he sent with it."

I read the note, which apologized and promised me an explanation of his "horrible behaviour." It also said he had stayed awake all night worrying, and while he was worrying, he made this pâté for me.

"Where's the pâté?" I said.

"Once it was tested, then it was tasted, and, well, everyone at the lab raved about it. There was very little left when I got back to the lab."

"That was pretty fast work," I said.

"They've been doing many tests for that poison. And they have a new machine that you can put almost anything in, and it will analyze it. The machine has just arrived. Two days they've had it."

"I mean it was pretty fast work eating my pâté. Do I have any recourse?" I said. "You people took something that belonged to me." I smiled.

But the smile froze on my face as J. P. talked.

"The second package was also a pâté," he said, "but there was no note with it, and it was deadly, but with a different poisonous mushroom."

I gulped. "Which one?" I was remembering the mushroom lesson from Laurence.

"Amanita phalloides. You have heard of it?"

"Yes," I said. "It's very deadly, isn't it?"

"But the symptoms do not appear immediately, so it can invade the body before its presence is known."

My fears were returning with full force. I could barely keep from crying.

"It was wrapped in the same kind of paper as Clement's was," J. P. said, "and was addressed to Madame Kirk and had your room number on it."

"Did you check it for fingerprints?" Annee and I asked in unison.

"The nurse's prints were the only clear ones. She had picked up both of them at the front desk. They had been delivered within an hour of one another by the same man. At least, the receptionist thought it was the same man."

"We'll be careful of what we eat," Annee said.

"Whoever it is is getting nervous," J. P. said. "Probably somewhat desperate. Maybe feeling we are closing in. Desperate people try many things. So be careful. And not just about what you eat."

I didn't ask him about M. Saverne, and he didn't say anything about him. Annee had told me that he was at the inn that day, but surely the police would question him after hearing my story. Or maybe they would be watching M. Saverne to see whether Denis would get in touch with him. Could he have helped Denis escape?

And who is making these poisoned pâtés? And why is the killer after me? It's too late to try to keep me quiet.

J. P. asked me what I intended to do the next day, and I was a little slow to catch on, reciting a list of domestic chores that I planned to attack and carefully omitting my list of people to see.

Annee piped up at that moment. "We're postponing the christening, so you are free to do whatever you want to do." She arched her brows. "And we can manage at the inn without you."

J. P. waded right in, as if on cue. "How about lunch? We can go to a restaurant in Melun where they never heard of pâté."

I didn't believe there was such a thing as a restaurant in France where they hadn't heard of pâté, but I didn't object.

Annee smiled as if she were part of some sort of conspiracy. Why do people get so smiley when they see two people being attracted to each other?

Annee and I stopped at the house, where I changed clothes and Annee nursed Fanny. The baby, Annee said, was getting used to eating when food was offered. Just the reverse of the way babies usually get fed.

After the baby was fed, Laurence said she would take care of the cleanup detail, and Annee cautioned her against letting in Denis or the man who said he was Denis. "If you see him, call the gendarmes," she said.

Laurence now was firmly in Annee's camp and swore she would do as she was told. She was far less sympathetic to the man who called himself Denis.

"The police may be watching the house anyway," Annee said. "Just keep everything closed and locked. I won't be gone more than a couple of hours. If you would feel better, I can get someone to stay with you until I get back."

Laurence assured her that she would be fine and would call the police the moment she thought there was anything wrong.

M. Saverne was in the kitchen when we got to the inn, and I wasted no time in confronting him. "Why did you tell me you were the one who hit me?"

The ladle he was holding splashed down into the cauldron. Annee led Vincent out of the kitchen and signaled to me that she would be right outside the door. I was taking a chance that he wouldn't get hostile and finish the job that Denis had got such a good start on. My take on M. Saverne, though, was that he was looking for a way out of the muck in which Denis had mired him.

He turned to me and shook his head. His big hands hung at his sides. "I wouldn't blame you if you never believed me again," he said.

"Try me," I said.

"Denis told me to take the blame. That was before I told you my story. The rest of the story is true. And you were so kind, I didn't want to change my story."

"And now? Does he still have power over you?"

"What do you mean?"

"Did you help him escape?"

"Denis escaped?" He looked surprised, but I already knew he was a good liar. Also a good cook, good enough to make a great pâté with deadly, delicious mushrooms in it.

"I told the police who really hit me. I guess they'll have more questions for you." I wondered if he'd flee. But I figured that the cops had had enough time to put a watch outside, and if M. Saverne fled, he might lead them right to Denis.

"You didn't know he escaped? That the prison guard may die? That a poisoned pâté was sent to me at the hospital?"

Again Jean Saverne looked surprised. "No, I didn't know. I don't know what Denis will do next."

"Who would be helping him?" I said. "That is, if you didn't."

His face registered a hurt expression, but I wasn't about to waste any pity there, not on such flimsy evidence of sincerity. "Clarisse, maybe."

"When did you find out that Denis was still alive?"

"The day you were beaten. Denis came to my house after work. He told me that someone had tried to kill him and he was hiding. He also said I should help him get a particular box out of the garden shed."

"Did you get it?"

"Yes."

"What was in it?"

"I don't know, but it was heavy. It was about this size." He indicated a cube slightly larger than a shoe box.

"You haven't told the police about this yet?"

"No."

"Maybe you'd better tell the cops what you know. Did you know where he was hiding?"

"I suspected that Clarisse was hiding him—that is, until she started to see Yves. But that may have been a ruse devised by Denis, too."

"So when he showed up at the inn that night calling himself Paul Rien, you knew who he was?"

I remembered the act M. Saverne had put on, how he said he thought the man looked like Denis.

"I'm sorry," he said. "I did not feel free to tell you."

"And now?"

The flicker of his eyelid told me there was more, that Denis still had a hold on him. "Now that he is free again," he said, "I still fear him." M. Saverne looked as if he would cry.

"Can't you go to the police and tell them?"

"I still would not be safe. Even when he was in jail, I

received messages warning me to be quiet."

"Where did you get these messages?"

"At home. At the inn. He had no trouble sending messages from the jail."

The cop connection again, I thought. Maybe Denis was blackmailing a cop. Jacques? I tried to get more out of M. Saverne, but he wouldn't say more. Would the police have any better luck?

"And the money that you said Clarisse stole?"

M. Saverne's face grew redder than usual. "I had to give it to Denis."

"I'll let you tell Annee," I said, and left the kitchen and got involved in the work of the inn. If someone were watching the place, I decided, he or she was using binoculars or some other vision-augmenting device. With my naked eyes, I could see no one keeping watch on the inn.

Where are the cops? Shouldn't they be looking for Denis? Wouldn't the inn be one of the places he might head for?

The gendarmes were not the only no-shows, however. Odette didn't appear at her regular time, either, which gave me more work to do with Clarisse in the dining room.

I began to feel sympathy for Clarisse, even though she probably wasn't aware of all the villainy that had been attributed to her. Clarisse was a dependable worker. She never hung back, waiting for someone else to do the work; she was always there and on time. The worst thing she'd done was to dally in the alley with Yves. Any dalliance she might have had with Denis, I was betting, was coerced.

We got through the first hour of dinner just about keeping up. The diners had to wait a little longer than usual, but we kept it manageable by juggling.

Annee came back after Fanny's next feeding and shouldered some of the load, and soon the crunch was over. During a few slack moments, I asked Annee whether she had heard from Odette.

"She called a half hour after she was supposed to be here," Annee said. "She said she was having terrible cramps, and apologized. Then she put Niki on the phone to apologize again." Annee frowned. "I don't know what is going on in that house. But I have not been easy with Niki for some time.''

''Maybe what's going on in that house is partly my fault,'' I said.

Annee put her hand on my arm and squeezed. ''You gave them a dose of truth,'' she said. ''It's bitter medicine. I know the taste.''

A gasp escaped from my lips. ''I'm sorry,'' I said, ''if I hurt you.''

''Don't be sorry,'' she said. ''I needed shaking to wake up. I think I've been asleep for twenty years.''

''Sleeping Beauty,'' I said.

''Well, sleeping, anyway.'' Annee chuckled.

At that moment Vincent came into the room from the kitchen, where he'd been helping M. Saverne. He went directly to Annee and spoke to her in French. I understood enough of the words to figure out that he was asking where Odette was.

Annee answered him in English since I was standing right there. I interpreted the language switch as a mild rebuke to him regarding his manners.

''She called in sick,'' Annee said.

''Oh,'' he said, his face coloring. I wondered whether the color was due to Annee's correction or because he was trying to hide his interest in Odette from me. ''She was all right earlier today.''

Annee and I both caught that. For how long had his interest in Odette been rekindled? When Vincent first showed up in town, he had been hiding somewhere, and Annee had suspected he was seeing Odette.

''Where did you see her?'' I said.

His color did not improve. ''In town,'' he said, gulping.

''Where?'' I didn't want to let him off the hook.

''Answer, Vincent,'' Annee said.

''Odette won't . . .'' he said. ''No, I shall not answer.''

''You'll get as bad as the Toutes with their secrets,'' I said.

Anger replaced embarrassment on his face. ''Odette told me about you,'' he said.

I looked at Annee, who seemed to be struggling with her emotions.

"Why don't you tell me what Odette said about me, Vincent? I can take it. I won't even get mad. And then I'll tell you some things about the Toutes that perhaps you didn't know."

"Why should I listen to you after all the trouble you've caused?" He was spitting when he spoke. Very French.

"Vincent," Annee said, "please come into the kitchen with me. Fran, give us a couple of minutes and then you come in, too." Annee was all business. Vincent went meekly.

They were no sooner gone from the dining room than M. Saverne came out of the kitchen. He was smiling and wearing a chef's hat, which made him seem enormous. He smiled at me and then went from table to table, speaking to the customers about the food, asking them what they liked, telling them how things were prepared.

When he passed Clarisse, he said a few words to her that sent her scurrying to the bar. She came back with a bottle of Armagnac and a tray full of small glasses, which she immediately started to fill at the small bar in the dining room that the waitresses used for everything.

I went to help her, figuring that M. Saverne had decided to furnish *digestifs* (after-dinner drinks) to everyone in the dining room. M. Saverne also came over to help pour and serve after a few more minutes of socializing with the diners.

"I think you'll be wanted in the kitchen," he said to me. "I'll help Clarisse with this."

Annee and Vincent were perched on stools next to the big stainless-steel table in the middle of the kitchen. Annee looked relaxed. Everything under control again.

"Vincent tells me that you upset the Toute family by telling the parents a lot of lies," Annee said.

"That's what Odette says?" I said.

"Yes," Vincent said. "That's what she told me."

"Where did you see her?" I said, returning to the question that got him riled before.

"In our usual place," he said, after a glance at his mother.

"Which is well hidden in the woods," I said.

He reddened again and examined the fabric on the front of his shirt. "Yes."

"I think you'd better show me the place," I said.

He looked at his mother and then at me and quickly away, focusing on the air above his head. A white area appeared around his lips. "I can't. I can't. Odette, she, she wouldn't like that."

I knew that if I was going to get any cooperation out of Vincent, I'd have to pry him away from his long-standing loyalty to Odette.

"Odette may have inherited her parents' disrespect for truth," I said. "She may have secrets you don't know about."

I don't know what inspired me to say that, but this idea, I could see, found a home in Vincent's awareness. Although he said nothing immediately to betray that change, his face told the story.

Annee leaped in with a mother's view on the seducer of her son. "She has caused you more trouble than you have ever caused her," she said.

The trouble, I assumed, had to do with the big blowup before Vincent left town.

"You don't know anything about it," he said, practically on the verge of tears.

"Maybe you should tell me," she said gently, coaxing. "Maybe I would understand you better and be able to help you."

My feeling was that Vincent was already having some difficulty with his relationship with Odette, and now he had two women who were being sympathetic to him and telling him, at the same time, that Odette the angel might have a bit of the devil in her.

"Maybe we should tell Vincent all the things we know." I spoke with some emphasis on the word "all," but I didn't know how much she wanted to tell her son.

Annee took a deep breath. "I was thinking the same thing," she said, and launched into the whole sordid tale.

It must have been difficult for her. But it was even harder on Vincent. When she stopped talking, he ran out the back door and started to retch.

He returned pale and stoop-shouldered, his eyes watery,

his hands hanging as if they didn't belong to him. "I have to talk to Odette," he said. "I'll show you the place tomorrow morning—I promise you."

"Are you going to warn her that I'm coming?"

He looked surprised. "No, oh, no. It's not that. It's something else. After the things she told me, and the things Mother told me, well, I have to straighten them out with her."

Annee looked on approvingly.

My mind was working like a buzz saw. I would keep my eye on Vincent and follow him tonight.

Twenty-six

I was pretty sure that Vincent would lead me into the woods at the end of the street where the Toutes lived. I wasn't so worried about going into the woods as I was about finding my way out. The methods I thought of for not getting lost were numerous: Lay a trail like Hansel and Gretel? Take a flashlight and a compass? Bend twigs over on the way in? Drip phosphorescent paint on the path? Hunker down till morning?

I kept thinking that the Toute girls would be able to help me find out where Denis had been hiding. They knew the woods, they weren't afraid of the woods. They ought to have an idea about where someone could hide. Surely Odette had found the place where Vincent had hidden himself when he returned to town.

But Odette was not going to cooperate with me. As far as she was concerned, I was a villain. Whatever her folks had told her, it wasn't the truth, or at least what I called the truth. Maybe they had some twisted kind of logic that could make a story that would sound true to one of their own children.

Niki and Jacques, who at first had seemed such wonderful parents of precocious children, now appeared to be more sinister. If Denis had a friend in the police department, as J. P. seemed to think was the case, Jacques might have been the one who helped with the escape. But why? And who made the pâté that was sent to me? Who clobbered the guard? Jacques? Clement? What was behind all the killing? Did it all start with someone who had a grudge against

Denis? Or did Denis do all the killing, including the murder of Marcel Gris?

I thought about the various crimes and sins that Denis had committed. He was a bully, a deceiver, a liar, self-centered in the extreme. But was he a murderer, too?

And Jacques—wasn't he all those things, too, but with different manifestations? And was he more or less capable of murder?

Niki? Was she a killer? M. Saverne? I thought about the people who had the slightest connection to Denis. All the Toutes and Niki's parents, the Bouchegrandes; the wife of M. Foyer, Monique; Pierre Bouton, the rival innkeeper. Then there were the people who had more than slight connections: Vincent and Laurence.

My most cynical self asked: Had I ruled out anyone?

Of course, I had ruled out Annee. Hadn't I? Then I remembered J. P. and his assessment of Annee as being a little thick. Could she have been playing dumb? Could she have been planning to kill Denis for a long time and pretending not to know about his escapades?

The work at the inn didn't require much attention that evening. Vincent's departure was the only thing I was watching for. Clarisse took the dinner orders and I cleaned off tables and got drinks. The French take ages to eat, and nobody ever hustles anyone away from a table or rushes to give the customer the check (*l'addition*) after the meal.

The evening was waning and there were people eating their main courses at only a couple of tables when in walked Odette, who had had such bad cramps she couldn't come to work.

She walked over to Annee and bussed her on both cheeks. Odette looked flushed and happy and was talking excitedly. Vincent, who was in the kitchen when she arrived, apparently had his antennae set for the sound of her voice, because he was out of the kitchen like a shot almost as soon as Odette started talking.

Vincent got both cheeks kissed twice each before Odette started talking again. Then Clarisse joined them and there was more excited conversation, which was joined by some of the diners and soon by some of the people from the bar and M. Saverne.

The crowd was so thick around Odette that I could no longer see her, but her voice was still rising in soprano enthusiasm. To my surprise, I found myself picking up a word here and there in French, and when I put the words together, it seemed that the discussion in the dining room that Odette had initiated was all about the TV people coming to Vaudoy. I didn't get the details, but I was happy to have understood anything in the patter and rumble of the many voices.

Since my French was anything but secure, I asked Annee, the next time I got the chance, what the excitement was about.

"The TV people are going to set up tomorrow to film Odette and Bernadette at their practice place. They want the townspeople to be there watching, the way it was before all the trouble." Annee's voice caught on the last phrase.

"It had to happen," I said. "Those two girls are wonderful together, there in that little natural theater."

"Yes," she said. "I hope that all that's happened doesn't change the way they are."

I could see in the faces of the people in the dining room a sort of unity. The girls whom they had appreciated and watched were now going to be shown to the rest of France. Were they wondering, as I was, whether fame would change them, or take them away from the village where their talent was nurtured?

Bottles of champagne materialized and Odette was toasted and cheered. Then Bernadette and the rest of the Toutes showed up, and the toasting started all over again.

During the celebration, Annee excused herself. As good a baby as Fanny was, she did have to be offered food on a regular basis.

"I'll be back in about a half hour," Annee said. "Probably this"—she waved her arm to encompass the dining room scene—"will still be going on."

"We'll be late cleaning up," I said.

"Yes, but how many times do we have celebrities in Vaudoy en Brie?"

It was relatively easy for me to avoid Niki and Jacques in the crowd of well-wishers. Clement was another story. He followed me around, carried trays for me, helped me clear tables and pick up drinks from the bar, all the while apologizing and explaining, some of which I listened to, especially when he was talking about what his parents said about me.

"They were upset," Clement told me, "and they said you were lying because you were trying to protect Annee because Annee has a new baby."

"Did that seem reasonable to you?" I said.

"At the time, yes," Clement said, but his eyes were full of questions that I knew he wouldn't ask. "And it seemed that the whole family had been attacked, except for Bernadette and me. I felt I had to do something to show that I was on their side." His eyes pleaded for a sympathetic response.

"And now?" I said. "How do you feel now?"

"I told you in my note. By the way, did you like the pâté?"

I told him what had happened to the pâté, and I was about to ask him when he made it and whether anyone else was around when he was preparing it. J. P. had said that the wrappings were the same in the poisoned and unpoisoned varieties that had been delivered to the hospital. The lethal one could have been prepared at the store, I reasoned.

But Clement got a signal from his father and I never got to ask the questions. Jacques was calling for quiet and had grouped his family around him. He was about to make a speech, but I didn't stay to listen.

I hadn't forgotten to watch Vincent, who was given a signal by Odette while her father was raising his voice and calling the group to attention. Vincent slipped into the kitchen as a hush fell on the room.

I made my exit in a nonchalant—I hoped—way to the bar and then from the bar to the front door. The bar was empty except for Albert, Georges, and Remi, the regular drunks for whom time stood still. Everyone else was interested in the Toutes and what Jacques had to say.

There was no sign of Vincent in the street. Had I lost him so soon? I was just about to dash out the front and up the alley when he appeared, coming around the corner from the kitchen carrying a bag, a rather full cloth bag. Food? For Vincent and Odette? For Denis?

I waited until Vincent had traveled far enough down the block so that he wouldn't be able to see me clearly if he turned around. My plan was to watch him, not to confront him or accuse him.

He headed straight for the woods and entered the darkness of the trees not far from where we had seen Bernadette crying. Could Denis be in the woods undetected by the gendarmes all this while?

I still had not seen a sign that the police were anywhere in Vaudoy watching the suspects or searching for Denis, but I felt that they had to be nearby. That was what the cops in the States would do, I told myself.

I saw Vincent switch on a small light that he kept trained on the path. I entered the woods where there was no path and the footing was uneven. My intention was to keep some trees between us. Every time I put a foot down, I wondered whether a snapped twig would give me away, but the forest floor was soft and noiseless. And luckily, Vincent was not moving fast.

The small light wiggled across the path, back and forth, as if he were looking for something. The air had cooled and I didn't have enough on to keep from shivering. But I wasn't afraid, I told myself.

All my senses felt sharp, and at one point I thought I heard Vincent breathing. But the keenness was soon dissolved in the slow rhythm of his pace and the swinging light. It was startling when he finally stopped and veered off the path, straight toward me.

I barely had time to halt and take cover behind a tree. He took no pains to hide or go softly, but barged through the trees purposefully, passing within a few feet of where I was standing, holding my breath and wondering whether his sense of smell was sharp enough to catch the lingering scent of toilet water or soap or cooking that clung to me.

I had no trouble picking up the hot grease smell that emanated from him. Probably from his spending the day in the inn's kitchen or from the bag he was carrying. I resumed my pursuit once he was safely past me.

He stopped in a small clearing and put the bag he had brought from the inn between two large rocks. He beamed the small light around, pausing when the ray picked out a group of large rocks that rose on the other side of the clearing.

The hiding place, I thought. The place where he had hidden when he came to town. I didn't see any entryway or mouth of a cave, but I felt that there was something there.

Good, I thought, I'll come back tomorrow and scout it out. Right now, I'll follow Vincent back out of the woods, since he has a light. And going over the route twice will help to imprint it on my mind.

I waited until Vincent had put some distance between us before I started after him. I had the feeling of having accomplished my mission and was traveling along lightly, again following the small light zigzagging across the path.

Was the bag of food for Vincent and Odette on their next rendezvous? Would Vincent be smuggling food to his father, even though they had a history of animosity and the latest events had done nothing to change that? It made sense that he would be keeping his meetings with Odette secret since her father did not approve.

I was lost in these thoughts when I heard another sound. It was behind me, and my skin began to prickle. Get out of here, my mind said. Forget Vincent. Move.

But I wasn't fast enough.

Twenty-seven

Someone grabbed me from behind; an arm pulled against my throat so tightly I could barely breathe. I thought that was it, I would be strangled. I felt a warm exhale on my ear and smelled garlic and something else that was familiar but which I couldn't name just then, because my own death preoccupied my brain. I was going to die this time.

I tried to wriggle out of the grasp; I tried to make a sound. Perhaps Vincent would hear me. But the choked sound I made was barely audible, and then a hand came over my mouth and I was pulled against a body. The body was male and he was aroused. I felt him against me. Thoughts of death were crowded out by thoughts of rape. My stomach was turning; my breathing was shallow. I told myself not to faint. Hold on, hold on. Fight, squirm, scratch, bite, kick.

I elbowed him in the gut. Since both of his arms were in use holding my mouth and my throat, my arms were free. I reached up and pinched the skin on his cheek and twisted. He gasped and tightened his grip on my throat. Tighter, tighter. The fear rose in my throat and then seemed to roll in a wave over my entire body. I couldn't breathe, and I passed out.

When I woke up, I was bound and gagged, leaning against what felt like a tree. Something, maybe a blanket, was wrapped around me, for which I was thankful. I didn't know how long I had been out or how far I had been taken from the spot where I had been grabbed.

One thing I was fairly sure of: I hadn't been raped, not yet. I lifted my head cautiously, but I couldn't see anything. Dark, very dark. And silent. The air was still and smelled damp and moldy. I was inside a cellar or a cave, I thought. There wasn't the slightest rustle of leaves; there was no light from the stars or the moon.

My neck felt hot where the arm had held me and my arms and legs were stinging. Had I been dragged and bumped along the ground and against trees and bushes?

I couldn't think what my attacker would do next. I wondered whether Denis was the one who had grabbed me. Did he intend to kill me this time? And was he aroused, as I had thought, when he grabbed me? Then I focused on the stinging sensation on my arms and legs. It was localized and in spots where I wouldn't have been scratched had I been dragged through bushes. I felt sick. When I was unconscious, he had bitten me, I thought.

The very thought diminished me, nauseated me, and started great waves of anger. I tugged at my bonds, gritted my teeth. Tears ran warm down my face. In my rage, I accomplished nothing except to exhaust myself.

As I sat there panting, frustrated, small sounds broke into the space between my breaths, which were hampered by the gag. I tried to get control of my breathing to listen.

Giggles? A woman's voice. A man's voice. Coming closer. Yes, voices. What were they saying? They were still too far away for me to pick up any of the words. But the tone was happy, friendly. Was it Odette and Vincent? Should I try to make noise over the gag? Closer still. No, the male voice wasn't Vincent's. The woman, was that Annee? What would Annee be doing in the woods? Or was that Niki? I couldn't tell. The man and woman were speaking French rapidly, and making little noises in between some of their sentences. Were they eating?

Suddenly a light flashed on a surface several feet in front of me. I dropped my head as if I were still unconscious, but I kept my eye on the surface where the light had been but was no longer. The voices grew fainter and then there was silence again.

I tried to take inventory of my body and keep a lid on the outrage and disgust lest it overshadow what my nerve

endings were telling me. The tingling, burning sensation
was strongest in two spots on one of my thighs and in one
spot on each arm.

If I get out of this, I told myself, I will make that man
pay. I gritted my teeth and held back the tears of self-pity
that were about to start rolling. I tested the rope or whatever
was holding my hands, which were bound in front of me.
Not the best way to keep a prisoner held securely, I thought,
and wondered why they weren't tied behind me. When a
reason occurred to me, I shook it off. I hated the idea of
my unconscious arms being around Denis's neck.

Perhaps he doesn't intend to keep me here long, I
thought. Perhaps he'll be back any minute to finish what
he started. Maybe the woman came and interrupted him.

I moved my mouth to check the tightness of the gag.
Yes, there was some give, and with my hands in front, I
would be able to pull it off. I listened for the return of
Denis or the woman or both of them, but heard nothing.
The gag was easy. It was down in no time and I was able
to breathe more freely and immediately felt stronger.

With my teeth exposed, I went to work on my hands. It
wasn't rope, it was some kind of strong string. As I put the
string in my mouth, I smelled that smell that I had noticed
when I was first grabbed. What was it? Some kind of food.

I worried the string with my incisors, picking away at
the knots—a lot of them, it seemed—and getting whiff after whiff of that odor. I got one loop off, but there were
others. I kept working and listening, hoping I wouldn't hear
anything, wanting with all my will to escape. The next set
of loops was joined together, and when they were untied,
I regained much more mobility. Also, I became aware of
how the tension of the string had burned my skin.

I ran my hands down over my ankles. Now that I could
move my fingers, maybe it would be wise to work on my
feet before freeing my hands entirely, and see if I could
walk away from here. My feet, too, were tied with the
string, but there didn't seem to be so much of it. I felt the
little knots and thought that teeth were better for untying
this string. However, I wasn't that supple. Touching my
toes was easy, but getting my face down that far was another thing. My fingers gradually figured out the little knots,

and the strings started to come undone. Actually, I had only two knots to untie to free my feet. Big knots of small string, but still, only two. And then my feet were free.

I stood up and felt unsteady. I inched my way toward the spot where I had seen the light, thinking that might be the way to get out of where I was. A cave—I was sure now I was in a cave. I moved my feet quietly, feeling my way across the uneven floor. The log that I had been leaning on angled in the direction I wanted to go. I lifted my arms, still bound together, and was surprised at how soon I touched the rough stone ceiling of the cave.

Careful, I thought. It might get lower. Keep your arms up and guide by the ceiling. It seemed to take forever, and I began to wonder whether I was still going in the same direction.

Then I felt a merciful breeze on my face and knew that I was close to the entrance. The smell of fresh air was a sharp contrast to the dank odor of the cave.

If I could just get out and behind a tree and be quiet. I sent up a prayer to whom it may concern. If you've been watching, I told the prayer-intake line, you know I'm not a bad person. I need a little luck right now, and if you could just give me a little, I'll investigate the source of your power and send you a thank-you note or light a candle or do a good turn or something that you would like.

Suddenly there was light, from the stars and the quarter moon, and after my being in total darkness, it seemed like a spotlight from which I ought to shrink. I wasted no time in getting myself away from the entrance to the cave and into the thickest part of the woods I could see. Then I put some distance between me and the cave, but I was lost. I didn't know which way to go to get out of the woods, because I had been unconscious when I was brought to the cave.

I made my way until I came to a thick mass of bushes, which seemed like a good place to stop and get my bearings, if I could. Also, I would work on the strings that still held my hands. This time, while I worked on it, I recognized the odor that clung to the string. It was like the *saucisson sec* (sort of like salami) that I had had at Annee's and at the inn. I especially liked the sausage with a piece of baguette and some *cornichons* (small sour pickles).

God, I was hungry all of a sudden.

Finally my hands were free and I rubbed the skin on my wrists where the string had made little ridges. I guessed I could go without food for a little longer, but I was very thirsty, and if I didn't do something about my thirst, I knew I would get tired.

I tried to remember where the river passed through the town and whether it ran through the woods. When I had seen the fountain, I remembered, the spring that fed the fountain ran off into the river. In one direction, the river snaked through the field and past the new school. In the other direction, it skirted the woods and maybe ran into the woods for a little way before it made its way into fields again.

I listened for the sound of water, sniffed for the smell of water, but I wasn't experienced enough to find it with ears and nose.

But then I heard sounds that made me hunker down into the thicket. It was the man and the woman again, coming straight toward me. I curled into the smallest ball I could make and held myself very still. The voices came closer, not speaking quickly and gaily now, but slowly, seriously, with long pauses.

They passed very close to me, and when they did, I again got a whiff of that sausage smell. Did Denis always smell like that? I wondered. Or wasn't it Denis?

I was thanking the anonymous power that had saved me again, and to whom I had made my desperate promises, when I suddenly had something else to add to my list of thank-yous. The man and the woman had stepped into water that was almost close enough for me to touch. Why hadn't I heard it? I thought, straining my ears to pick up the little lapping sounds. But I still couldn't hear the river except where the man and the woman were stepping.

Then there was splashing and small laughs and more splashing. Swimming? Were they swimming? I heard the sound of something hitting water, as if a swimmer were kicking and had broken the surface with one hard kick.

I raised my head to see. The moon had broken through the trees and there were two people swimming, naked as if in the Garden of Eden. I couldn't make out their features on the misty water, nor could I identify the voices, but I thought they were the two who had passed the cave earlier. And I was almost certain that the man was Denis, but I hadn't really gotten a good look at him at any time. All I knew was that I had been bitten while I was unconscious. And I knew of Denis's reputation.

The questions I was asking myself had to do with how I was going to get out of the woods. But now that I had found the river, I knew that all I had to do was to follow it and it would lead me out of the woods and into the fields. The trouble was that I was disoriented and didn't know which direction would be the safer way to go. In any case, I couldn't move just then without running the risk of being seen. I didn't want to be trussed up and put back in the cave to wait for whatever Denis might feel like doing next.

I was so intent on watching the two swimming that I wasn't aware of another sound coming through the trees until it was almost on top of me, and then it was too late for me to move. I stayed still, hoping that the third person would pass me without noticing. But I had stuck my head out of the brambles and I didn't look like a bush.

I thought that the third person was female and was dressed in dark clothing. I didn't know whether to call to her for help, either. Who was it that I could trust? She seemed intent on the swimmers and was almost past me when she saw me and yelped. At that I took off into the woods, not knowing which way to go, but trying to keep myself parallel to the river in case I got a chance to get to it and follow it.

Behind me were excited voices, shouting to one another in French. I didn't need a translator to know that all three of them would be after me. I suddenly realized that I was wearing a light blouse and would be easy to spot, so I tore it off as I ran, then realized that my bra, too, was white. Off it came, too. Then I remembered all the commando movies with the mud streaks on the white faces and wondered whether I dared stop to muck myself up.

I listened, but the voices had stopped. Were they still coming after me?

I slowed down and traveled quietly. Then I doubled back

toward the river, hoping that I would meet it before I met one of them.

I didn't hear anything, which worried me, because I feared they were lying in wait, ready to pounce. And I had been pounced upon once already that night. I stopped to listen and heard only my breathing. That could be heard far enough away, I thought, to bring them running. Luckily, my heartbeat wasn't as easily heard, because that pump was doing its work in pounding fashion.

As I stood there, I heard the ripple of the water and realized that it was only steps away.

If I could get to it. I must get to it.

I tiptoed silently and there it was, catching the light of the moon in the middle, but dark at the marshy edges. I grabbed a branch to steady myself as I stepped in. Splashes would give me away. The water was cool and the mud was deep and soft, but I finally hit bottom.

As I put my other foot in, I heard a sound nearby. Someone was walking slowly. Damn. I tried to keep the panic down and get myself into the water, all of me, without making noise.

Something made a huge splash back where the people had been swimming earlier, and I heard the footsteps change direction and head back toward the sound.

Then I finished immersing myself in the river, which was about two feet deep right there. I sat on the muddy bottom and availed myself of some of the muck to darken my face and shoulders. I was careful not to splash.

The footsteps came back toward me and I pushed myself against the muddy bank, hoping to blend into the marsh. I almost screamed when I saw the foot close enough for me to touch. And then I saw something that even in that extremity of danger made me feel sad and disappointed, maybe even betrayed.

Twenty-eight

The leg that stood on the bank catching a moonlit ray had dark teeth marks on it. It was like the leg I had seen sticking out from under a hospital gown. Annee. Annee, running around in the woods with Denis. What else had she done with him?

And her story about the night Denis was killed, all false. It must have been. She must have known all along that Denis was alive. J. P. was right to suspect her. And the killings of Arnaut and Foyer? They must have found out. And now me. They are trying to kill me. She and Denis. In this together. But . . .

I didn't dare let her know I was there. She'd tell Denis for sure. But did she know he'd bitten me? Was that all right with her? And who was the other woman?

The water rippled around my chin, which had acquired a long, slimy piece of vegetation. Good, I thought, better to blend into the scenery. The rest of me was covered in the muddy bottom. All I wished for then was that she wouldn't step out into the water, because she would surely step on me.

I heard a voice that I was sure was Denis's say, "*Pas ici* [Not here]," and he couldn't have been more than a few yards away. I shivered, not for the first time that night, but maybe with more reason, because Denis was coming closer and the water seemed to be getting colder.

They stood next to me, but the sounds they made were no longer those of two people looking for me. They were fondling, petting, groaning noises. I hoped they would go away, that I wouldn't be privy to any more of Denis's perversions than I already had been.

It seemed forever before they walked off, still in their rutting mode. It was time for me to try to get down the river to safety. I wondered briefly where the other woman was, but reasoned that if the two of them felt free to pursue their lovemaking, perhaps the woman had left.

I was glad they were distracted from the pursuit. And I wasn't about to make noise and distract them from their distraction.

While I had been lying in the mud, it had come to me which direction I should go in to get myself back to Annee's house. I felt pretty sure that I would get there before she did. That is, if I was right about which way to go, and if I was quiet, and if no one pounced on me.

I floated myself out into the current, and then I remembered which way the river flowed and was certain of my direction. In the middle of the river, the water ran a little deeper, and I dropped my shoes off, which were soaked and full of mud. It was easier going without them, and I swam along with the current.

I took off my skirt, too, but I didn't discard it. I would need to cover myself with something to walk the streets. I swam slowly without splashing, looking for the place where I wanted to climb out. There was a bridge over the road that led up to the *mairie* (town hall), and just before the bridge was the fountain where the overflow ran into the river. I remembered sitting there one day and listening to the water, which first splashed into the pool of the fountain and then quietly flowed into the big stone tub where the women used to do their laundry, and then splashed again as it tumbled from the tub into the river. Right near the fountain was a path to the road. That was what I was looking for.

But I was not out of the woods. I heard a lot of commotion and shouting and then a light cut through the air and a bright pool opened in front of me. Down, get under, was the message from my brain, and I submerged with a splash I hadn't intended.

Oh, God, they've decided to come after me in earnest.

I tried to keep down near the bottom, but I was getting

tired and cold, besides being totally panicked. Swimming along the deepest channel of the river, I began to wonder whether I would ever get home again to Cheektowaga; to my dog, Horace; to my tentative love affair with a Buffalo cop named Ted Zwiatek; to Polly, the leader of the battered women's group.

Damn, I thought, is this what happens? Is this the way one's life passes before one's eyes? Get out of this water, I told myself. Get to the bank on the other side from where you went in and get out.

My head came up first and I looked back and saw that a light was still shining on the water, but I was downstream from it and it didn't seem to be moving. Other lights were moving in the woods near the light in the water. I turned and swam to the edge and looked into the trees, waiting for my eyes to grow accustomed to the darkness again.

I almost shouted with joy when I saw the light coming through the trees. The lights from a house, not searchlights from people who were looking to put out my lights.

Just as I began to haul myself up onto the bank, I heard a shot. Motionless, I waited for another while I tried to run a check on my body to see if I was hit. But I was so cold, I wasn't sure whether I would know if I were wounded.

Another shot. Was it closer? I couldn't tell. Fear was blurring my perceptions and I couldn't get control. I sank down into the water and swam out to the middle of the river, trying to breathe regularly, trying to keep my arms and legs moving without making splashes that would call attention to me. I would go farther downstream, I thought, farther from the shots and the lights.

The current was suddenly faster and carried me along like a log. A shadow loomed, and as the terror rose in my throat, I bumped into something. I reached for the bottom with my feet, but it wasn't there, so I grabbed for whatever I had bumped into and found myself holding onto a log that had fallen over a good part of the river at that point. Lucky, I told myself, that this time I didn't hit my head. My head had taken enough lumps. But I had scratched my shoulder and arm when I hit the log.

There were branches spreading out from the tree, too, which blocked my way. I was reluctant to swim under it for fear that I'd get caught in the branches. But the current was tugging at me, and the water was cold. I had to do something.

I looked back at where the light had been and saw nothing. I couldn't hear any more commotion, either. No shouts, no shots.

Exhausted and still worried about being pursued, I swam across the current to the bank on the side where I had tried to get out before. I was gasping by the time I got there, and worried that someone would hear my breathing.

Bushes grew down to the water at that spot on the river and I gratefully pulled myself ashore in the sheltering shadows. I didn't know where I was or how far I'd have to go to get help, or where exactly to go to get help. Maybe going to Annee's was out of the question.

Warmth, I needed warmth. I couldn't stop shivering. How could I get warm? I looked for lights. Maybe there was a house nearby. But the French weren't ones to leave lights on at night, and there were few lights in the town. I looked up through the trees at the sky and realized that the trees were thinner here and that the moon wasn't shedding the light it had before. Clouds were creeping across the sky and covering the stars, too.

How was I going to find my way? And where was my way?

I crawled out from the bushes and stood up. Bad move. I almost fell over from dizziness. Head between the knees when you're dizzy, a voice from the past shouted in my head.

A few minutes later, I lifted my head and tried again, more slowly, and made it to my feet. I wrung out my skirt and wrapped the wet fabric around me with the waistline under my armpits. The trees were sparse in the direction I was heading, and soon I was out of the woods and in a field of sunflowers.

Good, I thought. They're tall enough to give me shelter if someone should come along. But I was still very cold, and no amount of moving was going to warm me up. What did hypothermia do? Would it knock me out? All I knew was that it was serious and that I should try to get warm.

Maybe, I thought, I'm safe enough here to turn my attention to getting warm.

I knelt down on the ground and it felt warmer than my skin. I pulled up a few sunflowers and laid them in between the rows. Then I pulled up some more, a blanket, something to hold in what heat I still had. I took off my wet skirt and underwear and lay down under the stalks and shivered. Without warning, I was crying, sobbing. Thoughts were running through my head with such speed, like a computer gone mad with its data all out of order.

I don't know how long I cried. But I think I stopped because I was exhausted.

Then something wet moved next to my ear and I yelped. Then more wetness. I tried to push it away and whatever it was pushed against me, harder.

My nose finally told me what it was. A dog. He was friendly and apparently delighted to find a human down at his level during the course of his night rovings.

I hugged him and felt his warmth. Yes, I'll try to keep him here, I thought. After some petting and rubbing and cooing, he snuggled against me. He was rapturous with all the attention. I curled around him, basking in his heat, and I could feel myself grow stronger.

He nestled with me under my little shelter of sunflower stalks, me thinking how lucky I was that he had come along. He snored and I almost giggled.

The next thing I knew, the sun was up and the dog was gone. The air was warm and my skirt was almost dry. What was more important, I was warm. I remember that dog as if he were the good fairy who came along when I was in need and then disappeared without waiting to be thanked when the good deed was done.

Voices nearby made me sit up and put on my skirt in a way to hide the parts that are most of the time hidden. My legs were dirty, as were my arms, dirt from the river and from the field. What my face looked like, I didn't know, but when I ran my fingers over it, flakes of dirt fell. Maybe it would be just as well to keep hidden, I thought.

But I was curious about the voices. Even though I wasn't sure what French farmers sounded like, I didn't think the voices were those of farmers. For one thing, there was a lot of talking going on, and quite a few voices. And I had never seen farmers in large groups going about the business of harvesting or plowing or spreading manure.

I lifted a bunch of sunflowers a bit higher than the rest and positioned my eyes to look through them. Trucks, TV trucks, were strung out along what must have been the road, which I had missed the night before. The sunflowers, I thought—they must be in the field near where the Toute girls practice. Of course; today was the day that the practice would be televised.

One thing for sure, I didn't want to be on television. Not in one of their color segments, not being asked my opinion, not at all. I would go to the other end of the field before I took to the road.

I hoped that when I got to the house, Marsha and Laurence would be there. I didn't want to face Annee alone. Maybe I could get J. P. on the phone before I had to talk to her.

I made my way on hands and knees to the far end of the sunflowers and stood up and walked through the next field, which was planted in wheat and had been partly harvested. Away from the TV trucks, the road was deserted, which suited me fine, because I didn't want to be seen in my disheveled condition. My bare feet hurt when I stepped on the cut stalks of wheat and then when I walked on the small stones at the road's edge.

As I got near to the house, I saw Annee's car and my heart took a nervous jump. What if Denis were at the house? If he was, would I be safer at the front door or the back door? I looked around to see if there were any police nearby. But again I saw no one, not a soul who could be an undercover cop, not anyone.

The front, I thought. I'll go in the front. When I rang the bell, my knees felt weak. The door opened as my nerves were vibrating with the tension.

Annee.

I turned to run.

"Fran. Come back," she said. "We've been so worried about you."

I turned at the foot of the steps to the front door. "You and who else?" I said.

At that second Marsha showed up behind Annee. I never thought I would be so glad to see my ex-mother-in-law. "What happened to you, Fran?" she said. "My God, you look like you've been dragged by wild animals. Where are the rest of your clothes?" Marsha came down the stairs and put her arm around me, and I could no longer restrain the tears and the anger.

I started talking and hollering and insisting that the police be called, especially J. P. I showed them the marks that Denis had made.

Marsha listened. Laurence joined us and listened, too. Annee didn't come close to me, probably because I was shooting angry glances her way.

When I got to the part about the marks on the woman's leg, Annee caught her breath. "You think that was me?" she said.

"Well, wasn't it?"

"No." She pulled up her slacks and showed me her legs. "Did the legs look like this?"

I looked, and looked again. Her legs were scarred, but there were no red marks, no bruises. Her marks were healing. The marks on the woman in the woods were still new. Like the ones on me.

"But," I said, "who . . ."

Annee came toward me now. "Come in, Fran. We'll run a warm tub for you. Then we'll get some food into you. And we'll call the police. And while we're doing that, we'll tell you what happened last night while you were gone."

Twenty-nine

The three women fussed over me, cleaning my wounds, undressing me as if I were a child, and getting me into the tub, shampooing my hair and combing the weeds out of it.

When I started to feel almost human, they started talking about the night before. They had sent the police to look for me, they said, and the police had gone to the woods.

"The police? Was that the shooting I heard?"

"But they weren't shooting at you," Annee said. "It was Denis. They found Denis."

"Found him? Only him? Not anyone else?"

"Just Denis. And they found a cave where he had been staying."

"The cave where I woke up," I said. "I was in a cave."

Marsha picked out my clothes, a skirt and a summer blouse. When I protested that the marks Denis had made on me would show, Annee spoke up.

"We're not going to hide what he did anymore." She kicked out one foot to show the scars visible on her legs because she wasn't wearing stockings. "If anybody asks what they are, I'll tell them."

Over breakfast, they told me how worried they had been. They said that the police had asked a lot of questions about me. J. P. had been there, and he had said that the police had asked Denis about me.

"Denis claimed he hadn't seen you," Annee said.

"Well, it was dark," I said. And we all laughed a little.

We speculated on who the women in the woods were,

who it was that I had seen swimming with the man I thought was Denis.

"Denis has been with many women," Annee said. "That gendarme who calls himself J. P. has a long dossier on Denis."

"J. P. was surprised that you didn't know," I said.

"I didn't want to know. Things are so much clearer now."

"Clear enough so that you could make a guess as to who was in the woods last night?"

"Who? Clarisse? Niki? The Toute girls? Any of the other women from the village? From another village?" Annee delivered her list with some heat. "I count myself lucky that I didn't catch some horrible disease from him." And that seemed to be as far as Annee wanted to go with that conversation, because she abruptly began talking about Fanny's progress.

And this woman who had been so unaware of her husband's activities showed that she could notice just about everything if she wanted to. Every little change in the way Fanny used her hands, in the way she followed with her eyes, in the length of her naps, in the intensity of her attention, was noted and commented upon.

As I was tucking into my second helping of croissants and coffee, the police arrived. J. P. was among them. He had deep circles under his eyes.

"So," he said, "you were playing detective."

"It didn't feel like play," I said.

He insisted that I tell him everything, and I started to, but Marsha and Laurence and Annee were there to help. So I only had to answer questions that they couldn't answer. It was actually a relief not to have to say the words again. Because, as I heard the women repeating what I had told them, it all sounded so horrid, so hard, so tiring.

It also gave me a chance to think, and as I thought about it, some things were clearing up.

Along about the time that J. P. had heard enough, Vincent came in, and J. P. started asking him about the bag he had taken into the woods, the one I had seen him hide.

Vincent mumbled and stuttered and finally confessed that he and Odette were going to meet after the televising and celebrate. There was wine, he said, and some pâté in the bag. "We often store food there. It stays cool between the rocks and the animals can't get at it easily."

"Does Jacques suspect," Annee asked Vincent, "that you and Odette are seeing one another again?"

"We're not seeing one another that often. She is so busy practicing and working at the inn and going to school. Mostly I see her at the inn." Vincent looked sorrowful when he spoke of Odette being busy. Obviously he wanted more of her time than he was getting.

Annee looked at her son with great pity and then gave a shrug. There wasn't anything she could do to make the hurt go away, I thought. It wasn't something she could kiss and make better.

J. P. then brought up the subject of the women in the woods and went down his list of possible suspects.

Vincent almost attacked J. P. when he mentioned Odette. And after he quieted down, Vincent ticked off a long list of reasons that Odette couldn't have been in the woods, first among them being that she needed her rest in order to perform for the TV cameras today.

"Who else knows the woods the way the Toute children know them?" J. P. said, clearly baiting Vincent.

Vincent took the bait. "Clarisse knows them; Madame Toute knows them," he said, and then he mentioned the names of other women, some of which I had heard once or twice at the inn, but I didn't have faces that went with the names. I might even have served them their dinners or drinks. But their names had never been tied to Denis, unlike Niki's and Clarisse's.

My respect for J. P. went up a couple of notches as I saw him take Vincent on an emotional roller coaster that ended with Vincent happily going along to the gendarmerie with J. P., ostensibly to tell him everything he knew about the woods. I guessed that J. P. had a few other questions to ask.

I was wishing I could be there when J. P. asked Vincent whether the bag of food was really for Denis. It was one of the questions I wanted to ask.

But I contented myself with asking Annee everything I could think of. She and I spent the next couple of hours—

and sometimes we were joined by Laurence and Marsha, who were busy tidying up the kitchen and packing lunches so that we could all get to the Toute girls' big place in the sun—recounting the events that had led up to this day.

Annee was a detective after my own heart. She liked to put facts down on paper and stare at them, a technique that I often used. It wasn't that great revelations came from staring at the bits of paper, but having the facts laid out kept my mind from speculating too far afield.

Annee did this while I kept eating. There was a tremendous hole that I was filling with croissants and coffee this morning.

As Annee wrote the names of the dead and the dates they had died, I called up their images in my mind and I tried to remember the last time I'd seen each one. M. Foyer. M. Arnaut.

Then I went through the nonfatal events, like my bop on the head, my wrestling match with Clement, and Laurence's dose of poison.

Then Annee made slips of paper for all the people who knew how to make pâté, a longer list than I had previously thought.

When Annee had made up slips for everything we could think of, I said, "What do you think?"

"I don't think we have been on the right track," she said.

I practically leaped out of the chair. "That's what I was thinking. Something's bothering me. Something I saw. A picture. Something."

"It's not over," she said. "I have this terrible foreboding."

As soon as she said it, I knew she was right. "What can we do?"

"Be careful, Fran. Just be careful."

"You, too," I said. "Do you still want to go watch Odette and Bernadette?"

"How could I miss something like that? And Laurence and Marsha have been outdoing themselves with preparations. They've even got a wonderful little carrying basket ready for Fanny."

Marsha walked in on cue. "We're just about ready," she

said. "We can get there early to get a good place."

"Everyone else will have the same idea, I'm afraid," Annee said. "But let's be on our way." Then with a wry smile, she asked me whether I was done eating.

"I guess I can stop for a while," I said, "so long as there's plenty packed up for lunch."

Marsha laughed. "Not to worry. We've packed with you in mind."

After Annee had given us all a lecture on keeping together and keeping safe and keeping our eyes open, we were off, each of us carrying a basket. Two with food, one with drinks, including wine, and one that had been fitted with blankets and covered with netting for Fanny.

We weren't the first to arrive. The hollow was half full when we got there and set out our blankets.

It would be at least an hour and a half before the Toute girls arrived. We planned to use the time eating lunch. Other people had planned to do likewise. Wine bottles were in evidence on many blankets, and the air was rife with hints of cheeses and sausages and vinaigrettes.

The picnic plan went fine except for the crowding. As time wore on, the spaces between the blankets kept shrinking.

At one point a few sharp words were exchanged, but the altercation was quickly muted when Jacques appeared.

He gave a little speech, which Annee translated for me, but which I had understood most of anyway. He asked the people to arrange themselves quietly so that the girls would not get nervous. Then he cleared a path to the center where the girls would pass. The path went right by our blankets. I saw him look at Annee, who was playing with Fanny's fingers, with such an expression of longing and regret that I almost felt sorry for him.

Vincent turned up just before Odette and Bernadette arrived, and we had him sit with a basket on his lap, because our space had been squeezed away.

He looked unhappy and I figured it had something to do with Odette. I guessed that their plans to celebrate had been canceled because fame had its demands.

"Did you see Odette and wish her good luck?" Annee said.

Vincent mumbled, "Yes," and his lower lip quivered. He managed to hold back the tears. Just.

The girls came in sight and the crowd began to applaud, ending Annee's attempt to cheer up her son. Some of the crowd stood and cheered; others waved handkerchiefs. In America, I thought, someone would have been selling T-shirts celebrating the Toute girls' debut. But that fad hadn't yet caught on.

Odette stopped next to our blanket as she and Bernadette were making their way down the path that had been cleared for them. Bernadette, behind Odette, stopped, too. Odette smiled at Vincent and Annee and greeted them—somewhat coolly, I thought: Vincent got only two busses in the air when he rose to greet her, and Odette barely stooped over to kiss the air somewhere in the vicinity of Annee's face. The rest of us she waved a greeting to with a little flip of the hand.

We lifted our glasses to toast her and I saw her stare at my arm. I thought Odette was going to ask me about the purple bite mark that I was sure she had seen. Maybe because she had seen the marks on her mother. Then she looked at Annee's uncovered legs. I couldn't read her expression, except to say that she noticed the scars. Then she and Bernadette thanked us for the toast, and Odette lifted her chin and made her way to the area that would be the stage.

The television camera operators were having a tough time with the crowd. Every time one of them stopped in front of a group, the people would shout for them to get out of the way. Jacques again called for order. Which he got.

Annee translated: "He told them that the cameras would not stay long in one place and asked everyone to please be quiet. And he added that the alternate plan was to film the girls at the gymnasium, where only a few people would be admitted."

Odette was doing some stretching and Bernadette was tuning up her flute. The cameras were already rolling, some catching the crowd. I saw Madame Foyer being interviewed and wondered whether she had been selected so that all the news in Vaudoy could be viewed at once. If they were going for the other big story, I figured Annee would be on their list of interviewees.

I mentioned it to Annee, and her response was, "I don't think they know what I look like. And I didn't give them much time when they called about talking to me."

"Unlike Madame Foyer," Vincent said.

"I am sorry for her," Laurence said. "But I don't like the way she has been acting since Guy was killed."

Odette clapped her hands and put her arms out to the side. I had seen her do that before at the practices and it silenced the crowd. It worked this time, too, but more slowly. Bigger crowd.

The notes of the flute began, slowly. A sad piece, I thought. Not one that I had seen Odette dance to before. But then I remembered hearing the music the day Marsha and Laurence and I had surprised Bernadette playing it in the woods. After the first few notes, Odette began to dance, and the mystical combination of the two sisters worked its magic. Everything was forgotten except the music and the movement.

I wondered how the camera people could remember to run their cameras, but they did. I guessed they were inured to everything but getting the picture.

A low-sailing rain cloud passed over and doused us all, but the dance continued and no one left. The only concessions some of the audience made to the brief summer shower were to lift blankets here and there. Most didn't even do that.

Odette moved in the air somewhere between the ground and the sky, while Bernadette's flute seemed to include the wind and the birds in its song.

It was hard to imagine that these were the same girls who walked the streets of Vaudoy, who worked at their grandparents' shop, who worked at the inn, who did such a mundane thing as go to school.

Odette wore speckled leotards, pink and maroon, and a pink chiffon scarf that sometimes trailed behind her, sometimes wrapped around her. Her feet were bare and her hair flew wild with the wind of the dance.

Bernadette hunched over the flute, her posture matching the downcast mood of the piece. So somber was the performance that when it was over and Odette was lying scarf-covered in the grass and Bernadette had lowered the flute from her lips, no one moved. Fifteen seconds passed and then one lone clap, then another, and then the applause rose to a roar. The cameras moved in tight on Odette and Bernadette, and some of the audience moved in on them, too.

Jacques and Niki waded in to the rescue, accompanied by a squadron of gendarmes. Where they had materialized from, I had no idea, but they did the job of crowd control, and only those who were invited into the circle were allowed to approach the new starlets.

The TV people looked ecstatic. They were interviewing everybody who was at all articulate, and some who weren't.

Vincent was turned back at the police line. I know Odette saw him trying to break through, but she did not instruct the police to let him pass. He ran into the woods clutching his face. Annee watched him go.

"Do you mind if we wait a bit to see whether Vincent will come back?" she said.

Since the rain had stopped and the air was warm, we were in no hurry to join the parade walking through the field.

"We didn't eat our dessert," Marsha said.

As the crowd thinned and we had more room to eat, the baskets were again opened. Marsha and Laurence still had a wine-and-cheese course and a *tarte* and coffee for us to tackle.

Fanny, who had slept through the performance, now protested that the next one to eat would be herself. We waited while Annee served up Fanny's lunch.

Since we were by the path that everyone was using to exit, we got to see who was there.

Clarisse stopped to say hello and to ask Annee something about what was to be done at the inn. She spoke in French, and this time I didn't get much of it. What I did get, though, was a look at her legs, which were bedecked in four places that I could see below her skirt with plastic bandages.

On the pretense of scratching my leg, which was closer to her legs than my head at that moment, I leaned toward her to get a better look. The telltale scars, though faint, were there, but the bandages seemed too small to cover up teeth marks. If I made sure she saw the marks on my legs, I thought, maybe she would say something that would tell us whether she was the woman in the woods.

I was wishing I had arranged a signal with Annee, because I wanted her to pay attention to what was said. Signal or no, I barged ahead, making sounds and lifting my skirt and rubbing my thigh and saying, "I'm going to have to put something on this. I think it's getting infected."

Annee shot me a look, and I knew she was in the game. She said something to Clarisse, and Clarisse looked at my leg and blanched.

The exchange took no more than a few seconds and then Clarisse left, rather abruptly, I thought.

"What do you think?" I asked Annee when she was gone.

"She seemed more startled than angry," Annee said.

"You think," I said, "that the woman in the woods would be angry and jealous?"

"Yes, I think so."

Marsha and Laurence concurred.

"From what you told us," Marsha said, "the man and woman were acting like they were madly in love. If I were that woman, I would be furious if I thought my lover was messing around." I thought Marsha could have stopped sooner and spared Annee's feelings, but that's not Marsha.

While Marsha belabored the obvious, my mind was filling in some of the spaces that had been blank up to then. Scenes that I played back seemed more significant now, and I got a sick feeling in my gut that scared me.

That was why, when I looked up and saw J. P., I dreaded what he was going to say.

Thirty

J. P. didn't look like his usual well-groomed, collected self. His blond hair was stringy and greasy and his suit was rumpled. There was no flashy smile, either; his expression was grim, to say the least.

"Madame," he said, looking at Annee, "we have failed."

Annee's face registered alarm. "You let him escape again?"

"That would have been better," he said. "No, Monsieur Rien is dead. Really dead, this time."

"But he was in jail. What . . ."

"He had a visitor this morning. She said she was Madame Rien and the guard let her in."

"Annee has been with us all morning," Marsha said.

"We know that. The woman did not fit your description at all. Forgive me, but she was younger."

Annee smiled, but the quivering around her eyes and mouth said much more than her smile. "I'm sorry," she said, "but my feelings about my husband are mixed with so much bitterness that I don't know what I'm feeling."

"I understand," he said.

We all did.

"How did he die?" I said.

"Shot," J. P. said.

"But didn't someone hear the shot?" I said.

"Didn't they come running and catch who did it?" Annee said.

"The guard at the desk heard only a slamming cell door.

252

The young woman appeared shortly thereafter and seemed angry, the guard told us. When he asked her what was wrong, she told him that Denis told her to go away so that he could sleep. The guard thought it was funny and didn't check on Denis until it was time to make his rounds.''

There was silence for several seconds.

Then Annee said, ''Clever.''

''Very astute,'' J. P. said.

In the midst of the subdued atmosphere, Vincent returned with his face all lit up. He didn't notice the glumness in everyone else. I knew what that meant, and so did Annee. She frowned briefly at J. P. when he started to tell Vincent about Denis. J. P. got the message and said nothing.

''Can you do without me at the inn until dinnertime?'' Vincent said, smiling broadly.

''Of course,'' Annee said. ''But be on time. I think we'll be busy tonight.''

Vincent was off without any further discussion. He walked almost as lightly as his lady love danced.

We were watching him go when Odette paid us a visit. She spoke cordially to us, standing next to me, so that I had to look up at her. It was difficult to think of her as the same person who flitted like a moth when she danced, who expressed such a range of emotions when she moved her lithe body.

There in the grass next to the blanket, she was just a girl who had been giving Vincent a hard time, a girl who worked at the inn with Clarisse at suppertime.

We told her how wonderful the performance was, and she thanked us and said that she was very nervous today because the TV people were there. ''And Baba insisted on playing that sad piece that she just composed,'' Odette said.

I remembered the day in the woods when I saw Bernadette crying and I thought about the music she played that afternoon. What could have made one so young so horribly unhappy?

''Baba?'' J. P. said. ''Who's Baba?''

''Bernadette,'' Odette said. ''I've always called her Baba.''

''Where is she now?'' J. P. said. He was friendly, but I thought his questions were leading somewhere.

"She went home," Odette said. "She's very tired."

Odette seemed to be in the mood for small talk. I kept thinking that Vincent would be waiting for her, and was wishing that she wouldn't keep him waiting. She bent over and looked closely at Fanny. "*Ooh là là*," she said. (They really do say that.) "*Est-elle mignonne*? [Isn't she cute?]"

When Odette left and strolled leisurely toward the woods, I said to J. P., "Why did you ask about Bernadette?"

"Because she fit the description of the woman who visited Denis this morning."

"Bernadette?" I said.

"It may not have been Bernadette. I'll have to question her."

"Wait," I said. "Bernadette didn't pass by here. If she went home, she went the long way, through the woods." My mind was really buzzing now, and the sick feeling was returning.

"I think you should get your men and go through the woods—*now*," I said. "Find Bernadette."

"Vincent is in the woods with Odette," Annee said, fear drawing the blood from her face. "I want to go with you." Then, turning to Marsha, she said, "Please take Fanny home right away."

Marsha turned white and started gathering up the blankets. Even Laurence was moving rapidly.

Annee, J. P., and I set out toward the woods, going across the stage area, where Niki, Jacques, and the Toute boys were still talking to the TV people. I saw Jacques take note of us and wondered whether he should be told about the woman matching Bernadette's description. When I looked him in the eye, I saw his face lose its composure.

We weren't far into the woods when Jacques and Niki joined us. J. P. stopped and told them to go back.

"We will be quiet," Niki said. There were tears collecting in the corners of her eyes.

What do they know? I thought. Or what do they suspect?

At that point J. P. told them about the woman who had visited Denis. "Was Bernadette gone at any time this morning?" he said.

''The girls went to practice,'' Niki said. ''They were doing a new routine, they told me.''

Niki, I remembered, knew her way through these woods. ''Can you lead us to the places where they go?'' I said. ''Do you know where the cave is?''

Her face flushed, and I knew then that she was still hiding something. J. P. saw it, but I wasn't sure who else had noticed.

''I know where there is a cave. It's not far from the river,'' she said, turning on one of her radiant smiles. What a weapon for dissembling, I thought, a smile like that.

''Hurry,'' I said.

''Wait,'' J. P. said, ''there are too many of us.''

He was right, of course. Even though each one of us had an interest in chasing down Bernadette, there would be no way to sneak up on her if we all crashed through the woods together. He directed all of us to go back except Niki, who would show him to the cave.

Annee, Jacques, and I started back, but Jacques turned in another direction. ''I know the way back to the road near my house,'' he said. ''It's still shorter for you than going back to the field.''

He led the way and gradually maneuvered himself to be walking in front with Annee. I knew what he was doing, but I didn't feel that I had to protect her from Jacques's advances.

As we went along, the terrain became familiar. I remembered seeing Bernadette weeping somewhere near that spot. The prickly sensation at the back of my neck made me turn. It seemed to me that I was in the place where I had been grabbed the night before. My breath was coming in short, violent gasps and my heart was contracting in corresponding thumps.

I stopped and held onto a tree, waiting for the panic to subside.

It was then that I saw Odette and Vincent through the trees, not exactly in flagrante delicto, but close. I didn't want to call out to Annee and Jacques, who by now were far ahead of me and probably continuing the argument that they had begun as soon as they were walking without me.

Getting as close to the tree as possible, I peered through

the foliage. No Bernadette. Was she somewhere behind me, waiting for a chance to pounce? Or was she innocent and had simply gone home through the woods?

Vincent and Odette were straightening their clothing and smiling at each other. Then Odette went over to an outcropping of rock. Yes, I thought, that's the rock where Vincent left food the night before.

Odette pulled out the bags that Vincent had put there and a couple of others, so I figured both of them had planned for this little celebration. Get out of here, I told myself. This is a private moment for these kids. But I stayed, the pins and needles on my nape still active. I kept looking around me, not wanting to be caught from behind again. Even though Denis was dead, I didn't feel safe.

Vincent went off a few steps into the woods. Thank heaven he chose the other side of the little clearing from where I was huddled by the tree. Odette busied herself putting out the food. She said something to Vincent about champagne, and I assumed that his job was to open the bubbly.

Vincent zipped up and walked farther away. The champagne must be somewhere cooler, I thought.

Odette put the food on the plates, and I watched her cut up a couple of pâtés and serve them, along with bread and pickles and olives.

Vincent returned with the champagne and eased the cork out of the bottle with a small pop. Odette was standing by with a couple of fluted glasses. I didn't see where the fancy glasses had been stashed.

They toasted and kissed and then sat down on a log to eat. They had forks and knives and regular plates, there in the woods, as if they were in a dining room. It was time for me to leave, I thought, but I didn't. I kept staring at the plates that Odette had fixed.

No. My mouth dropped open.

Did I see what I thought I saw? My brain began to catch up. The aura of young love through which I had been watching the scene suddenly turned dark and sinister.

Vincent lifted his fork.

I shouted from my spot in the trees. "Vincent, don't! Don't eat that."

Odette stood up, looking wild. Vincent dropped his fork. "What's the matter? Who's there?"

"Me. Fran. I saw Odette."

I raced toward them.

Odette picked up Vincent's plate and flung it into the trees.

"Odette," Vincent said, "why did you do that?"

I was almost to the little clearing when Odette, her eyes blazing, picked up her knife and came at me.

"Odette, stop," Vincent said.

Odette lunged, the knife aimed at my chest.

I kept my eyes on the knife and moved to one side, catching her arm as she slid by me. I felt like I had made an advanced move in one of those Oriental self-defense disciplines.

Her arm twisted and she screamed with rage and pain.

Vincent, in his addled state, shouted, "What have you done to Odette?" And he came running at me.

Odette I thought I could handle, but the two of them posed a problem. Run, I thought. Probably I could outrun Vincent.

But before I could put that thought into action, Bernadette appeared from nowhere, carrying a gun that shook menacingly in her hands.

"Stop. Do not move. I will shoot."

Odette spoke to Bernadette in French, and I understood some of it. Basically she was telling Bernadette to shoot me and giving her reasons why it was necessary.

"Stop," Bernadette said. "Don't move. Odette, Vincent, don't move." Then she said the same thing, but in French. I think I understood every word. Talk about heightened awareness.

"But, Baba," Odette said in English, "what is the matter?"

By now, Odette and Vincent were also alarmed by Bernadette's manner. Not to mention the gun she was waving around.

I took a chance, then, to see what the mood was. "She was trying to poison Vincent," I said to Bernadette.

At that moment J. P. and Niki, who had apparently heard the disturbance, appeared behind Bernadette. They must have been moving silently toward us in the past minute or so.

Just as Bernadette realized they were approaching, probably because we were all staring at them, J. P. grabbed the gun from Bernadette's trembling fingers.

Bernadette crumbled into a weeping heap.

Niki said, "You said Odette was giving poison to Vincent?" She looked at her older daughter. "Odette, haven't you done enough?"

"Maman, I wouldn't poison anyone, especially Vincent." She looked fondly at Vincent. "I told you, Baba is having a nervous breakdown." She said this in English, although she was speaking to her mother.

"*Non, non*," Bernadette said through her tears.

"There are two pâtés in those bags," I said, grabbing the bags from the niche between the rocks. "She put slices of one of them on her plate and a slice of each of them on Vincent's plate."

Niki took the packages and opened them and looked at them.

Jacques and Annee came back looking for me about that time. The range of feeling that ran over Jacques's face was hard to decipher.

Niki spoke quickly in French to Jacques, too quickly for me to catch, but Annee had no trouble and she gasped as the long tirade that Niki delivered ran on.

Then J. P. pulled his gun and handed me the gun Bernadette had brought into the woods. "I'm sure you know how to handle this," he said. "Keep them all covered."

By then, some of what Niki had said was sinking in. She and Jacques had been covering for the girls, because they suspected that one or both of them had been involved in the killing of Marcel Gris.

Niki turned to Odette. "*Dis-le moi. Tu les as tué tous*? [Tell me. Did you kill them all?]"

"Maman," Odette said.

"*Et toi* [And you]," Niki said, looking at Bernadette.

Bernadette and Niki exchanged long looks. I don't know what they were saying, but some information was being exchanged through their eyes.

Niki moved so quickly and unexpectedly that not one of us could stop her.

Bernadette screamed. Odette shrieked. Niki stood there chewing, her face taking in her daughters' reactions.

Odette pulled the rest of the pâté away from Niki and tried to open her mother's mouth to get at the pâté she was still chewing.

"*Pourquoi* [Why], Odette?" she said, then started to vomit and gasp for air.

Odette sobbed.

J. P. pulled a phone from his pocket and called the ambulance and some backup gendarmes, who were positioned near the TV trucks.

J. P. ordered everyone to sit and wait, including Jacques, who was insisting that he carry Niki away to get help.

"The ambulance will be here before you can carry her out of the woods," J. P. told Jacques.

I knew what was going to happen next, but every one else gasped when J. P. pointed his gun at Jacques and told him to give up his weapon. Jacques's face quivered.

The whole scene was captured on TV moments later when the camera crew followed the gendarmes into the woods.

Thirty-one

We were standing by the graveside, burying Denis Rien. It was the funeral that Marsha and I had come to France for weeks before. And now not only was he dead, but so were M. Foyer, M. Arnaut, and Marcel Gris. Two others, Niki and Laurence, had escaped death, and a prison guard was hanging tenuously to a wisp of life.

Odette, who had become famous one day for her dancing, was infamous the next. But the French were fascinated by her for her passion. Her passion for dance and her passion for Denis.

All the killings were for her love of Denis, she told the police. She killed Denis's double because he found out about their romance. She said she went to the shed with him, pretending she thought he was Denis, and offered him her pâté.

According to J. P., when the lab finally got some of the pâté in its uneaten state, the chemists there said she had minced the Inocybe de Patouillard very fine and cooked it down so that it was very concentrated and much more deadly than it would have been if someone had put it in a pâté accidentally. The mushroom, they said, has a sweet flavor and a strong fruity odor, which made the pâté smell very appealing.

The pâté that she had made for me was from the more deadly mushroom and didn't require any fancy cooking. In the case of that mushroom, Amanita phalloides, she didn't need to add as many mushrooms to do the job. A single mushroom cap, the lab said, would be enough to kill.

The dogs of the press swarmed through Vaudoy, sniffing out the scraps of the story. And the villagers suddenly remembered all kinds of things that became significant.

Madame Foyer told them that her husband had seen the bite marks on Odette's arm that night at the inn. Later, Foyer and Arnaut argued about the marks and Odette heard them. They were dispensed with by the same method Odette had used to silence Marcel Gris.

The guard at the jail was a pushover for a pretty girl, especially one whose father was a police official. Odette admitted to hitting the guard over the head and helping Denis escape.

The police were going ahead with the charges against Bernadette as well, because the younger sister admitted that she knew what Odette was doing. Poor Bernadette. She did as her sister told her. But because she tried to help me when Odette and Vincent came after me in the woods, she would get clemency, J. P. told me.

J. P. also told me that Odette thought I was getting too close to the truth, and therefore, I, too, was added to her list of expendables.

"But what about Laurence?" I said. "Why was she to be a victim?"

"That was a miscalculation on Odette's part. That pâté was intended for Annee and Laurence. She made it before you arrived. When she realized her mistake, she went into the house and retrieved the pâté."

"But why Annee and Laurence?"

"With them out of the way, Odette would have a shot at a lot more money."

"So it wasn't just love that motivated her."

"No. It was passion, control. That sort of thing."

"That sort of thing," I repeated, and wondered whether passion and control were what had motivated my ex when he tried to kill me after I left him.

Denis was slated for death, J. P. said, when Odette found out what Denis had done to me. Either she caught him at it or she spied on him. And that was enough to convince her that he was up to his old tricks, which he had probably sworn to her he was done with. She probably had believed him because she wanted to. She told the police that she sent

Bernadette to dispatch Denis, but I wonder whether Bernadette wouldn't have thought of it sooner or later all by herself.

My guesses as to why she tried to kill Vincent are too far afield. She had loved him once, too. Maybe she had developed a taste for death. Maybe Vincent had followed her or had guessed the truth. Maybe it will come out at the trial.

As for Denis and his various larcenies, J. P. found out much more from the notebook and the boxes confiscated from the shed. J. P. only wished he had had time to prosecute Denis using the information. There was money in many bank accounts, and those bankbooks were in the box that M. Saverne had helped Denis retrieve from the shed. That box was found in the cave.

My suspicions about Jacques were right on the money; he did have his own agenda. He was in Denis's notebook, J. P. told me, and Jacques was relieved when it seemed at first that Denis was dead. He and Niki suspected that one of their daughters or both were behind the first murder. But when the killings continued, they retreated into denial, and hoped that Odette and Bernadette had nothing to do with them.

J. P. had a theory about Odette and Denis, which he revealed to me at length when he took me on a whirlwind tour of Paris.

"She may have been revolted and angry when she found out about her mother and Denis. But revulsion turned to passion when she confronted him, the man who defiled her mother. Odette and Denis were made for one another," he said as we sat on the steps of Sacré Coeur, with Paris at our feet.

"Denis may have been attracted to her because he liked the idea of stealing his son's girlfriend," I said.

"Ah," he said, "you understand the deep meaning of covetousness."

I shrugged. I had never thought of it that way.

"Anyway, it took a girl detective from the States to help us solve this," he said.

"Girl?" I almost said, but then let it drop. I thought of the ways I had blundered through the events that led up to the denouement, and then thought about how many times the gendarmes had dropped the ball. "Thank you," I said, and dropped the other shoe.

As Denis was lowered into the ground, I was wishing that my first trip to France had been more conventional. Notice that I said "first"; I do intend to go back.

I did get some photographs to show my boyfriend, Ted, and Delia, Natasha, Polly, and my paperboy, Wally Klune—pictures of me smiling next to the Eiffel Tower, in front of Notre Dame, on the steps of Sacré Coeur, and at a café on the Champs Élysées.

But one great thing I did take home with me was Annee's promise to move back to the States with Fanny, my very own namesake.

She had been christened the day before her father's funeral. Vincent hadn't made up his mind whether he would come to the States after he had straightened out his part in Odette's adventures. He was feeling too rotten to speak at length to anyone.

Laurence was positively in heaven, because she had decided that she would spend six months of every year in the States.

I never did find out what else Denis had on M. Saverne, but J. P. knew and wouldn't tell me. Anyway, M. Saverne was going to buy the inn and Clement was going to work with him. Yves and Clarisse got a lot of comfort from each other and continued to see each other, but not in the alley behind the inn.

When we were leaving the cemetery, Clement came over to wish me bon voyage, since Marsha and I were to board the Air France plane only a couple of hours after the funeral. He handed me a small package and the corners of his mouth turned up in an impish grin.

FAST-PACED MYSTERIES
BY J.A. JANCE

Featuring J.P. Beaumont

UNTIL PROVEN GUILTY	89638-9/$5.99 US/$7.99 CAN
INJUSTICE FOR ALL	89641-9/$5.99 US/$7.99 CAN
TRIAL BY FURY	75138-0/$5.99 US/$7.99 CAN
TAKING THE FIFTH	75139-9/$5.99 US/$7.99 CAN
IMPROBABLE CAUSE	75412-6/$5.99 US/$7.99 CAN
A MORE PERFECT UNION	75413-4/$5.99 US/$7.99 CAN
DISMISSED WITH PREJUDICE	
	75547-5/$5.99 US/$7.99 CAN
MINOR IN POSSESSION	75546-7/$5.99 US/$7.99 CAN
PAYMENT IN KIND	75836-9/$5.99 US/$7.99 CAN
WITHOUT DUE PROCESS	75837-7/$5.99 US/$7.99 CAN
FAILURE TO APPEAR	75839-3/$5.50 US/$6.50 CAN
LYING IN WAIT	71841-3/$5.99 US/$7.99 CAN

Featuring Joanna Brady

DESERT HEAT	76545-4/$5.99 US/$7.99 CAN
TOMBSTONE COURAGE	76546-2/$5.99 US/$6.99 CAN